KATY

THE WOMAN WHO SIGNED THE DECLARATION OF INDEPENDENCE

BETTY BOLTÉ

ALSO BY BETTY BOLTÉ

Becoming Lady Washington: A Novel

Notes of Love and War

Hometown Heroines: True Stories of Bravery, Daring, and Adventure

Snow on Magnolias

<u>Fury Falls Inn</u>

The Haunting of Fury Falls Inn

Under Lock and Key

Desperate Reflections

Fractured Crystals

Legends of Wrath

Homecoming

<u>Secrets of Roseville</u>

Undying Love

Haunted Melody

The Touchstone of Raven Hollow

Veiled Visions of Love

Charmed Against All Odds

KATY

Betty Bolté

Mystic Owl Publishing
Huntsville, Alabama

Mystic Owl Publishing, Huntsville, AL 35815

www.MysticOwlPublishing.com

www.bettybolte.com

Digital ISBN: 979-8-9860450-6-1

Paperback ISBN: 979-8-9860450-7-8

Cover design by Sweet 'N Spicy Designs (http://sweetnspicydesigns.com)

CHAPTER 1

PROVIDENCE, RHODE ISLAND – 1762

*T*he ship bumped against the wharf, rattling Katy's nerves even more than the alarming and uncomfortable trip from Connecticut. If only the ship could turn about and go back to her childhood home, but she held out no hope of such an event. She clutched the railing, her gloves soaked through, the sharp tang of fish and salty sea masked by the scent of rain. Seagulls cried out as they drifted overhead. Providence loomed before her, its bustling streets evidence of the population that had attracted her brother's flighty interest. An interest in the printing trade he'd apprenticed to learn and now was striking out on his own. Well, with her and her mother's help.

The British colonies were slowly gaining in both population and respect for the exports they produced. The resulting influence and clout the colonies enjoyed continued to be a source of pride across all thirteen colonies. In her native town of New London, Connecticut, the merchants and artisans also continued to multiply. Home. How she'd miss it.

She hummed a ditty to herself, a means of calming her agitation, as she scanned the streets swarming with coaches pulled by gleaming horses, and wagons by lumbering oxen. People dressed in lightweight linen beneath various outer garments dodged among the vehicles, avoiding the biggest of the mud puddles from the seemingly ceaseless rain. Her stalwart mother stopped beside her with a gentle smile on her face, her dark cloak glistening in the rain.

"My darling, don't fret. All will be well. You'll see. We'll have the men bring the trunks and meet us at our new home." Sarah Goddard was tall, graceful, confident.

Everything Katy tried to be but failed at miserably.

"Yes, Mother." Widowed but still a strong and attractive woman at fifty-six years of age, her mother had earned Katy's admiration more than she could say. "I'll adjust."

"We both will." Sarah huffed an impatient sigh. "I have a little surprise for you since I know how difficult this move is for you. We'll have our own place instead of accepting William's offer to live with him."

"Difficult" barely served to describe her feelings. Indeed, Katy had lived in New London the entirety of her twenty-four years on earth. She knew everyone in her neighborhood, having grown up and socialized with them through various church and community activities. She never thought to live anywhere else. She'd even found herself expecting to spend her entire life living in the house she'd been born in and had grown up within its walls. In the city where everyone knew who she was and her relations so she never had to introduce herself. The last several years had been so peaceful and calm, what with her brother away from home.

Then William, her younger brother by two years, finished his apprenticeship at the print shop in New York. She hadn't thought his choices would impact her life. But when he decided to start his own shop in Providence, because there wasn't any competition there and the town needed a decent printer, everything changed. Until William set up his press, the only other one in the colony was in Newport, owned by Benjamin Franklin. But her brother had apprenticed with one of the best printers in the colonies, so he'd give Franklin some competition. How William had convinced their mother to give him three hundred pounds to start such a venture was beyond her. No, that wasn't entirely true. It really wasn't as unfathomable as one might hope. Her mother loved her son to distraction and would do anything in her power to help him.

Never mind that the move meant giving up everything and everyone she'd ever known. That was an entirely different matter. When the idea had been raised months earlier, she'd even considered staying in New London where she felt safe and welcomed. But her mother had immediately insisted on supporting William every way she could. Katy loved her mother too much to be separated from her by such a distance. So, eventually, she'd reluctantly agreed to make the move as well. Really, when she took a hard look at her options, she had no better choice.

"When did you have time to arrange for a new home just for us?" She resisted humming during the conversation with her mother, but her anxiety hadn't abated. She was very relieved she was not to be forced to live under her brother's roof. He could be a might difficult, to say the least. The man tended to push her beyond her patience more often than not. One of her failings when it came to being a dutiful sister. She really shouldn't have wished for him to continue to live elsewhere when his apprenticeship ended. The thought evoked a flash of guilt at her unkind desire.

"I had William find a suitable place and make the arrangements for me. I'd rather we have our own space, instead of living with the young men apprenticing under him."

"Yes, a very good consideration." Katy turned to investigate a sudden commotion on the dock in front of her. Two men in rough dock workers clothing were rolling a hogshead, an immense barrel containing merchandise from Spain by the labels pasted on its side, up the ramp to the street. Or at least trying to. She couldn't help but notice how mismatched they appeared. The closer man with his black hair and beard pushing the barrel up the ramp had to be six inches shorter than the other shaggy haired man, with a similar difference in sheer size. "That doesn't look particularly safe…"

Just then the larger man slipped on the wet dock, falling to his knees. He cried out in pain. The hogshead listed and then teetered backwards as the other man narrowly missed being crushed under the weight of the barrel. The hogshead bumped and bounced down the wood ramp to the dock and splashed into the river. Katy gave an involuntary start forward, as if she were capable of providing any help whatsoever. She held still with an effort.

"Those poor men. I hope they're not injured." Sarah clasped her gloved hands together as she watched the scramble of men to help get the shaken men back on their feet and fish the hogshead out of the water.

The group of men exchanged several coarse words of frustration and effort over the next minutes while they worked to right everything that had gone wrong. Some of the words were new ones to her, but they also entertained her distracted mind for a moment. Language and words were dear to her.

Katy slid a glance at her mother to confirm the humor she heard behind her mother's comment. Her mother managed to find mirth in the most unexpected places. "Perhaps a lesson has been learned today."

Sarah nodded, a twinkle in her eye. "Perhaps, indeed. We should be able to start for our new home shortly." She turned to the two men in hunting shirts and pants who approached where they stood on the deck, their ruddy skin glistening in the damp.

"Mrs. Sarah Goddard?" The taller of the men pulled his cap from his head as he stopped in front of her mother.

"Yes. Did my son William send you?"

He nodded. "We're here to carry your trunks and what-have-you to your new home."

"You have this address?" Sarah stated the address clearly and waited until they nodded their understanding. "We'll meet you there shortly."

Katy didn't know the men her brother had hired to meet them and help with their move. She was glad her mother confirmed that her brother had given them the same address he'd told them. She hoped they could be trusted to deliver their belongings safely and without undue delay. Everything and everyone seemed new and foreign even though Providence wasn't terribly far from New London. At least by boat. Trying to go across country would have taken much longer. Roads linked the various towns and cities of the American colonies, but many were little more than a deer path through the wilderness of forests and underbrush. What with all of their belongings they'd brought to their new home, they elected to travel by ship up the coast and into the harbor.

"Mother, should we let William know we have arrived before we go to the house?" Katy didn't want his ire to get het up. "I really wish he'd met us himself, but I suppose he's busy at the printing shop."

His quick temper was famous despite his youth, only twenty-two years of age and already known as a firebrand. Yet now that their father had passed a few years before, he was the man of the house. Katy and her mother had come to Providence to help him run the new print shop. Would he appreciate their sacrifices made on his behalf? Would he even consider they'd had to make any? Not only had they left behind family and friends, but her mother had given up being the postmistress in her husband's stead. A position that ensured she engaged with many of the people in the community and thus always knew what was happening in town. Her father had served in that position until his death five years ago.

That thought rushed long-buried emotions to the surface, choking off her next words for a moment. How she missed her gentle, loving father! A religious, compassionate, strong soul who looked out for his community as a doctor and the postmaster for the town. Until that blasted gout took hold and didn't let go. Her doctor father didn't have any way to treat it. After years of suffering with the pain and inflammation, he'd collapsed and died. They would never know from what exactly, but the specifics didn't matter. Only his loss mattered.

"Going to see your brother first thing is a good idea, dear. We'll hire a cab to take us round there and then on to the house. By that time, our baggage should have arrived."

Her mother's soothing voice brought her back to the moment. "I am rather anxious to see our new house and begin to make it our own. Let us hurry to William and then on. It's wet everywhere and I'm tired after this difficult journey."

They hired a cab near the docks and soon found themselves alighting at the print shop located near the Great Bridge that crossed the river not very far from where they'd arrived. A fine location, in the heart of the growing city. They went inside and were immediately accosted by chaos and disarray, the sharp tang of ink, and the *clickety-clack-thunk* of the printing press. Katy halted, her mouth falling open. What had they gotten themselves into?

She drew in a long breath. Her brother was not known for his organization skills, but even she was surprised at the lack of order within the shop. He also harbored an aversion to recording of details, such as would be required to manage the revenue for the fledgling press. Thus his sending for their mother to help him with the financial records and supplies. Sarah had been doing a fine job of managing the financial reports in place of her deceased husband for years.

Two young apprentices were staring at an immense printing press, listening to William cursing on the back side of the machine. His tone suggested annoyance not anger, but the language was definitely not what he'd normally use with his mother in the room. She should do something to warn him they'd entered the shop. She pushed the door closed with a loud *thump*.

William stepped out from behind the press at the sound, wiping his inky hands on a rag as he hurried toward his mother. "Mother! I am sorry you heard all of that. I am so glad you've arrived safely."

William's light brown hair brushed his shoulders, his hazel eyes squinting as he grinned at them. He'd grown and matured into a rather good-looking young man while he'd been away in New York. He even managed to look like a respectable person in his dark blue suit coat and white working shirt over knee breeches and white stockings. If only his temperament had matured along with his appearance, then the transition wouldn't be so difficult. Hope swirled but didn't settle inside. She'd wait and see just how much her younger brother had actually matured.

"Yes. I'm sure." Sarah swept an assessing look around the large room crammed with the press, work tables, composing stands, and a tall table by the front door. Several young men, some little more than boys, worked at stacking reams of paper and refilling the ink vats. "I hope you've been expecting us and all is readied?"

To Katy's mind, the apprentices in the room seemed slow,

inept, and slightly troubling. What had her brother seen in them to take them on as apprentices? One thing was apparent. Not a one of the men or boys in the room knew a jot about housekeeping. Bits and strips of paper lay about on the floor and the tables. Ink had spilled over the edge of one table onto the floor, leaving a black puddle by a leg. Cobwebs draped like dirty lace across the upper corners of the room. She sneezed as dust floated past her nose despite the high level of moisture in the air. An unseemly situation for them to work in and for customers to witness.

"Yes, Mother. I've hired staff for you, too. But, of course, if you don't like any of them, we can find someone else." William made a show of tossing his hair out of his eyes. He'd let it grow too long again, probably through neglect rather than intent. "Let me take you to the tavern this evening for a fine meal. A welcome, if you will."

"That is a kind offer, but one we are too tired to except." Sarah approached William and gave him a quick, affectionate embrace. "We will return tomorrow and we can sort out how we can best help you. Be thinking on that subject in the meantime. I'll have the cab take us to the house you located and we'll see you tomorrow."

"As you wish, Mother."

Relief swept through Katy's core as they emerged back outside into the lessening rain. The hustle and bustle on the street seemed less chaotic than the shop. "Oh, Mother…"

"I know, but we'll sort it out tomorrow. Come, we'll take a gander at the house, shall we?"

"I do so hope it's in better order than the shop." Katy shook her head as her mother flagged down a cab.

Not fifteen minutes later the cab dropped them off in front of a two-story frame house, with a central door on the first floor flanked by windows. The second floor boasted two windows above the others, and all the shutters had been painted white. A chimney sprouted from either end of the comfortable dwelling, a fine column of smoke dissipating into the rainy afternoon. The front stoop stood barely two steps above the muddy street. Katy inspected the new house and nodded. Not as fine as their previous home, but it would suffice.

"At least he found someplace moderately suitable." Her mother echoed her thoughts.

The front door swung open and a young man wearing black slacks and coat with a plain white shirt greeted them. He towered over Katy, his red hair and green eyes hinting as to his Irish heritage. Behind him a young woman in an iron gray maid's uniform stood silently, her eyes curious and gentle. Katy offered a smile in greeting, which the maid returned.

The man indicated for the women to enter through the door he held open. "Welcome to your new home, Mrs. Goddard. Miss Goddard."

"Thank you very much. And you are?" Sarah sauntered into the modest entranceway and paused to await his answer.

"My name is Trent McTavish, ma'am."

"I assume my son hired you as the…?"

"Yes, ma'am. I'm your butler. He also arranged for a cook, Mrs. Lauren George, who is busy in the kitchen, and this maid, Patsy Smythe, to attend you both."

"Very well." Sarah glanced past the butler to smile at Patsy. "In a minute, I'd ask that you show us around the house and we'll identify our bedchambers."

"Yes, ma'am. I've ensured all is ready for you." Patsy dipped a curtsy and then folded her hands in front of her to wait for her next orders.

Katy peered farther into their new home, curiosity mingling with her inner anxiety. A central hallway with gleaming pine floor led to the back of the house with doors set opposite each other at intervals. A dainty table stood to one side with a spray of flowers and reeds in a vase on top. A gray striped cat with yellow eyes stalked toward her slowly, apparently judging whether she was friend or foe. The walls showed signs of where frames once hung but were now barren. Serviceable but in need of some attention. She reached out a hand to the cat, letting it sniff her fingers before she stroked its head.

"That's Ceasar. He's cook's mouser." Trent nodded at the tom cat with a small grin on his lips.

"Every house needs a cat, in my opinion." Katy patted Ceasar's head again and then straightened. "Cats not only serve a purpose but also provide a certain underlying energy to a home."

"Yes, miss." Trent nodded once then noticed her mother's expectant expression. "Now, what can I do for you, Mrs. Goddard?"

"Something smells divine." Sarah leveled her gaze on Trent. "Cook must be whipping up a tasty supper for us. Please show me to her as I wish to speak with her on a few matters of importance."

"Yes, ma'am." Trent pivoted and led the way down the hall to a distant door at the rear of the house.

Katy took her time following them down the hall, peeking into each room as she went. Most of the rooms had little or no furniture. Some crates and barrels hid behind a door leading to a small work room close to the kitchen where her mother had disappeared moments earlier. She eased back out of the serviceable space and continued toward the kitchen. As she drew closer, her mother burst through the doorway, stopping Katy in her tracks.

"All right. I've informed Miss George of our preferences and things to avoid in her menus. Cook is preparing our supper accordingly. We'll go pick out our new bedchambers and begin to settle in. Tomorrow, we'll sort out the mess at the print shop. Agreed?"

"Yes, ma'am." Katy smiled at her mother. She was in command. Some things were as consistent as the sunrise. "Let's begin."

They spent the evening settling in, eating a fine welcome home meal, and then collapsed into their respective beds for a good night's exhausted sleep.

The next morning, Katy rose to the smell of bacon cooking. She quickly recalled that her mother intended to depart for the print shop as the sun rose. So she threw back the quilt and performed her morning ablution. Dressing in a simple but flattering pale yellow linen day dress with light green trim, she slipped her feet into sturdy leather shoes. She brushed her long chestnut hair with a soft brush, then pulled it up into a simple bun at the back of her head. Best to keep the long locks out of the way while doing whatever chores she was assigned.

After a quick breakfast, the two women ventured out the front door into the early morning sunshine. The streets seemed a mass of mud and slop from the churning of carriage and wagon wheels, of hooves and boots. Katy picked her way carefully beside her mother to the waiting cab and climbed inside. She was thankful yet again for the efficiency of their new butler, knowing they'd need a cab this morning to go to the print shop with the roads in such a state.

The sun was barely above the horizon when they arrived and went inside, after Sarah requested the driver to return to pick them up at four in the afternoon. Katy withheld her true opinion with an effort. The apprentices, whatever their names might be, seemed not to know how to function together. It only took a heartbeat for Sarah to take charge.

"You there, what are your names and what are your

assigned tasks?" She folded her fingers into a single fist in front of her and waited.

Katy could only grin as her mother made order out of chaos. As the boys—she really couldn't call them men at that age—buckled down to work, her mother turned to her. "Now, how about you put this place to rights?"

Housekeeping. Of course. At least it was something she knew how to do and could do without any instruction.

"I'll get started, Mother."

"And I'll confer with your brother about my role here as well." Her mother winked at her. "Don't worry, my darling, we'll make this work. You'll see."

Katy wasn't worried about how her mother might settle in to the new routine. Nor how she might do so as well. No, the bigger concern was, how long would her wandering, easily distracted younger brother stay in one place this time?

Katy stowed the straw broom beside the rear door of the print shop, letting it bump against the doorframe. Swiping a hand across her damp brow, she dried the sweat on her apron. She'd finally finished straightening and cleaning the shop. The ink spill had proved the biggest challenge, but she even managed to conquer its dark puddle staining the wooden floor. Once the mess had been mopped up and the rags discarded, she'd used vinegar and more rags to blot up the remaining stain. It was messy and took longer than she'd figured, but now the floor was clean. The apprentices continued to create their messes as they went about their work, but at least one could walk across the floor without stepping on a sundry of scraps.

"It's nearly time to go home for the day, my dear." Her mother's voice carried across the room from where she stood by the counter. She'd been reviewing the ledgers for the past hours, making adjustments and notations. "Have you finished?"

Katy bobbed her head as she started across the floor to join her mother. "I've done as much as I can for today. I'll tackle the windows tomorrow."

She eased toward the front door with its little bell dangling above to announce customers. The work tables as well as the slanted composing tables gleamed in the late afternoon sunlight filtering through the grimy windows. She'd labored to ensure every piece of furniture was clean and ready for use, working around the apprentices and her brother as needed. It wasn't always easy, and she had to wait to work in certain areas at any particular moment. Ultimately, she'd succeeded in sprucing up the cramped shop to be more inviting for customers and the workers alike.

"Very well." Sarah looked to where William, muttering under his breath, was working on realigning the carriage of the press so it would slide smoothly. "William, we are leaving. Do you need for us to see to anything else prior to our departure?"

With a heavy sigh, William straightened. He fixed a distracted glare at her before blinking the glaze from his eyes. "I'm sorry, Mother. This apparatus is being rather difficult at the moment and we're under deadline to have this ready to go to print in the morning. Word of the continued fighting in the Ohio Country is troubling, and the myriad calls for an end to the French and Indian War are clamoring to be heard. But this press is making that difficult. As for you and Katy, you may as well go on home. I can't imagine either of you could help fix this mess. We'll wrap up everything here in preparation for printing it on the morrow." He half-bowed at her with a smirk on his lips.

Sarah bristled but remained calm. "Thank you. We have

much to do to settle into our new home." She surged out from behind the counter to join Katy by the door, the long skirts of her dark gray day dress swishing agitatedly around her ankles as she came to a halt. Somber brown eyes filled with suppressed ire leveled on William. "Until tomorrow then."

William tapped two fingers to his brow and then turned back to his repair.

How rude of him. Not even wishing them a good evening. And what was it with his comment about them not helping fix a mess? The tone he used rankled her last nerve. But then, it was William. He tended to feel his wants and desires, his issues and concerns, were all far more important than any others. She'd really hoped he would have outgrown such immature behavior.

Katy opened the door for her mother to precede her outside to look for the expected cab driver. The large coach was pulled by a pair of chestnut draft horses, stamping their shaggy hooves on the muddy street. Her shoes pinched her tired feet as they picked their way around puddles to where the burly man held the door open for them to step up and inside. Katy couldn't stop the long sigh from escaping her lips as she sank onto the thinly cushioned seat. At least she hadn't been required to work until sunset like the apprentices. Sunup to sundown made for a very long day in the summertime. Her mother eased onto the facing seat and the driver closed the door.

Sarah regarded her for a long moment and then nodded. "I can fairly hear your thoughts, Katy. I know he can be brusque at times, but men are not as polite as we might wish sometimes. I tried to instruct him on being genteel, but you can only do so much. Now, on to other matters. When we get home, my dear, I'd like to speak with you about our plans for the house. And another topic." Sarah smoothed and arranged her skirts with both hands.

The way she'd said "another topic" sounded like something serious. Was she in trouble for something? She had not suffered her mother's ire in many a year. When she was a child, she'd earned her correction frequently, but she thought she'd outgrown such chastisements now that she'd reached her twenties. But her mother's tone suggested she had a weighty subject to discuss.

"What other topic?" She worried her lips for a brief moment before reclaiming a sense of calm.

"That can wait until we're home." Her mother winked at her with a grin on her face. "It's not something I wish to discuss when there is a possibility of being overheard and perhaps misunderstood."

With that enigmatic statement, the coach lurched into noisy motion. She softly hummed a hymn. Katy pondered what her mother might be about to broach with her but couldn't fathom where her thoughts may have strayed. Plans for the house, that was an entirely different subject. She had ideas for furnishing and decorating her room, for instance. She could envision improving the furnishings in the dining room, too. What had been installed by the landlord was serviceable, but since they planned to live there for some time to come, it made perfect sense to make it comfortable and reflective of their status in society.

However, perhaps their status changed when they moved from where her father had established his residence and presence in the community. As the doctor and postmaster, he'd commanded respect and deference. Her mother's role as postmistress after her husband died ensured the continuation of the same status for the family. Moving to a new city, a larger city, meant they were not known by the society nor therefore as respected. The money Sarah inherited from her husband would keep them living comfortably for a while. And of course, William was paying the rent on their new home. But was moving to help her brother actually a step down? Is that why William found barely adequate accommodations for them? She'd have to wait and see whether William could follow in their father's footsteps by establishing the level of acceptance, if not deference, they once enjoyed.

Katy kept her musings to herself as she didn't want to potentially upset her mother with her imaginings. Especially if she were in fact making a fuss about nothing or being foolish. One thing she'd learned from her mother was how to put on a brave, serene countenance. The result of doing so seemed to encourage others to like and perhaps even admire her to some degree. Such regard paved the way for stronger relationships since one didn't appear weak and needy.

The cab stopped then rocked as the driver dismounted from his seat to open the door for the ladies. Sarah accepted his hand to assist her to the street. Katy trailed after her, her mind still all a spin with her ponderings. If only she had a friend to confide in, to sort out the muddle in her brain. How she missed her friends back in New London.

"First, let's get settled for the evening and then we can discuss our thoughts on how we want to change the furnishings in the house. We need to make it our own." Her mother led the way briskly to the front door, which opened with a slight squeal as she stepped up on the lone step serving as a refuge from the muddy street.

Mr. McTavish waved them inside, stepping back to allow them to pass. Katy smiled at him with a dip of her head. "Thank you."

"Miss." His deep voice echoed in the mostly barren entryway.

Her mother started up the staircase to go to her

bedchamber. She glanced over her shoulder. "Katy, meet me in the sitting room in a few minutes. I'd like your opinion."

"Yes, Mother." Katy hurried up the stairs after her mother's retreating figure, and on to her room to change into a clean dress suitable for relaxing at home. She'd have Patsy clean the one she'd just removed so it would be available for later. After all, she only had a half dozen or so dresses in total. Instead of her leather shoes, she slipped on a pair of satin slippers, which her tired feet thanked her for. Then she made her way to the room where her mother waited for her.

"There you are." Her mother swept an arm to indicate the contents of the entire room. "We can't replace everything, since it's not ours, but we can store some items in the attic and add some pieces here and there. Ones that we find attractive, comfortable, appropriate."

The furniture in question—a loveseat, two cushioned chairs, several low tables with candlesticks on them—was worn and faded. Indeed, the side tables had marks where hot wax had marred the dark wood surface. She let her gaze travel around the room, noting the chipped white marble mantel over the cold fireplace. Like the entry, the walls showed signs of where framed portraits once hung. Heavy maroon drapes hung at the two front windows, while the glass had rippled from the flow of the material over time making it hard to see through the panes.

She brought her regard to her mother's patient expression. "There is much we could do here to improve the presentation. Like a runner on the mantel to hide the chip at the end, and put some flowers or statues on it to decorate it. Plus some portraits on the walls, which will hide most of the tracings of previous ones until we can arrange for the walls to be repapered or repainted."

"Yes, those are fine ideas. What do you think of adding some flowered wool slipcovers to hide the faded seating and make a more pleasant appearance?" Sarah moved to touch the upholstered chair nearest to where she'd been standing.

"That would serve us well, I believe."

"Yes, I'll make some inquiries into a seamstress who can make some for us as soon as possible." She met Katy's gaze with a tilt of her head. "I think that's enough to begin with since we cannot upturn the entire house at one time. As to the other matter... Follow me." Her mother turned and strode out of the parlor, down the long hallway, and out the back door into the rear yard.

She didn't stop until she was standing on a path that wound around and through the plentiful garden. A combination of vegetables, flowers, and herbs created a blend of scents to assault Katy's nose as she stopped beside her mother. While not as knowledgeable about plants as she might be, she could identify bean poles and asparagus mounds among many other plants and supports. Rosemary and mint bushes also added their familiar aromas. She hadn't ventured out back of the house and so found the garden lovely to look at and delightful to inhale.

"Now, before anyone comes looking for us, my dear, I have something I'd like to suggest to you."

"Yes, Mother?" It would be rude to start humming, but she could think of the tune at least.

Her mother gave her a sharp look and then allowed a gentle smile to grace her mouth. "Life has taught me how important it is for us to be capable of managing our own affairs if the need arises. I had your father to look after me for many wonderful years, but once he passed I had to manage his affairs, the estate, and still care for you and your brother. Thankfully, I had learned how to do so from your loving father who planned ahead for that possibility. So I'm suggesting to you that you do the same. Begin to learn a trade. The one most readily at hand is the printing business.

You already have some experience helping in a post office, with the books and the management of an office in general. But I believe it would behoove you to consider being more actively involved in operating the press itself. Knowledge is the foundation of everyone's future. The more you know, the better off you'll be in this world."

Katy stared at her mother for several long moments, jumbled thoughts rattling around in her head at the suggestion. A woman printer. Was that even possible? Wouldn't she be laughed out of the building if she were to suggest such a thing to her brother? He had little regard for her abilities, after all. Then again, she'd never really applied herself to learn a trade. Come to think on it more, it didn't look that complicated though operating the bigger press was physically challenging. The other tasks associated with the process she could handle easily. Composing the text being both intriguing and relatively easy to perform. She might need to let the men handle loading and closing the press to print the pages. Maybe. Why not?

"So what do you think?" Her mother folded her arms and tapped a finger on her elbow.

"I think you have a good idea. I'll have to really think about it, though, before I say anything to William. He may not take it well. He's reluctant to admit that I am quicker to catch on to new things. But it would give me something more useful and perhaps important to do than sew and clean. And do charity works." She hesitated for a second before continuing. "I would like to find some local good works to become involved in so that perhaps I can start making new friends here. I really miss my friends in New London."

"I understand. We'll see if we can find something fitting." Her mother drew in a long breath and released it. "I'm glad to get that all out in the open. Now, shall we go in and enjoy Cook's delicious meal?"

As she strode arm-in-arm with her mother back toward the house, Katy wondered what had prompted her mother's concern on her behalf. Her suggestion wasn't a bad idea but she'd have to think about—if she really wanted to get elbows-deep in ink and paper and books—how on earth she'd raise the idea with her volatile and often jealous brother.

CHAPTER 2

PROVIDENCE, RHODE ISLAND – 1762

few busy days passed with Katy working alongside her mother and brother to keep the print shop inviting to customers. A steady stream of businessmen and government officials came and went. Her mother took charge of receiving the various orders from the clientele, whether an advertisement to promote another merchant's business, or blank forms to use for a government department, or to print a pamphlet. Essays related to the ongoing war, its high cost in both lives and money, also were submitted by residents to have printed for them to pass out to spread their opinions with others in the community. William oversaw the apprentices as the guys worked on typesetting the gallery forms using the racks of upper- and lower-cases of type available. The large mechanical press at the back of the room was kept busy all day long. A flourishing business and yet William had expressed his displeasure at the lack of sufficient customers to sustain it. Would he never be satisfied?

Katy dried her hands on her smudged cream-colored apron after rinsing them off using the bucket of water kept by the back door for that purpose. She'd added the small table with its bucket and ladle, a small stack of towels beside it for the others to use instead of their pants. She couldn't tolerate seeing them be so uncouth as to leave wet handprints on their pantlegs. Not a good look for the boys when customers ventured inside.

She looked around the crowded room, seeking any small cleaning tasks she might have overlooked. Not finding any, she crossed the room to talk to her mother between customers.

"Mother, I've been thinking about what you suggested the other day." Katy didn't elaborate further since her mother had wanted that conversation kept between them. She'd thought about the concept nonstop since her mother had suggested learning a trade. "I agree."

"Good choice, my dear." Her mother nodded as she dipped the quill pen into the ink pot on the counter. Adding some notation on the paper before her, she then put the quill in the stand and addressed Katy directly. "What convinced you?"

Many thoughts had crossed Katy's mind over the past several days. One thing she realized was the importance of the press to the community. Having the ability to share information, government proceedings, news from around the globe, as well as literature all improved the people and society in general. She wanted to be part of such a positive influence.

She'd also thought about how her mother had always seemed to be in control of herself in such a way as to instill confidence in those who worked with her. Which was most apparent when she stepped into her father's shoes to run the post office in New London. After watching and learning how her husband had managed the affairs of the office, she seamlessly took over the operation. Her father, too, had effectively carried his respectable weight in the community to bear on both his medical practice and his work in the post office. Unlike her short-tempered brother, her father had maintained a calm demeanor and approach to everything he did. Her parents provided a solid example for her to follow. With her mother's advice in mind, Katy had made her decision.

"I want to be capable of providing for myself. I don't wish to rely upon a husband or even my brother to provide for me." Katy stepped closer to her mother, leaning closer to whisper her next statement. "I want to be as independent as possible. I don't know that I'll ever marry as a result."

Her mother whispered back, "Does that have anything to do with...?"

Richard. Poor, poor Richard. The memory of his last day on earth swept through her with a rush of pain straight to her heart and soul. He'd been expected at her house to escort her out for what he had called a "special" dinner but he never arrived. Instead, his younger brother came to the door to convey that Richard Smallwood had been murdered by highwaymen, beaten and robbed and left by the side of the road. A horrific way to die. The love of her life was no more. The brother told her, through his own tears, that Richard had planned to offer for her hand over that special dinner.

She couldn't contain the sobbing and tears that erupted with the shocking revelation. She'd attended the funeral days later with her parents, crying tears of devastation at the realization their loving future together would never happen. His family had tried to console her, but nobody could bring him back to her so she was inconsolable for months. She'd finally cried herself out and vowed to honor his memory stoically. Live her life cherishing the love they had shared. Her eyes smarted now but she swallowed back the tears. She'd stilled the inner voice longing for a loving husband and decided marriage simply wasn't her destiny.

Lifting her chin, she cleared her throat and nodded. "A large part, yes. But also seeing how you have conducted your life inspires me to mimic your example. I wish to be like you."

"That's sweet of you to say." Sarah embraced Katy for a long moment before stepping back to peer at her. "Have you told William of your intent?"

Katy swallowed the nervous lump in her throat. "Not yet. Do you think he'll accept my suggestion?"

"We'll make sure of it. Come, let's inform him, shall we?"

Katy strode beside her mother, a soft murmur vibrating her throat, clasping her hands together before her skirts. When they reached William, who was composing the galley form of a broadside, she stopped beside him. Also on his desk was the text of the 1763 Almanack to be printed and distributed later in the year. She could tell the almanack was a big job. Maybe he'd let her help with completing it. Her mother stayed at her side but remained quiet, gesturing with a wave of her hand for Katy to proceed.

"William, I wish to speak with you for a moment." She waited until he laid down the composing stick, a narrow length of wood with channels for placing the bits of type. She swallowed the nervous lump in her throat. How would he respond to her request?

"I only have a moment, so please speak your piece." William crossed his arms over his chest and waited, his eyes darting from Katy to her mother and back again as he tapped a finger on his elbow. "Quickly if you please. I need to finish this broadside to release tomorrow."

"What are you working on?" Sarah edged closer to peer over his shoulder at the text written on a sheet of paper. "The news that just came in?"

"Yes, indeed. The fall of Morro Castle in Havana, Cuba."

William frowned as he cast a glance at the handwritten notice of the tragic event.

"Important news to share with our community." Sarah straightened so she wasn't peering over her son's shoulder.

"Oh my, that's going to make many people either elated or dismayed, depending on whether they're rooting for the British or the Spanish." Katy shook her head slowly. Why was there so much fighting around the world? Why was her king and country trying to expand their presence in so many parts of the world? Didn't they already have enough territories and possessions? "I know we should be rooting for the British, but Spain will suffer because of that defeat."

"British influence is spreading across the Caribbean, and defeating the Spanish will enable them to grow even more. Just watch. The British win will lead to Spain being ousted from Cuba and Spanish Florida. But we'll have to wait and see if that actually happens. Now, what did you want to talk to me about?"

Her brother's dismissive attitude toward the dramatic shift in the politics of the southern regions rankled. She couldn't help but think of how such a change would impact the residents of the areas being fought over. Just like what was happening in the Ohio Country not all that far from where she now lived. From what she'd heard, there was a new push to end the war but still it kept going. But like all of those watching from the outside, she had no control over any of it. Perhaps that's why her brother brushed it aside. Maybe he wasn't actually dismissing it so much as choosing to focus on matters he had some measure of control over. Like her desire to learn a trade.

Katy stiffened her spine and lifted her chin a tad. "I would like to learn to do what you are doing." She indicated the boxy composing stick and galley form on the slanted table in front of William. "I want to help with everything and not just clean up after everyone all the time."

William blinked at her slowly several times, his head tilting to one side as he regarded her silently. "Well, now. What would you want to do that for? You've got it easy as is."

"I need more to occupy my time, for one thing. And I'd prefer to be more useful to you and Mother. Please? Teach me? You know I learn new things quickly."

They'd both been taught by their mother the basics of a solid education: mathematics, world history, an appreciation of literature, penmanship, music, and art. Additionally, because Sarah had a French tutor as a girl, they'd learned French and Latin at her side. She'd even attended public school to learn science, too. Katy had devoured every book in her parents' library, reading many of them several times until the history or geography was stamped in her memory. William had struggled more but eventually equaled her in having a stellar education. Though he never did enjoy working with numbers and equations.

"I don't know about whether it's a good idea." William inhaled and exhaled before replying. "If you're serious, then let's just see how readily you can learn to compose text. But I won't stand for any sloppy work, you understand?"

"I'll do my utmost to please you, William." Elated he'd accepted her request so easily, Katy grinned. "Show me what to do."

"Pay close attention. I'll only tell you this once." He sighed heavily as he studied her. "Understood?"

"Yes, William. Please tell me."

"So this is a composing stick," William said, showing her the tool while picking up the tray. "And this is where you put the type." He pointed the tip of the stick at the individual pieces of the type. "Notice that they are in backwards? That's because when the type is inked and applied to paper, then you'll be able to read the words left to right as usual. Understand?"

"Yes."

"Now, the type cases hold the more frequently used letters—a, i, s, e—in the large center part, and less frequently used letters—like z, q, and x—in the smaller sections around the outside of the case. If you run out of any particular sort of letter, you'll need to wait until one of the lads has finished printing their job in order to have more of that sort. Got it?"

"Yes. Can I try?" Her fingers itched to take hold of the instrument and begin. To prove to her brother that she could do as well or better than his apprentices.

"Do you even know how to hold the composing stick properly? How to empty it without dropping the type on the ground?"

His tone suggested he didn't think she knew anything about what he did. But she'd been watching him and the boys for a while now and it seemed simple enough. Hold the stick in her left hand and use the thumb to secure each bit of type as she added the type with her right hand, being sure the type was upside down and in mirror image of the desired result. Then once the composing stick was full, put the lines of text into the galley and repeat the process until the page was all type set. Then tie the full page of text with twine to hold everything together, slide the unit off the galley, and type set the next page of the quarto or whatever size paper being used until the entire sheet was type set. Then add the decorative bits and headlines, lock the pages into the chase, a metal frame, using a mallet to insert wooden wedges into the space between the page and the frame to keep the type from shifting in the printing of the full sheet. Then off to the press it went. Many steps, but nothing onerous for goodness sake.

"I believe so. Like I said, I'm a quick study."

In answer, William rose from his stool and handed her

the composing stick before pointing at the draft text he was working from. "Continue from there."

She sat on the stool and quickly perused the cases of the type for various fonts used in the documents and other forms. Selecting a capital letter from the upper case, she placed it into the galley and then chose the next letter, a lower case one. As she grew more familiar with which letters were located in which little boxes holding the type, her fingers flew faster and faster. Speed helped them keep on schedule with the jobs in the queue.

After a few minutes, William cleared his throat, a scowl on his face. "I think you've got the idea. You finish this sheet while I start the next one."

"Very well." She put a hand on his arm to stop him from turning away. "Thank you, William."

Joy swelled in her heart as she continued filling the galley and creating the page units to use for the actual printing of the document. The more she did the quicker she could select and place the type in the composing stick. The more accomplished she felt, thoughts of what other tasks she'd learn to do filled her head. But most importantly, she'd taken the first real step to being in charge of her own life. What would the next step be?

"There are several different fonts you can use for any given project." William jabbed with his forefinger at the multiple frames holding the cases of type. "This font is used for headlines, this one for subheads, and then these others for the body of text. Then there are also decorative bits and separator bars."

Katy leaned closer to the divided cases, each small box containing a quantity of individual letters and numbers.

The pungent tang of the ink in the bottle nearby flooded her senses. She was grateful that it was the job of one of the apprentices to "rub" the lampblack into the varnish each morning to create the ink for the day's work. The smell was noisome to her. She hoped it wouldn't cause her head to ache, which would impede her from keeping her wits about her. "How do you decide which one to use for the body?"

He shrugged. "It depends on the desired end result. You will hopefully develop an eye for what looks pleasing as you grow more accustomed to using the different styles. We'll see."

His tone suggested she would fail in acquiring such an eye. She'd prove him wrong. "I wish I had that ability now."

"You've been composing for a month, so the concept may escape you." William tapped the table with his forefinger. "If you keep your eyes open and pay attention to how other documents are composed, perhaps one day you'll succeed in comprehending how to make the layout pleasing."

"Yes, William, I will do that and strive to meet your standards." She kept her hurt feelings to herself given the lack of support and charity contained in his observations of her ability.

The last month had flown by. Each day yielded a new challenge with different projects being brought in by the customers. She'd worked on completing the many galley pages for the almanack. Also several pamphlets and broadsides. But she had more to learn to be completely trained on how a print shop operated. His denigration only spurred her to reach higher in her efforts.

"Do you think I could start doing the business and legal forms? They seem fairly easy and that would take some pressure off of you with the bigger jobs."

"I suppose. If you can manage them, then I'd have more

time for my other pursuits. Including the new newspaper I plan to start publishing."

"A newspaper? What would you put in it?" She suppressed a sigh of annoyance. A new venture for her brother. He was always looking for another thing to work on. "I mean, will you be seeking the information yourself?"

"I will keep my eyes and ears open, yes. But also I plan to subscribe to other newspapers across the colonies and around the world, then share pertinent information from them." William studied her for a long moment. "You might assist with gleaning information from your daily life as well."

"Me? I have yet to make any connections in this place. But if I do, I'd be happy to contribute to your new venture." She angled her head as she peered at her brother. "What are you going to call it?"

"I've been debating that for some time. What do you think of, '*Providence Gazette, or Country Journal*'?"

She nodded in agreement with the proposed title. "And when do you want to publish this paper?"

"I've been working on a broadside announcing all of my plans for the new paper. Here, look at what I've drafted so far."

He pulled a sheet of paper from the edge of his desk and handed it to her. It read:

To the Publick. As the Colony of Rhode-Island from its first Institution to this present Time, has been remarkable for maintaining the Spirit of true British Liberty, I purpose to carry on the Printing Business in this Town, provided I meet with Encouragement as it is universally acknowledged a Printer is much wanted in this Place, very considerable Sums being annually sent into other Governments for Printing, to the Impoverishment of this town.

Gentlemen and ladies, As soon as possible I purpose to print a Weekly News-Paper, under the Title of the Providence Gazette, or Country Journal, to be publish'd every Wednesday Morning. The Price will be only Seven Shillings Lawful Money, per Annum. It is intended the Paper shall make its first Appearance on Wednesday the Twentieth of October, in Case a sufficient Number of Subscribers shall offer the Publick's Devoted Humble Servant, William Goddard.

She looked up from reading the announcement to see him smiling. "When do you intend to print this?"

"The last day of the month, Tuesday, August thirty-first. That will allow seven weeks to acquire subscribers before we publish the first edition."

"That's a smart plan." She clasped her hands together as she thought through his intention. "And you'll have time to obtain other newspaper subscriptions in the meantime."

"I've already begun doing that so I can start gathering information to populate the pages of my paper."

"What will the colophon say? Something like, 'Printed by William Goddard at Providence, Rhode Island,' perhaps?"

"I've thought about that, too. I plan to be more precise than that as a form of advertisement for the press." He held up his hands as if bracketing the text between them. "Thus, 'Printed by William Goddard, at the Printing-Office near the Great Bridge, where Subscriptions, Advertisements and Letters of Intelligence, &c. are received for this Paper; and where all Manner of printing Work is performed with Care and Expedition.' What do you think of that?"

She started to reply when the little bell above the front door jingled. Katy turned to see a man and a woman come into the shop. Her mother greeted them as per her usual friendly custom. The woman looked to be about Katy's age, so she deduced the man must be her father.

"Good afternoon, sir. How may I help you?" Sarah greeted them.

"Good afternoon. My name is John Wythe and this is my daughter, Miss Joan Wythe. We represent a troupe of actors who will be performing at the town square. Can you print up a play-bill circular to announce the performance?"

A play? How intriguing. Katy had enjoyed going to the theatre in New London with her friends. She'd not had an opportunity to do so since moving to Providence. Didn't know there was a theatre, for that matter. Was there one? Either way, she couldn't ignore the chance to learn more about the upcoming performance. Katy walked across the shop to stand beside her mother at the counter. She smiled at Joan who returned the gesture.

"Of course, sir. How many do you want us to print?" Sarah wrote in a small notebook the details of the order, pausing for Mr. Wythe's answer.

While the man completed his order with her mother, Katy moved to address Joan directly. "Will you be attending the play?"

Joan moistened her lips before replying. "Yes, I am looking forward to it. You should come."

"What will they be performing?" Hope fluttered inside as she waited for the other woman's reply. Could she possibly attend given the amount of work coming into the shop? But curiosity wouldn't let her remain silent.

"William Shakespeare's *The Merchant of Venice*. It should be wonderful. I hope you can make it. Several of my friends will be there as well. If you can get off from work, of course."

Katy looked up when her mother cleared her throat. The smile encouraged Katy to accept the invitation. She really would like to accept, to have the chance to make some new friends. She glanced at William and he nodded in agreement. Love for her family swelled her heart. Very well.

"Thank you. I will look forward to joining you and your friends tomorrow for the performance."

"That's wonderful. Meet me at the southwest corner of the square half an hour before the stated time." Joan pointed to the draft of the playbill on the counter. "I'm happy you will be able to attend."

"I am, as well. Thank you for the invitation."

"I'm glad I came with Father today. I have a feeling we will be good friends."

"I would like that." Katy wiped her right hand on her apron then reached out toward Joan, who clasped it with her own. "My first friend in Providence."

"I'm sure you'll make more. Indeed, I imagine my friends will all want to be friends with you."

"You're very kind to say so. We shall see." She squeezed Joan's fingers and then released her hand. "Until tomorrow."

"Yes. Until then, my new friend." Joan's pleased expression confirmed her sentiment.

"Ready, Joan?" Mr. Wythe said as he turned away from the counter, tucking a folded paper into his pocket.

"Yes, Father." Joan preceded her father out of the shop.

Katy's smile lingered on her lips for several beats. She finally turned to go back to the project at hand, but her inner joy continued to buoy her mood for the rest of the day.

CHAPTER 3

PROVIDENCE, RHODE ISLAND – 1762

The next afternoon proved hotter than she'd expected. She trudged as gracefully as her over-heated person could toward the rendezvous location on the town square. She'd donned her prettiest summer-weight dress, its long, light blue skirts swishing around her pragmatic leather shoes. She hoped the sweat trickling down her back didn't show through the fabric. Dust floated up with each hurried step she took. It hadn't rained in a week, and everything was covered in dust. Her cream-colored bonnet shaded her face from the harsh sunlight but nothing could protect her from the summer heat. Perhaps standing outside in the sun to watch a play wasn't the best of ideas on such a steamy afternoon. But she had promised, and she always kept her word. Besides, she wanted to make some friends. Life would be boring if she didn't have anyone to enjoy it with.

As she neared the specified corner, she saw Joan standing with a cluster of three young women, all wearing pastel linseywoolsey dresses that brushed the newly paved street. She picked up her pace, glad to enjoy the benefits of the firm surface. Her brother had made a point of telling her about how the main streets used to turn to mud and potholes, making them nearly impassable, before last year's lotteries raised enough money to finally fix the highest trafficked streets in the city. Providence was a progressive place.

Katy lifted a hand to wave at the women, and Joan waved back. Off to one side, Katy noticed another group of people, all men dressed in dark suits, black bibles in their hands. They must be broiling in the sun, wearing such dark attire. With their grim expressions and stoic clothing, they were probably with one of the local churches. Deacons, perhaps? Or ministers? Why were they hanging out on the corner?

"I love your pretty dress, Miss Goddard." Joan stepped forward to greet Katy as she joined the group of friends. "Let me introduce you to everyone. I'm pleased for you to meet Miss Susan Norris, Miss Mary Allen, and Miss Patrice Williams."

The three young ladies smiled at her as Joan introduced them. Susan's dark eyes danced with mirth, like she knew a particularly juicy secret. Mary's pale countenance was serene and calm, more standoffish than the others. While Patrice, a petite waif of a girl, surged forward to give her a quick hug before stepping back. Becoming acquainted with each of them would surely be quite pleasant given their friendly behavior.

"It's nice to meet all of you." Would they all become friends as Joan had suggested? She hoped such a boon would come to pass. "Thank you for inviting me to join you for the play."

Mary stepped closer to squeeze Katy's hand and then released it. "I'm so pleased you could come. I hope we'll be good friends."

"Yes, indeed." Patrice nodded briskly and clasped her hands together. "We get together often to play whist or to attend a concert or have a picnic lunch in the park. You must join us for those pastimes as well."

"That sounds very enjoyable, but it will depend on whether I am needed at the print shop." Katy shrugged lightly, slight regret sifting through her. "I moved here specifically to help in my brother's shop, but I'll do what I can."

"Of course," Susan said. "We'll always invite and you do what you must."

"Yes, I'm sure she'll try. Come, let's find a spot where we can enjoy the performance." Joan motioned to the others and they started walking down the street.

Before long they joined a growing number of people just off the town's square. An area had been roped off with a makeshift stage taking up the center of the space. Some actors milled about the gathering crowd, talking and laughing, apparently acting as living advertisements for the upcoming performance. Their costumes harkened back to the past with rich colors and embellishments. Katy rather envied them. To be able to step outside of your own life and inhabit someone else's. What must it be like to become someone other than yourself?

She would never know, of course. Her mother would not condone such behavior. Actors had an air of decadence about them. And they were typically men and boys, as well. But she could enjoy the efforts of others to entertain through their playacting.

"Miss Wythe, do you know who those men are over there?" Katy inclined her head toward the group that had just moved closer to the stage. "They don't seem like they're enjoying themselves."

Joan turned her head to see who Katy meant. "Oh, they always attend in the hopes of dissuading people from watching. The Puritans around here object to theatre, and won't allow one to be built. Which is why the troupe is forced to perform outdoors like this."

"But it's Shakespeare. Why would they object to such a revered playwright's work?" Katy cast a quick glance at the dark-clad men. "I don't understand."

"Nobody really does. Ignore them." Joan waved them off with a dismissive gesture of her hand. "They're getting ready to begin."

A gray-bearded man in a bright blue suit with flashy yellow shirt and white cravat appeared from behind the stage. A pair of burly stage hands maneuvered a glossy harpsichord into place beside the stage. A stool was produced and the man sat down and began to play a lively tune.

"Who is that?" Katy asked Patrice.

"Mr. Johnson. He travels with the troupe and plays the musical pieces for them." Patrice kept her eyes on the older man as he continued to play. "Once he starts playing, it lures others out to find out what is happening, and so the audience continues to grow."

"He plays beautifully." Katy couldn't keep a smile from her lips as the music filled the air around her. The upbeat tune was quite catchy, too. She'd add it to her own private repertoire. "Oh, those three men are stepping onto the stage. Let's listen."

"Have you seen this one before?" Joan asked. "Do you know who the characters are, I mean?"

"I've read the play but I haven't seen it acted out before."

"That's Antonio, Salarino, and Salanio to open the play. Shh. Here we go!"

Katy rocked up on her toes for a moment to better see, over the crowd, the three actors as they began reciting their lines. The story was familiar to her and yet seeing real people on stage acting out the words, their movement and sound of their voices, always made a play truly come to life. Merely reading plays would never be enough of an experience. She was besotted by their performance. She couldn't wait to share her experience with her mother. But she didn't want to rush through the play either.

Then it struck her that this was an experience worthy of putting in her brother's new paper. She paid even closer attention so she could relay specific details to him when she returned to the print shop. She'd become a sponge for any and all information she could glean from the world she lived in. Joy filled her soul. She had found her life's purpose.

With great care, Katy selected the title font to begin laying out Governor Samuel Ward's proclamation as a broadside. She squashed the errant shaft of pride that made her hand tremble. No time for such feelings when she needed to do the best work possible. History was in the making, by her efforts to compose the words of the governor so that it could be printed and copied, shared all around. The invention of a printing press had revolutionized communication and the need for literacy around the globe. She felt the weight of the importance of what she created with each choice she made. She didn't want to embarrass herself or her brother by doing a poor job. Who knew what historic documents she'd have a hand in making. Maybe even this simple proclamation would prove important. She paused in her composing to read the draft of the proclamation again, the better to plan the flow and layout.

> By the Honorable Samuel Ward, Esquire, Governor, Captain General, and Commander in Chief of and over the English Colony of Rhode-Island, and Providence Plantations, in New-England, in America. A Proclamation.

She'd already placed the device for the coat of arms for George III at the top center of the galley. Then she'd composed the main heading. Now she just needed to fill in the rest of the text in nice orderly rows. She had chosen to mix the English and long primer types in a way to provide a contrast to the contents. She continued her work, all while aware of the intense effort on the other side of the room. William and his new lead apprentice, Bartholomew Wyatt, were feverishly composing the first edition of the newspaper.

Shortly after Katy and her mother had arrived to help at the print shop, changes had been made to the slovenly crew of apprentices. Her mother had kept one of them but urged William to replace the others with more able boys and young men. Now the print shop hummed with a steady flow of work. Composing the galley form for various sizes of output, inking the tray, laying the paper on top of the galley, then operating the press to imprint the type onto the paper. Then another lad would hang the wet sheet over one of the ropes strung across the ceiling to dry. And so on. But they were still learning their trade.

"No, not like that." William roared his disapproval at the unfortunate lad. "Here. Give me that." He grabbed the composing stick from the stocky boy and dumped out its contents and began again. "You must pay attention to the finer details to ensure the finished work is as polished and refined as possible. The press's reputation is everything and we do not want to provide an inferior product. Even Miss Goddard does better than that. Be precise and careful. Understand?"

"Yes, sir." Bart stoically stood straight beside her incensed brother, his attention firmly on the demonstration of how to properly compose the type for the multi-column newspaper.

Katy silently applauded the lad's brave stance in the face

of William's unnecessary ire. Even though she rather resented the backhanded compliment. "Even" she did better? She huffed to herself in disgust. He'd never learned to control his temper, and one day it would land him in real trouble. The thought of what might occur between William and a customer he objected to, perhaps for what they wanted to put into the new paper or even if they refused to pay what was owed, made her feel bad. She hoped she was wrong.

She turned her attention back to the broadside and soon was finishing arranging the type. She scanned her final efforts with a keen eye for any misalignments.

> Given under my Hand at Newport, this Fifth Day of November, in the Year of our Lord One Thousand Seven Hundred and Sixty-two, and Third of the Reign of His most Sacred Majesty George the Third, by the Grace of God, King of Great-Britain, and so forth. Sam. Ward. By His Honor's Command, Henry Ward, Secr'y, God Save the King.

Satisfied, she laid down the composing stick and turned to call to her brother. "William, it's finished. Do you want to approve it?"

With a sharp nod, William handed back the composing stick to Bart who remained waiting at his side. "Continue in such a manner and don't be sloppy about it." Then he rose from the stool and marched across the room to peruse her work.

She waited with bated breath, confident in the quality of her work but yet fearful he'd find fault nonetheless. Was her brother capable of actually giving her praise for her efforts? After a few moments of his close inspection, he nodded slowly as he met her gaze.

"That will do. The Governor will be pleased, I'm sure." He patted her shoulder briefly before summoning another of his new apprentices. "Mr. Hollis, prepare this for printing. One hundred copies. They must be ready for the Governor on the ninth of November. So let's get busy."

The strong young man tapped for the job quickly moved to carry the unit closer to the press. Fred had come to them from a widowed woman in need of a proper education for her son. His blond hair was pulled into a queue tied with a black ribbon. Fred's wide shoulders stretched the fabric of the tan work shirt he wore. Moreover, the youth had a pleasant demeanor and positive attitude. Her mother was very pleased with how quickly Fred had taken to the printing trade.

"How's the paper coming along?" She wiped her hands on her apron, adding fresh ink smears to the fabric. "Will it be ready on time?"

"I won't tolerate not having it ready, so yes. The first edition of the *Gazette* will go out on October twentieth as promised." William frowned as he watched Bart working on the last page of the paper across the shop floor. "I think we're close."

With that, he marched back across the room to peer over the lad's shoulder at the galley he was quickly filling in with the final text of the newspaper. After a minute or two, the lad sat back and looked up at William. Her brother inspected the boy's work and then nodded once.

"Let's get this to the press so we can print out the copies and assemble the paper for distribution to our subscribers." William motioned for the apprentices to gather around him. The four lads quickly gathered in a half circle in front of him. "Now, listen to me."

Was he going to chastise them yet again? It seemed like they could never do anything the way he wanted it done. Katy felt bad for the boys. Most were under fifteen, though one young man, Nick Butler, had reached the age of seventeen. Being apprenticed meant living far from home and family. William had been so very lonely when he first started his apprenticeship. It took years before he really settled in and felt like the master and his kin were another kind of family. But that first year had been vastly difficult. He'd written many a letter filled with sorrow and fear of being so far from home. How did these young men feel about their situation? She was not in any position to inquire about their personal feelings. The only thing she could do was to be kind to them.

"You all have been doing a good job, but I want to teach you how to do a great job. It will take diligence and attention but I believe you're each capable of meeting my expectations." William paused to slide his gaze over the lads, then met Katy's eyes. "You all are fully able to do the best job this town has ever seen. I can tell from your efforts to date. Thank you."

The compliment shining in his eyes as he regarded her for a long moment warmed her heart. In that moment, she wanted to further her usefulness to the press, the paper, and her brother. What more could she do? Her gaze drifted to the small shelf of reference books in the corner by the back door. Books. Of course! She'd expand her knowledge through reading a larger variety of subjects in books. Then she'd be better able to contribute to the content of the newspaper with an educated perspective. That would also boost the importance of the paper to the community. Yes, a better education was the answer to her question of how to be more useful. Time to make a plan of attack to accomplish her aim.

CHAPTER 4

PROVIDENCE, RHODE ISLAND – 1764

Over the past two years, Katy had devoted several hours a week to reading everything she could lay hands on. She'd become more fluent in Latin and more familiar with the current literature flowing out of Britain. Of course, she'd also become far more proficient in composing the newspaper and had expanded into operating the smaller press as well. She'd slowly, step by step, earned her brother's approval and confidence, allowing her to be more involved in every aspect of the printing business. Her growing number of friends and acquaintances also fueled a steady stream of contributions to the newspaper. Speaking of friends, time for her to wrap up the last touches to the broadside she was working on so she could go home and prepare for her mother's planned entertainment.

Her mother had declared that it was high time they engaged in some merry-making, complete with music and dancing. She'd invited everyone she knew to the Petticoat Frisk and encouraged Katy to do the same. Lauren, their creative and talented cook, had worked closely with her mother to ensure a pleasing array of goodies to have on the banquet table. William had located a string quartet to entertain the expected crush of people. Mr. McTavish had overseen the storage of the bulkier items in the parlor to allow for the clearing of a dance floor. All her friends planned to attend as well. The event promised to be quite an enjoyable one.

Katy perused the completed sheet, pleased with the three-column layout topped by the title "Buy the Truth and Sell It Not." She'd inserted the image of a bible between the two lines to emphasize the religious nature of the sheet. The old gentleman who had commissioned the piece was, he'd said, "anxious for the Welfare of his Fellow-Creatures." She smiled to herself at the sentiment as she read over the contents of the three lessons in poem form. Satisfied it suited the purpose, she wiped her hands on her apron and turned toward her brother, sitting at the next slanted table.

"What are you working on?" She rose from her stool to stride closer, peering over his shoulder at the small frame on his table. "Is that some kind of invitation?"

He nodded as he laid down the composing stick. "Just finished, in fact. In time to have this printed and sent round to a lady friend. What do you think?" He slid back so she could center herself in front of the small frame. He'd aligned several type ornaments across the top, with the headline declaring "Providence, (Tuesday Morning) September 25, 1764." She couldn't stop her lips widening into a grin as she read the full text.

Madam, As the Close of this Day is devoted to social Mirth and Gaiety, and the Ladies being esteem'd the only real Promoters of it,--I take the Liberty to request YOU to make one a Petticoat Frisk, to be held in the Afternoon, at Mrs. Goddard's, where your Company will greatly brighten the Felicity of the Evening, and be very agreeable to all, and in particular Manner to one, who will think it an Honor to wait on you there, and is, with the utmost Respect,

Your very humble,

and most obedient Servant,

William Goddard.

P.S. The present lowering Sky, it is hoped will be no Discouragement to You, --for You may be assured of a pleasant Afternoon, should the Sun be obscured in Darkness, while the Ladies cheerful Presence united, can supply that Want of its hidden Rays.

"How humorous. Who is this mysterious lady you're inviting?" Katy stepped back to allow her brother to resume his place.

"You know her. Miss Sally Kennicutt." He wiped his hands on a rag and then stood. "I need to have this printed and sent around to her home."

"After, we should probably make for Mother's so we can receive our guests this afternoon."

"I'll be around later, I have some other business first." He shook his head at her wide eyes. "Nothing much so it won't take but a minute. I merely need to ensure the paper I ordered has arrived. I wish we could make our own and control the amount we had on hand, but that's not possible right now."

"Make our own paper. I imagine that would be quite an undertaking." She hesitated as a thought entered her head. "But I shall enjoy having time to talk with Miss Kennicutt this afternoon, and find out just what is happening between the two of you." She laughed out loud at the horrified expression on her brother's face. "See you later."

Midafternoon Katy stood in the open doorway to their home, ready to greet people as they arrived for the merriment. After a quick luncheon, she had changed from her work dress into her nicest gown. She inspected the garnet skirts with an embroidered bodice, a creamy scarf tucked in as a collar. She had been delighted by the flowered design the seamstress had fashioned for her, twining ivy with red and yellow roses. Her maid, Patsy, had helped her with the upswept hairdo that made Katy feel particularly feminine. She tapped her gold satin-clad foot on the porch with barely contained delight. She was ready for the party to begin.

As the number of people inside grew and expanded to the garden out back as well, she realized how well they'd been accepted in the community over the years they'd resided among them. Why? Because of the services they provided to the second largest city in Rhode Island. William had given them not only the first print shop in the city but also the first newspaper. In not-altogether-friendly competition with the one from Newport run by Samuel Hall.

"Katy!" Joan hurried up the steps, her pale yellow gown with white trim brightening the entryway. Like Katy, Joan's blonde hair was swept up into a smooth bun. "I've missed you the last few weeks. But I'm glad we're able to catch up today."

"I've missed you, too." Katy gave her dear friend a quick hug and then stepped back to assess her from head to toe. "You're looking lovely. Mary and Patrice arrived a few minutes ago and are inside. I haven't seen Susan yet, but I expect she'll arrive before long."

Beside Joan stood a young man in a fine suit, wearing a polite expression. He was tall and stout, looming above the women.

"Who is your escort? Katy hoped it was a relative, but the look Joan gave him said otherwise.

"I'd like you to meet my new beau, Mr. Harold Edward Langley."

New beau? Why hadn't her friend told her anything about him?

"Welcome, sir. Oh, I see Miss Kennicutt arriving with her parents. Excuse me, Joan, but I'll find you in a few minutes after Mother takes over here."

"Of course." Joan smiled at her and then walked farther into the house with Harold to where William stood with several other people.

Katy waited for the pretty young woman to climb the steps up to the front door. She wore a beautiful dark blue gown with cream trim and a matching bonnet, tan heeled shoes peeked out from under the long skirts.

"Miss Goddard. How delightful to see you looking so well." Sally held out a gloved hand to clasp with Katy's. "How kind of your brother to invite me to this gathering."

The new arrival conducted herself with comportment and confidence. As she should, given her standing in society. Her father owned one of the largest mercantile shops in the city, furnishing the day-to-day necessities at a reasonable cost. Sally's pretty features and grace made her attractive not just to young men but to everyone who had the pleasure of knowing her.

"Indeed. You're very welcome. I believe..." Katy looked over her shoulder to where her brother was watching the exchange. She raised a brow at him and he started toward her. "My esteemed brother is right here to greet you properly."

Sally shifted her attention to the grinning young man approaching. "Mr. Goddard."

William stopped beside Katy and took Sally's hand to kiss the back of it. "Thank you for coming, Miss Kennicutt."

"Perhaps you'd like to show me around? I would enjoy some punch on this warm evening." Sally folded her hands together as she smiled at William.

Katy saw the subtle exchange between them and realized they'd struck up a cozy relationship. "Yes, William, do show her about. And please ask Mother to take over here for me."

With a tilt of his chin, William proffered his arm to Sally and the couple strolled into the house.

"Good day."

The deep voice surprised Katy into spinning around a bit too fast, her long skirts tangling about her ankles. Strong hands gripped her upper arms. Highly polished black boots and tan breeches led up to an elaborately embroidered vest and coat, and on to a snowy white cravat. Then her flash of a gaze met the amused amber eyes of a very handsome man.

"Oh. Um…"

"Are you all right, miss?"

Katy realized she remained within his grasp and swallowed back the dismay. She straightened her spine, severing the connection. "Yes, thank you, sir." She drew in a shaky breath and let it out slowly to steady her nerves. "I appreciate your assistance."

The man doffed his top hat with one hand as he half bowed to her. "I'm afraid we haven't been properly introduced. My name is Robert Marshall. I am an acquaintance of William Goddard, here at his invitation. And you are?"

"Mary Katharine Goddard, his sister." She studied the laugh lines around his eyes, the dimple on his chin, and the smooth shaved jaw. "Thank you for coming. William is inside, if you'd like to go in and enjoy the banquet and the music which should be starting soon."

"Indeed, I should." Robert didn't move, merely gazed at her with a soft smile on his lips. "May I ask a personal question, Miss Goddard?"

Surprised, Katy hesitated before responding. "As long as it's not impertinent, yes." Now why had she agreed to let him ask her a question when she'd just met him? Something about his expression suggested sincerity and honesty, two traits she valued in her friends. Would he become a friend? Did she want him to? "Please, ask."

"Miss Goddard, would you allow me to court you if you're not seeing anyone else?" He pressed his lips together briefly and then smiled. "I'm as surprised as you seem, my lady. But I believe I'd like to get to know you better. If you'll permit me?"

The man had impeccable manners which spoke volumes about his character. He was also very pleasing to look at, broad, strong shoulders and narrow waist, muscular thighs likely from riding horseback. What kind of work did he do? How did he know William? All questions that would likely be answered were she to allow him to court her.

She hadn't entertained the idea since the tragic death of her beau years before. She'd planned to live and work and play as an unmarried woman. She would devote her time to the print shop and paper, to her studies, to her friends. To fulfilling her promise to support her brother any way she could. She'd stopped dreaming of a day when she might become a mother. She no longer wanted that path through life. She enjoyed her work and the people in her life too much to want to change it. Though, she supposed if the right man came along, she could change her tune on that score.

"You've only just met me, sir." She searched his eyes, looking for any sign of his making a mockery of her. "Why would you seek such permission on such a slender acquaintance?"

He held out a hand, waiting for her to meet him halfway. When she didn't, he dropped his hand back to his side. "I ask because I know your brother and I can see you have the same quality of forthrightness and purpose, but a gentler demeanor. I admire that." He inclined his head and then met her gaze. "I wish to find out more about you. Please?"

Footsteps approached behind her but she kept her eyes forward, pondering the startling request. What should she say? Torn between walking away and an admitted curiosity to know more about him too, she hesitated.

"Go on, Sister. I can vouch for him. Rob's a decent sort. He's a physick and has developed quite a fine reputation hereabouts." William shook hands with the other man, then glanced at Katy. Sally eased into place beside William, her expression encouraging as her brother continued. "He's helped me a time or two with minor issues. He's all right. But if he does anything you don't approve of, tell me and I'll take care of it."

Her brother had never offered to be her champion. She peered closer at him, seeking his assurance. When he nodded slightly, she could tell he trusted Robert. Surely, as a man of medicine he'd be trustworthy and honest. She still didn't know much about him, but her brother's confidence persuaded her to take the chance. After all, what could it hurt to endeavor to become better acquainted with the gentleman?

Katy moistened her lips as she looked between her brother, his lady, and the would-be suitor. "I suppose that is acceptable."

Robert half-bowed and took her gloved hand, gently pressing his lips to the back of her hand. "I am delighted."

"Perhaps you should show this gentleman around, Miss Goddard?" Sally prompted with a nod toward the dining room and its refreshments. "Before all the delicious food is consumed by these masses."

Robert crooked his arm for her and she slowly placed her hand on it. "Please lead me wherever you wish to go."

"Very well." Feeling somewhat foolish, Katy stepped forward with Robert in tow. The quartet struck up a dancing tune as they neared the parlor. "Do you dance, Mr. Marshall?"

With the furniture removed, the parlor seemed larger than usual. The quartet occupied the corner near the cold fireplace, the two violins, cello, and flute filling the air with lively music. Couples moved in tandem around the room, their feet thudding on the pine floorboards. Candles filled holders scattered about the room, creating a welcoming atmosphere for the guests. The scent of baked oysters and steamed crab competed with the sweet aromas of tea cakes and bread pudding. Katy returned her attention to the man beside her, her hand resting on his muscled arm.

"Yes, I do. Shall we?" Robert tilted his head as he waited for her response.

Without a word, Katy proceeded into the parlor where the other couples were already dancing. She espied Mary with an older man, and Patrice with a man who might be her father, dancing. She waited for Robert to move into position and then they followed the steps of the country dance with the others. As they danced, Katy could only wonder what the future might hold should this man become part of her life.

"What do you think of Robert Marshall, Mother?" The day seemed to take forever to pass so that the time for her new beau's appearance would finally arrive.

She and her mother had retreated to the comfortable seating in the parlor to work on their sewing. A cheery fire kept the chilly air at bay. She could hear coaches rumble past the front of the house every few minutes. She inhaled the delicious aroma of sweet buns baking in the small brick oven in the kitchen, her stomach grumbling at the delay in their Sunday afternoon tea. Rob should be arriving in a few minutes, which made her cast glances out the front window to see if he were walking up the front steps.

Over the last week, Rob had called upon her every afternoon for a stroll around town. Sometimes they stopped in at the tavern around the corner for a bite to eat and to talk. Or he'd take her to some hidden gem of a place in town to browse artifacts from around the world or to watch an acrobatic performance by a troupe of circus performers. One afternoon he'd surprised her by taking her to listen to a concert in the town square, delightful music played by an ensemble. He turned out to be very easy to talk to because he was so well-read and knowledgeable about a variety of subjects. She really liked that about him. Conversation with such an educated and experienced man proved not only refreshing but informative.

"He seems like a fine gentleman. Why do you ask?" Sarah kept her eyes on the knitting in her hands.

"I am unsure where our courtship might be headed. Would you approve of it becoming more serious?" Did she want it to? Yes…and no. She stopped the knitting needles in her hands to concentrate on her mother's response.

Sparkling eyes regarded her for a moment before she leaned forward to peer more closely at her. "It's wiser to wait and see how things evolve rather than jumping ahead to unanswerable questions, my dear."

Perhaps, but she couldn't help but wonder where their friendship might lead with time. "I know, but I find it difficult to not wonder."

Sarah chuckled as she leaned against the back of the small sofa. "You're curiosity and intellect naturally lead you to question and ponder the future. It will unfold as it should."

Lauren strode into the room, bearing a silver tray with the tea service and cucumber sandwiches and tea cakes. "My apologies to you both for falling behind this afternoon, ladies." She placed the tray on the low table between where Sarah and Katy sat.

"An occasional lapse is understandable, Miss George. Thank you for preparing such a delightful and I'm sure delicious repast for us."

"My pleasure, ma'am." Lauren inspected the contents of the tray one last time, then with a sharp nod, spun around and left the room.

"Will you pour, my dear? I'd like to finish this row before I stop for tea." Sarah indicated the tea pot on the tray with a tilt of her head. "If you don't mind."

"Of course—" A flash of movement outside drew Katy's attention in time to detect Robert hurrying up the front steps. "He's here."

Sarah grinned at her as she continued her knitting. "Just in time to join us, then."

Travis strolled purposefully past the parlor doorway on his way to answer the knock at the front door. A murmured exchange between the two men was soon followed by Rob hesitating in the parlor door to gaze at her for a moment. His bemused smile had her returning his silent greeting in kind.

"Mr. Marshall," Sarah said, breaking the silence, "how kind of you to take time from your busy day to call upon us. Please, come in." She laid her sewing on the table while she addressed the new arrival.

Rob quickly entered and sat down beside Katy on the sofa facing her mother. "I apologize for being later than promised, sweetheart, but I had to tend to a last minute patient."

"No apology is necessary, sir." Katy met his smiling but serious gaze. "Tending to your patients must be a priority."

He inclined his head in acknowledgement and gratitude. "Thank you for understanding. Now, might I join you ladies in your Sunday tea?"

Katy reached for the tea pot to pour the steaming amber liquid into the cups on the tray. She smiled to herself as she handed out a cup to her mother and then to her beau, keeping one for herself. Miss George had obviously anticipated Robert's visit.

"What have you been doing on this pretty fall afternoon, Mr. Marshall?" Sarah settled her cup on the saucer and placed it on the table beside her knitting.

"Other than treating a bad case of… well, never mind. I won't trouble you ladies with the maladies of others." Rob took a long swallow of his tea and then eased the cup onto the saucer he held in his other hand. "I did have luncheon at the tavern and was happy to learn that a new college has been founded in Warren. They're calling it the College in the English Colony of Rhode Island and Providence Plantations and will be open to all religions. I believe it's been founded by the Baptists, but they are not limiting students to that singular denomination."

"That's quite remarkable." Katy had never heard of such an open-minded approach to educating people, but such an endeavor seemed very worthwhile. "I hope it flourishes."

"I believe that I heard they hope to enroll students by next year." Sarah placed her tea cup on the tray. "So they are serious about creating a college in this colony. We didn't have one until now, so that is a welcome addition."

"Our colony is progressing in a very fine direction." Rob nodded as he swallowed the last of his tea and set the cup and saucer on the tray beside Sarah's. "Miss Goddard, would you care to take a short walk with me? I'm expected at a patient's house for dinner, my payment for healing his ailment, in an hour, but I would enjoy walking with you on this lovely afternoon for a few minutes."

What a busy man. Busy but very conscientious and caring.

She'd have to adjust her expectations as to his waiting on her accordingly. Of course, he had to work around her schedule at the printing house as well, so it was only reasonable for her to remain flexible to meet his availability. Indeed, perhaps she should not count on his appearance at a particular time since he would likely be called upon at a moment's notice to see a patient. Perhaps not let herself become too attached or reliant upon his presence at all. Especially given her indecision about their relationship. Yes, such an approach would protect her from inevitable disappointment. Even so, she would enjoy whatever time they might have together.

"I'll get my wrap."

A couple of weeks later, Katy checked on the dining room table setting for the dinner party her mother was holding that evening. Lauren had done a fine job of ensuring the silver shone and the crystal sparkled. The flowered plates and silver utensils were laid out with precision. The aroma of roasting chicken and fish wafted into the room, teasing a rumble from her tummy. In addition to the meats, the cook had already roasted asparagus and potatoes, baked hot rolls and set out a pot of jam. Her tummy muttered again. Katy shifted the matching branched candlesticks to align in the center of the table, flanking the low floral arrangement. October had ushered in the much colder air that New England was renowned for, so a blazing fire in the hearth warded off the chill.

The front door opened and banged shut. Katy could tell from the heavy footsteps it was her brother arriving. She cast one last glance around the room and turned to greet him as he stopped in the arched doorway. His happy expression suggested he bore good news along with the fresh scent of outdoors.

"Good news?" Katy folded her arms across her waist.

"The best." William unbuttoned his overcoat as his eyes sparkled. "I was informed today that my appointment as Providence's new postmaster is now in effect."

She blinked at him several times as she assimilated this bit of news. "Following in Father's footsteps? Congratulations are definitely in order."

"Yes, quite a boon. I've been angling for this appointment as it makes sense given that we send out the newspaper via the post. I'll have better access to incoming news and the local gossip as well. It's brilliant."

The arrogance of the man never ceased to confound her. His role as a public servant should not cause such boasting. But that wouldn't be her brother if he didn't. He'd always held a high opinion of his abilities. Indeed, he acted as if he could do no wrong and that his opinions carried the weight of righteousness. Rather than encourage him to continue in such a vein, she elected to change the subject.

"Mother's guests will be arriving very soon. Were you planning to stay for dinner or do you have business to attend to as the new postmaster?" She shouldn't, but she rather hoped he had to go elsewhere. His news irked her. Not that she wanted to be in charge of the Royal Post for the city. No. She hated the feeling of being of less worth than her younger brother. For a time, she felt more equal to him because they worked together daily. Now he had a new role, one only a man could perform. Unless, like her mother, the man died and the widow stepped in to fill the void. But that of course could never apply to her own future since she straddled the fence when it came to the idea of marrying in the first place.

"Of course I'll join in and we can celebrate my good fortune." He peered at her for a moment and then frowned slightly. "Don't be upset. This is a boon for all of us as my income will increase and you and Mother will benefit as well. I will always look out for you both."

"Yes, you do." An aggravating eventuality given that both Katy and her mother worked with him. Why wasn't it called their salary or pay instead of an allowance? Made her want to gnash her teeth but she refrained. Doing so wouldn't serve any useful purpose. "I'll set another place for you."

"Grand. And one for Rob as I saw him on my way here and invited him as well." William removed his coat and started toward the hallway, where Travis received the heavy garment. "Thank you, Mr. McTavish." He looked back at Katy. "I'm going to freshen up and I'll be back in a while."

"Don't be long. The others should arrive momentarily." Katy smoothed her skirts with both hands as she followed her brother out of the room.

A knock at the front door was answered by the butler. The rush of chilly air flowing down the hall ushered in her suitor. Rob looked fine indeed in his burnt sienna breeches with cream vest and black cravat. His polished black boots shone in the candlelight as he strode to her, taking her hand and kissing the palm. She smiled up at him, delighted to see him again. They'd grown quite close in a very short period of time. Close enough that she could see he also bore good news.

"What has happened? I can tell you're about to burst at the seams with some news." She held his hand for a moment as he led her down the hall and into the parlor.

She glanced around the refurbished room, cheered by the flowered wool covers and the snapping fire removing the chill from the air. Patsy had placed several vases of flowers around which smelled divine. She and her mother had managed to make the house a comfortable and inviting home. Rob stopped and smiled down at her.

"Let's sit and I'll tell you." He pointed to the small sofa near the fireplace. "It's rather shocking, so it's best you're comfortable."

She settled onto the seat as he sat down beside her. "I'm prepared for whatever you have to say." She hoped so, anyway.

"My darling, I have just received a letter from the University of Edinburgh welcoming me to study medicine. Isn't that amazing good fortune?"

"Edinburgh? Scotland?" Shocked by his revelation, she could only stare at him for a long moment, grappling with the ramifications. They'd only just begun to feel comfortable together, though not so much that they'd been even hinting at a future together. Still. The faint resurrection of the miniscule hope of a husband and family crumbled into nothing. "You're going away. For how long?"

"Several years." He gripped both her hands, tugging her attention to meet his gaze. "My darling, I am so very grateful to have had the opportunity to meet you and spend time with you. I'll always remember our time together as some of the happiest days of my life."

"But...?" She could tell he had more to say. Could tell that he was ending their courtship without any remorse. The break in their friendship was sad, naturally, but she'd survive. She should be more upset. She frowned at the fact she wasn't remotely distraught, merely surprised and startled by the suddenness of the revelation. She could go back to the more comfortable approach to her future, of living on her own terms. If nothing else, she always could rely upon herself.

"I am sure you will find someone who will make you happy." He squeezed her fingers one last time and then let her hands go. "I just cannot turn down this excellent opportunity. I have worked long and hard to be accepted to study medicine in Scotland. I cannot turn my back on the chance presented to me. I do hope you understand."

Overthrown for a profession. Of course she understood, wanting the work more than the relationship. After a moment more of sorrow for what might have been, she let it go. After all, she felt the same way about her own endeavors.

She squeezed his fingers and then rose to her feet. "I do. Now how about some dinner for old times' sake?"

CHAPTER 5

PROVIDENCE, RHODE ISLAND – 1765

Spring had finally arrived, permitting the print shop to leave its windows and doors open to catch the floral scented breeze. The relief from the cloying pungent scent of the ink proved immense. Katy worked on the layout for a book brought in by Mr. Timothy Allen. William had laid out the flow of the fair copy text, resulting in a document that would be sixty-six pages when complete. A big job but she welcomed the challenge.

She scanned the others working at various tasks around the room. Her mother moved from station to station to check on progress on the apprentices. Thank goodness they'd been able to find a journeyman to help with the press operations. The physical nature of the heavy machine had proven too much for the women to handle on their own. And with William unavailable more often than not, the task fell to the younger apprentices. Speaking of her brother, where was he on this pretty spring morning?

She turned back to the book galley she was composing. The title, "The Main Point; or, Saving Faith Distinguished from Counterfeits: As Delivered publicly in several

Discourses," was a touch unwieldy but adequately described the content of the book. The colophon William had penned for her to include rankled, given his frequent absences. She read the line, pleased with the appearance if not its message: "Providence: N.E., Printed and sold by William Goddard, at the Post-Office." Like he had any hand in the production of the book. She'd had far more hand in it than he did.

The process of compiling such a document involved many steps and many days' worth of effort. First the layout of the text in the eight page folio so that when the resulting two sheets were folded and quired, or gathered, the page numbers flowed consecutively. Each folio of eight pages of text had to be composed in a galley form then imposed, proved, and printed. Those freshly printed sheets were hung to dry on ropes hanging from the ceiling that stretched across the room. While those dried, the next galley form needed to be composed with the appropriate text and the process repeated until the complete text resided on paper. The stack of sheets of paper then had to be built up by a series of such gatherings, a task for the apprentices, and then folded, stitched, and covered. William preferred having leather covers for the books, but some of the smaller pamphlets only received a paper cover. This one he'd declared would have a leather cover with a bit of ornamentation to set it apart from the ordinary works.

Without any warning, William strode in, his hair tousled by the light breeze. His serious countenance didn't bode well. He marched into the center of the room and whistled, stopping the chatter of the apprentices and the *clatter* and *thump* of the press. All eyes turned to see what the owner of the print shop had interrupted their work to say. Katy's mother watched from where she'd been straightening a display of books on a shelf by the front door.

"Everyone, if I may have your attention. I have an

announcement that will impact our efforts from here on. Effective with the May 11 issue, the *Gazette* will suspend publication for six months."

Sarah tensed and took a few steps closer to her son. "What has occurred to warrant such a sudden end to your newspaper? We have subscribers who have supported us for years who rely upon it."

"To be blunt, the expense of publishing it has increased, especially the threat of duties as a result of the dreadful Stamp Act that is to be unfairly, and I believe illegally, levied upon us in a few months. I'm sure my fellow colonists will not tolerate such an abuse of power by the Parliament." William waved a hand back and forth in the air as he pivoted to fully address her question. "More to the point, I'm sure they will find their news elsewhere, Mother. My very real hopes have exceeded any success we are currently having. But I have been asked to be a silent partner with Mr. John Holt in New York. Therefore, I will not be present to continue to compile the news."

The apprentices stilled as they waited for the rest of the announcement. Katy understood the concern in their eyes. Without the newspaper business, would they still have a role? Were they to be let go? What of the agreement between the parents and her brother to train them to a trade? Her jaw hurt from clenching her teeth together to prevent saying something out of turn.

"Are you shuttering the entire enterprise, then?" Sarah asked, interlacing her fingers in a tense fist in front of her.

"No, Mother. The good news is that the print shop and book bindery business will continue but under your management. If that is agreeable to you?"

Sarah nodded slowly and then shifted her gaze to study Katy's carefully blank expression. "If Mary Katharine will be my first assistant?"

The fury simmering in Katy's gut eased at the offer. Something of a promotion. She didn't fathom why her brother had to shift his focus to another venture in a distant state. The subscriptions for the *Gazette* were enough to sustain it. Why cease publication altogether merely because his interest had waned? But the bindery was something she had worked hard to master and since her mother stated her willingness to step up, then so would she.

"Yes, Mother, I'll be happy to assist you."

"Then it's all settled. I'll pen a notice for the May 11 edition to inform our readership of the change. Carry on, everyone."

Katy stood rooted in place for several long moments. She loved her brother. She did. She wouldn't be helping him, working alongside him and for him, if not. But she did not understand him. Not at all.

"Mother, how can you tolerate such a high collar on such a warm afternoon?" Katy waved her fan in front of her perspiring face. "It's very warm even for July."

"Perhaps these old bones don't mind the heat as much as they once did." Sarah smiled gently at Katy. "Why don't you step outside under a tree and see if you can't cool off a tad?"

"No, I dare not. This Rhode Island Almanack is a big job and I know you want to have it available next month. Even with the apprentices' help, it will take us a month to complete it. Indeed, I need your help determining the best layout and flow, if you have some time?"

"Of course." Her mother peered closely at her. "Have you begun yet or are you asking for confirmation of your proposed layout?"

Honestly, she had not managed to work out exactly

where to break the text for each individual page. Seeing the pattern, the placement of each page, for the folio to ensure the page numbers emerged from the printing and binding process consecutively as required still eluded her. Something about having to flow the text out of order in a seemingly random pattern so that it ultimately ran in order still confused her. But she'd work it out yet.

"I believe having you talk me through it will help me to understand the flow better. William had been most impatient to leave for New York when he attempted to instruct me on it."

"Let's have a look then." Sarah motioned for Katy to lead the way back to the work table.

"I've sketched out a rough draft of how I think it should flow, but am not certain of exactly where to stop and start the text. How does one estimate the number of words per page?" Katy lifted a sharpened pencil from the table and frowned at the draft of the layout she'd attempted. "William said something about a number and how to calculate it but I didn't follow his process. Plus have you seen the number of tables and lists Mr. West included? It's going to take a lot of time and effort."

"It's easy once you grasp how to estimate the contents. And Mr. Lancaster can help with the tables. He's very good at those. It's one of the reasons William took him on as journeyman. Now, let's talk about the layout." Sarah went on to break down the entire process, including how to decide which ornamental type to use to decorate the title page and other key pages in the finished book, as well as how to create the lines for the many tables included in the almanack. "You'll need to be judicious on using the special symbol types, but I think we have enough to do a page at a time. Does that make sense?"

Katy could only glare at the crammed and detailed pages

of tables of the sun and moon's movements, tides, and more. But the almanack was an important tool for the people. "Indeed. Thank you. I'll redo my estimation and ask for your concurrence before we begin the galleys."

"It's a good thing that you also know how to layout books since it's just us now operating the bindery and press." Sarah hesitated and then addressed Katy. "For the colophon on this one, William wants us to use a certain line. Here, let me write it down so you can include its length in your estimation.

"You already have the title but your brother wants the credit in a specific way." Sarah took the pencil from Katy and jotted down, "By Benjamin West, Philomath. Providence, in New-England: Printed and sold by Sarah and William Goddard, at the Post-Office."

Katy nodded even as she objected to the inclusion of her brother's name. Still, he remained the official owner of the shop. She couldn't object to him having a continuing say in his own business. She just wished he actually deserved the credit.

"I'll add that to the title page. Thank you for your help, Mother. Now I can proceed."

She spent the rest of the afternoon determining the exact content of each page of the almanack. The next morning she began composing the title page. The title was, typically, long but descriptive. It took her a little while to select the correct letters of type and design elements to layout the title page. Just the title page. Not one of the tables. She tried to ignore the daunting prospect they posed. As she worked, memories of Joan and Harold's wedding a few days before flowed through her mind. Joan had worn a beautiful dress and fancy shoes, baubles at her ears. A small family and friends affair she hoped would lead to a good life together.

When she'd put in the last of the type, she set down the composing stick and read over her work, which of course meant having to read it in reverse since the letters appeared backward to normal reading. The fact that she could read the backwards type amused her. When inked and impressed onto the paper, they would read correctly.

The New-England Almanack, or, Lady's and Gentleman's Diary, For the Year of our Lord Christ, 1766. Being the second Year after Bissextile, or Leap-Year; and the Sixth of the Reign of His Majesty King George the Third. Containing, A short History of the Travels of the Eclipse of the Sun that will happen this year, by way of Preface; an Ephemeris; Sun and Moon's Rising and Setting; Time of High-Water at Boston; Lunations; Eclipses of the Sun and Moon; the Planets Aspects; Judgment of the Weather; Spring Tides; Courts in the New-England Governments; Feasts and Fasts of the Church; accurate Tables of Roads; a Paper on Fear; a Piece on Comets; with a Variety of Things, both useful and entertaining, and all that is really requisite in an Almanack. Calculated for the Meridian of Providence, in New-England, Lat. 41 Deg. Min. North, and 4 H. 42 M. West from the Royal Observatory at Greenwich, but, without any sensible Error may serve all the Provinces adjacent.

Mr. West had left the colonies to visit London a couple of years ago, but he never returned. She'd heard the young man had made a name for himself with his oil paintings of various prominent men while over there. While she was happy for him and his good fortune, did he have to create so very many tables? She flipped through the twenty or so handwritten pages replete with tables of various kinds. The common thread among them was the use of ruled lines, symbols, brackets, and other special pieces of type.

She glanced across the room to where Paul Lancaster worked on another rush job. His burly frame hunched over his work, dark blond hair obscuring his pockmarked face. He was a quiet sort, but proficient in his work for the press. Her brother had made a fine choice with Paul's work ethic and polite manners.

"Mr. Lancaster, can you come here, please?" She waited for the hefty young man to make his way quickly across the room to her. "Mrs. Goddard would like for you to help with these tables. Can you do that?"

She showed him the small stack of pages and watched him lift the first and pore over it. He nodded silently to himself as he read over each of the tables. Then he tapped the pages into a neat stack and set them back on the work table.

"Yes, miss, I'd be happy to." He indicated his slanted composing table where the unfinished galley awaited his return. "Soon as I finish with the other piece."

"That will suffice. Thank you." Katy turned her attention to the last of the handwritten pages that didn't include tables.

The last page of the submitted book included an essay, one of a political nature. Mr. West had titled it, "A Short View of the present State of the American Colonies, from Canada to the utmost verge of His Majesty's Dominions, July 1765." The author of the essay—was it Mr. West himself?—spoke of the "ill temper" the people felt about the lack of representation in the levying of taxes. One sentence really struck a chord. "Such being the deplorable Situation of this Country, once renown'd for Freedom, it is hoped a Review thereof will excite such a universal Spirit of Patriotism in every Inhabitant, that our Liberty and Property may be yet rescued from the Jaws of Destruction." He then specifically cited the hated Stamp Act that had been passed the previous March, alluding to those who had spoken out against it already. She read the piece with avid interest and agreement, but then a sense of alarm filled her at the tone of the piece. The final three points hinted at drastic potentialities.

1. 'Power, like Water, is ever working its own Way; and, wherever it can find or make an Opening, is altogether as prone to overflow whatever is subject to it.'
2. 'Though Matter of Right overlooked, may be re-claimed and re-assumed at any Time, it cannot be *too soon* re-claimed and re-assumed.'
3. 'And if the Representative Part of Government is not tenacious, almost to a Fault, of the Rights and Claims of a People, they will, in a Course of Time, lose their every Pretensions to them.'

She re-read the essay twice more before setting down the sheet of paper on the work table. The reference to the Stamp Act raised yet again all of the concerns her brother harbored about the increased costs. Concerns she shared, of course. The women in the city might agree with her, but their opinion was not important to the men in charge. At least, not openly, though she suspected the women influenced the men's opinions.

The British Parliament first passed in 1764 a Sugar Act, which taxed sugar and other goods to raise revenue after all of the expense of the Seven Years' War with France had ended in 1763. They wanted to use some of that money to support several regiments of British soldiers to keep the peace between the Indians and the white men in the colonies. Violators of the Stamp Act, which was passed in March 1765, would also be tried and convicted without a jury trial, leaving the question open as to how fair a process would result. While it was understandable to a point that they'd need to replenish their coffers, the fact that it was at the colonists' expense, literally, without having any say in the matter, made people very angry.

The Stamp Act was a tax slated to start being collected

on November 1, 1765, on all legal documents and printed materials. A tax collector would issue the stamp in exchange for the taxes collected. What upset William—and herself— the most was that it applied to wills, deeds, newspapers, pamphlets, and for some unknown reason cards and dice. Thus they'd have to raise the cost of all their printing work to cover the new tax. If the Act was allowed to go into effect.

What angered everyone was the supposition that the colonists were virtually represented in Parliament even though they had no actual person designated to represent them. And then to deny offenders a jury trial on top of that was a dangerous precedent indeed. She'd read where some of the more radical men thought the tax was a gradual effort to take away the colonists freedoms and place them under a tyrannical regime. Why else would the Parliament want troops in North America after they'd removed the threat from the French? Why else, indeed.

It was one thing to live under the rule of a good king and his parliament. It was an entirely different animal when the king became a tyrant. Forcing his will, his desires, his demands on the people he governed without them having any recourse, let alone say. Sentiment ran high in town over the impression that the king was doing so.

She stared at the inflammatory essay. Should she say something to her mother about its inclusion? She mulled over the idea and then dismissed it. She agreed with the message, which was presented accurately and rationally. Besides, her mother had probably already read it or she wouldn't have merely handed over the closely written pages to be typeset. In fact, the people who bought the almanack would most likely appreciate the perspective and the call to action.

"Katy, dear, are you finished for the day? I think it's time we head for home." Her mother strolled slowly toward her, her fatigue evident. "You can sort that out tomorrow."

She straightened the stack of paper and placed a weight on it to hold it until the next day. "I've been thinking, Mother. Since I have read and reread all of the books in William's library, what if we visit the Redwood Library across the river and see what they have to offer?"

"The Redwood is supposed to be a very prestigious library. Perhaps we can find a day when we're not too busy and we can go explore." Sarah smiled as she gestured toward the door. "For now, let's go home and enjoy some supper, shall we?"

Katy rose and picked up her purse. "We shall."

Tomorrow she'd buckle down to work on the almanack. For tonight, she'd simply enjoy the summer evening.

Over the next month, William came and went, usually with little notice. Katy worked on perfecting her skills at typesetting and broadening her knowledge about all forms of printing. On one visit, William announced he was working on setting up a paper mill, then he was off to New York again. How did he keep so many competing ventures going?

In late August, he showed up once more. Breezed right into the print shop on the twenty-second day of the month. Katy was in the middle of composing Stephen Hopkins' treatise entitled "The Rights of Colonies Examined." The pamphlet extended to twenty-four pages and contained what seemed to be somewhat inflammatory language. But it was Mr. Hopkins' right to state his views. She was nearly finished, but needed to verify the layout was accurate before handing over the galleys to the apprentices operating the press.

William strode through the open door and marched over to where Paul was working on another broadside. "Mr. Lancaster, I have a special project I need to put together to release in a couple of days. Will you help me?"

"Of course, sir. I'm nearly finished with this one." Paul set his composing stick down on the table. "What are you planning?"

"A special publication. I'm calling it 'A Providence Gazette Extraordinary.' It will be mostly of Benjamin Franklin's essays he wrote from his post in London putting forth his opposition to the passage of that infernal Stamp Act. There are men who believe he supported it when I know for a fact he did not. So I want to prove that."

"Very good. Do you have it written out?" Paul glanced over at Katy, who had continued observing the exchange. He raised one brow in question and then turned back to William. "I can begin on it next if so."

Katy left the two men to their conversation, now that she'd determined her brother wasn't going to task her with something else. Within the hour she put the last of the type into place and took time to review and confirm everything was ready to be printed. She lifted the form and headed over to the most recent and youngest apprentice, one Tom Braverman. Only he was very shy and not so brave at the tender age of fifteen.

"Mr. Braverman, I have a pamphlet typeset and ready for you to print. Please print and assemble forty copies and let me know when you're finished."

"Yes, ma'am." Tom's pale blue eyes stared at her but he didn't say anything more.

"If you need assistance, also let me know that. Can you do that?" She watched his Adam's apple slide in his throat before he screwed up the courage to speak to her.

"Yes, miss." He took the form from her and turned to place it on the large work table near the printing press.

She studied him for a moment longer, aware of his uncertainty and yet good-faith efforts to perform the jobs he was tasked with. What kind of home had he come from? Did they miss him? She couldn't imagine being sent away from home even to learn a trade. Gratitude filled her soul as she realized how fortunate she was to be learning at home.

"Katy, are you finished for the day?" Her mother called from her post at the counter at the front of the shop.

"Yes, I am. Why?" Katy walked over to stand on the opposite side of the counter, facing her mother.

"I recall your idea of going to the Redwood Library. I know you've read everything we have multiple times, so let's take a cab across the river and see what might please you. I'm sure we'll find something different to interest you."

"Oh, do you think they'd permit us to even browse their collection?" Katy pressed her palms onto the counter. "I mean, will they let us in?"

"My understanding is that they will, dear. Mr. Redwood and others built the library as a community project. I'm told they wanted to ensure an educated citizenry in order to support a prosperous and compassionate society." Her mother laid her hands on top of Katy's. "I would be very surprised should you decline my offer."

While she didn't know much about the collection, she had heard snippets about the library itself. Joan had mentioned something about the amazing assortment of books, portrait paintings, and even concerts and lectures. Her mother was indeed correct that she'd grown tired of rereading the same tomes and longed to expand her reading.

"Let's go see what they have." Katy smiled as her mother squeezed her hands and then straightened.

"I'll have Mr. Braverman flag down a cab while we gather

our things." She turned and crossed the room to ask the boy to run outside and hail a cab for them.

Within a few minutes, Katy joined her mother in the waiting cab and they trundled off across town to the connecting bridge over Easton Bay. Summer heat created mirages of water vapor in the air. The sound of seagulls crying overhead competed with the sounds of horses hooves and wheeled vehicles. Excitement and anticipation swirled inside Katy as the team of horses hurried them through the busy streets. With all of the carriages, coaches, wagons, and dog carts going hither and yon, she found it difficult to understand how Providence wasn't the largest city in the colony instead of second. Maybe one day the city would become the largest.

"Mother, I am curious about something."

"Yes, dear? You know you can talk to me about anything." Her mother's calm expression showed her openness to discourse with her daughter. "What is it?"

"William." She hesitated to say exactly what was on her mind. After a moment of wavering, she drew in a deep breath and let it out slowly. "I'm confused by his coming and going so much. Why is it he is unable to focus on any one thing for long?"

"Aah. That is not something I know how to answer." Sarah gazed at Katy with a slight frown dipping her brows. "I think that losing his father when he was only sixteen came as quite a blow to him. He lost the man who was teaching him how to be a man in his own right."

"I was only eighteen myself."

"But you've always been more mature for your age than your brother. I think he lost his guiding star when his father died. I think he's struggling to navigate still."

"His going back and forth to New York, and joining the Sons of Liberty, and then starting to rail against the Stamp

Act in his paper, all concern me as to what direction his life is heading. I mean, the Sons of Liberty are talking about assaulting the stamp distributors in each colony. Someone is going to get hurt, and I hope it won't be my brother."

"I share your concern, dear, but he's master of his own ship. It is not up to us to set his course. We can only assist when necessary." Her mother pressed her lips together and then nodded to herself. "As for assisting William, that is something I promised your father before he passed. He'd seen William's tendency to switch attention from one project to another and asked me to always look out for his best interests any way I could."

"Father asked you to support William?"

"Yes. And now, I'm asking for you to make the same promise to me." She smiled gently as she reached out to clasp Katy's hand. "I am not going to be on this earth for much longer and I need to know you'll do all in your power to help and support him after I'm gone."

"Don't speak of dying, Mother." She shook her head, alarm shooting through her soul. She studied her mother's calm demeanor and let out a sigh. "Of course, I'll promise to help him as I can."

"Thank you, my dear." Her mother sat back in her seat. "I know I'm asking a lot, but I believe it is necessary for us to support his efforts."

"I do hope he'll not want to leave Providence now that we've settled in and have been so welcomed by our neighbors and the community in general. His dashing off to New York worries me on that score. I don't want to leave my friends, either."

"I would not want to move, not at my advanced age. I don't want to be farther from my sisters, for one thing. At least they write me often, and I them. Besides, at sixty-four, these old bones are beginning to complain when I stand for too long."

Katy studied her mother's face, detecting fine wrinkles around tired eyes. Katy hadn't thought much about her mother's age, but the reminder prompted concern. Her mother was her own guiding star and confidant in addition to being her teacher of how to live life well. Should she be concerned about her mother's health? She seemed to be well and strong. For how long?

The cab came to a halt and the driver jumped down to open the door. Her mother dismounted the vehicle first, Katy close behind her. The sun beat down on their bonnets as they faced the welcoming Neoclassical façade of the Redwood Library. The building appeared to have been built with stone, but in fact the architects used rustication techniques to shape wood into what looked like blocks of stone. Then they'd painted them with red paint, probably to reflect the name of the library. The entrance featured several steps leading up to a porch with four columns, a single door centered between the middle pair, open to permit visitors. On either side of the door two windows were also open to allow any stray breeze to cool the interior.

Katy preceded her mother into the large entryway of the library. Wood floors stretched throughout. Tables and chairs were arranged in groupings to facilitate reading or quiet discussion. An older man greeted them and invited them to look around, ask any questions they might have. In awe of the book-lined walls before her, Katy strolled through the rooms, peering at the titles of the thousands and thousands of books. Topics included just about everything she could ever want to know more about. Medicine. Science. Ancient History. Law. Apologetics. Astronomy. Latin. Theology. She went back to the titles about medicine and found one of interest. Titled

"An essay on regimen. Together with five discourses, medical, moral, and philosophical: serving to illustrate the principles and theory of philosophical medicine, and point out some of its moral consequences." She smiled to herself at yet another long title, but perhaps it could answer her new concern regarding her mother's constitution. Published more than twenty years previous, she hoped it would still be of use.

Holding the book carefully in both hands, she carried it to the desk in the front room of the library. A whole new world of education had just opened up to her and she intended to experience all of it.

PROVIDENCE, RHODE ISLAND – 1766

"I'll do my best, Mother, to have this completed as quickly as possible, but it's many, many pages." Katy flipped through the book in her hands, one published in London and now her mother wanted to be the first to print it in the colonies. Going to the last page she gasped. "Did you see this?"

"The total page count is somewhere around two hundred. But, darling, think of what this will mean for the reputation of the Goddard Print Shop." Sarah's smile widened, her light brown eyes twinkling with anticipation. "I'm so honored to be publishing the first American edition of Lady Mary Wortley Montagu's famous and popular letters. Just try to imagine the amazing experiences she must have had traveling all around Europe, Asia, and even into Africa."

The Englishwoman was notorious as a result of her lifestyle and marriages as well as her writings. She was the daughter of the fifth Earl of Kingston and Lady Mary Fielding. Her first act of notoriety was to elope with Edward Wortley Montagu, a Whig member of Parliament, in defiance of the marriage her father tried to force on her. After that marriage failed, she spent more time writing various essays, letters, and poetry. In fact, she'd gotten into a poetical spat with Alexander Pope, who had made sport of her in his poem *The Dunciad*. She replied in kind but the spat soon died out.

Lady Mary Wortley Montagu, the gossips reported, had proposed living with an Italian writer named Francesco Algarotti, but that idea fizzled out. But eventually she met and supposedly married Count Ugo Palazzi and lived with him in Avignon, France, for ten years. After her husband died in 1761, she returned to London to live with her daughter. Sadly, only seven months later she died from cancer. Everyone knew this woman as a brilliant, versatile writer, but she also advocated for women's capabilities despite the general cynicism.

"Her letters and poetry have been well received everywhere." Katy peered closer at her mother's eager expression. "Why are you so anxious to see this published? By us?"

"Oh my dear, because women publishing women is the most powerful statement we could send to our community. Doing so builds upon our revival of the *Providence Gazette* back in March, succeeding where a man did not. Having a woman's name as publisher in the colophon sends a powerful message. Though it does pain me to see my son fail at anything." Sarah pulled the book from Katy's hands to grasp her fingers. "I believe it is important for us to learn from Lady Mary's example. To live our lives on our own terms as much as possible."

"She did live an extraordinary life. It's sad to think of her passing on to heaven just four years ago." Her daughter must have been heartbroken at her mother's demise. A thought which invoked Katy's concern with regard to her own mother passing on. "I suspect her death left a very large hole in her family and friends' lives."

"I am sure. Now, back to us honoring her memory by

publishing her letters. I'd like to have it out early in August. I feel it's important to not delay issuing our edition this summer."

"A month from now?" Katy did a swift calculation in her head and then nodded. "I think we can manage that if I start on this very soon."

"I'll let you begin." Sarah started to turn away, then pivoted back to briefly embrace Katy's shoulders. "This publication will be a wonderful addition to our contribution to society and the colonies in general."

"Yes, I can see it being well-received as an important collection."

Katy opened the book to the title page and suppressed a sigh. Quite a long title followed by a longer description. Plus the colophon to be added at the bottom. Another three lines of text. But at least Katy's role at the shop was now included in it, with the updated "Printed and sold by Sarah Goddard, and Company." No William in sight.

He'd left in June, mere months after the repeal of the Stamp Act on the eighteenth of March. Freedom from additional taxes on printed materials meant he could start a new print shop. This time with two men as partners in Philadelphia, Pennsylvania. Mr. Joseph Galloway was speaker of the Pennsylvania Assembly and had promised her brother he'd receive the government's printing jobs. Mr. Thomas Wharton was a successful merchant. Both were Quakers, which rather concerned Katy since she wasn't very familiar with their religious leanings. One thing she'd noticed was just how much calmer the print shop operated in his absence. She often missed her brother's presence but not the disruptions his comings and goings created.

She turned the page to the first of the letters. Well-spaced lines of text filled each page, with extra white space around the beginning of each missive. A pleasing layout but one she could improve upon. Perhaps with a bit of a nicer embellishment to separate each missive. And a cleaner font with plenty of space to make reading easier. She'd taken William's advice and studied what other printers had created, and then worked to improve on their designs with her own. As a result, she received many compliments from the customers of the busy shop.

The little bell over the door announced a customer. Katy glanced at the door to see Joan sashaying inside. Leaving the book on the table, Katy hurried to greet her friend.

"Good afternoon. I am so pleased at your visit." She inspected her friend's appearance to evaluate her well-being.

Dressed in a pretty lightweight gown of pink muslin, Joan seemed to be bubbling with verve and liveliness. Her blue eyes twinkled as she approached, a happy look on her face. All seemed to be well with her, a relief. Katy had been so busy ever since William left, she'd neglected her friends.

Joan reached out to clasp hands with Katy. "I wanted to invite you to afternoon tea. We can catch up on all the gossip in town."

"I would enjoy that very much." Katy grimaced as she squeezed her friend's hands. "Unfortunately, I have a very big project to begin which needs to be finished in a very short time."

"Surely you can spare a few minutes to have tea. You must keep up your strength." The mischievous grin on Joan's face suggested she had an ulterior reason for her visit. "Please inquire with your mother whether she can release you for a mere thirty minutes."

The temptation proved great indeed. To have the luxury of spending dedicated time with her close friend, to share the various observations and happy moments. Her mother would most likely encourage her to do so. Only the responsibility of the large job of printing a book in only a month weighed down her enthusiasm.

"I am sorry, Joan, but really must decline. We will soon, though. I promise."

~

The warming fire in the fireplace snapped and popped. The chill of the autumn season continued to deepen into colder temperatures. Grateful for the heat emanating from the fireplace, Katy continued working on some new blank forms for the government.

"I cannot believe this." Her mother marched across the floor, her long brown skirts brushing her shoes with each stride. She stopped to point at the newspaper in her hand. "Look at this. This press claims it has the same *New England Almanack for 1767*. That is not possible. We have an exclusive on the pamphlet."

"Let me see that." Katy took the paper from her and studied it. Apparently several Boston firms—R. and S. Draper, Edes and Gill, T. and J. Fleet, and Green and Russell —advertised the same Benjamin West almanack as what the Goddard print shop offered. "They cannot say such things when they are untrue. We must let our readers know the truth of the matter."

"Yes, we'll write a notice for Mr. Inslee to include in the next edition." Sarah retrieved the paper and sighed. "Will you help me draft something immediately?"

Over the next twenty minutes, the two worked on putting the strongest objections possible together to be included in the next *Gazette*. The final notice concluded with, "Charity bids them hope, that those Gentlemen have more Virtue and Honor, than to pursue under-handed Measures to obtain the Property of others, and that Mr. West could not be deluded by any consideration to deviate from the Paths of Rectitude, and risque the Loss of his Credit by selling a second-Time what he had already disposed of."

"That should stop their false claims, Mother."

"Yes, it should. Mr. Inslee, please come here and prepare this notice for the next edition." Sarah held out the scribbled draft. "Use your talents to make this stand out so everyone is forewarned of this chicanery."

The lanky man ambled over to casually accept the paper. Katy didn't know what her brother had thought of this helper. Samuel had apprenticed under Benjamin Franklin and then worked for William for some time on his new paper in Philadelphia. Young Tom Braverman had not suited for being an apprentice and was terminated, so the Goddard shop in Providence needed some help to meet demand. Thus her brother had sent Samuel Inslee to work with them. He was good at his job but exhibited little in the way of industry and energy.

"The other thing I need to do is to seek tanned sheepskins for the book binding side of things. Also rags are desperately needed so we can make paper now that the paper mill is turning a profit. These shortages are starting to impair our ability to keep up with our customers' needs."

"I'm sure we can write something up without any problem, Mother." Why was her mother so worried? Katy hadn't heard of any immediate shortages. "How urgent is your need?"

"I'm looking ahead based on the jobs in the queue." Sarah started to say more when the front door opened. She looked to see who had entered.

Katy jumped up from her stool when she recognized Joan. Chagrin flooded through her at the lapse of time since her last visit with her friend. After Katy had declined her offer of tea back in July, it had been several weeks before she'd found time to join her in August. Now, she'd come again, two months later. What a terrible, negligent friend Katy had become. So many jobs had swamped the four people working in the shop that she'd neglected everyone, not just her dear friend. Hopefully, she could still call her such.

"Joan! I'm so, so sorry I have been such a terrible friend." Katy quickly embraced Joan's shoulders and then stepped back. "How have you been? Let me look at you."

"I'm well. I know you've been very busy but I fear for your health. You work so much. I think you need to take time to enjoy your life as well as your work." Joan clasped her hands together and aimed serious eyes at Katy. "Please, my friend, come join me and the others for afternoon tea. I think you deserve to also have some free time to enjoy things."

Katy looked to her mother, who stood tensely by the counter. They did have a lot of work to do, but nothing needed to be completed that day. She glanced to where Paul and Sam were working on composing pages for the newspaper. Her own work table awaited her to finish the playbill. The play wasn't scheduled for weeks, though, so why couldn't she spare some time for her friends? After all, nobody could work without some kind of pause to relax and refresh.

"Very well. Let me ask Mother if she agrees first." At Joan's nod, Katy took her arm and ushered her toward her mother. Understanding lit in Sarah's eyes as she stopped near her. "Mother, would you mind sparing me for a spell to have tea with my best friend?"

"I think that is a fine idea. But please return ere long so we can meet our deadlines."

As Katy and Joan strolled out of the shop, still arm in arm, Katy vowed to herself to find a way to have time for both work and play.

"Who might you be?" Patrice teased. "I can't recall your name…"

Katy laughed as she took her seat at the table at Miss Jenny's Tea House. "Well deserved. Shall I introduce myself to you?"

Katy glanced around the half-empty establishment. It looked like most every other eating place that served ladies in the city. White cloth-covered tables with a center candlestick were scattered about the large room. An immense stone fireplace occupied the side wall, a roaring fire inside. Quiet conversations murmured throughout the room. Several windows looked out onto the street, gold drapes hanging on either side of each. A comfortable and pleasing place to yet again while away some time with her friends.

Joan settled on the last open chair at the square table. "That's enough foolery, ladies. Shall I pour?"

"Oh, please, let me." Katy reached for the silver tea pot sitting on a matching tray near her. "It's the least I can do after neglecting all of you for so long."

Patrice pushed a stray lock of her light brown hair behind her ear with a graceful movement of her fingers. "At least you're looking well. I feared like Joan that you would work yourself to death."

Katy poured the fragrant liquid into four cups, sliding one to each of her three friends. "I'm sorry Susan couldn't join us, too." She set the pot down on the tray and then drew her cup toward her to sample the delightful mint-flavored black tea. "What is taking up her time these days?"

"She has a new beau, so spends most of her time with him." Mary held her cup between her two hands, peering over the steaming rim with laughing eyes. "It's quite shameful that she's thrown us over for a mere man."

Having a man in one's life could indeed make priorities change. Katy smiled at her good friends, glad Joan had insisted she leave work to spend a few minutes with them. With more help in the shop, she'd not be needed quite as much. She wanted to be needed, but perhaps a little less than she'd let herself commit to over the past years. Life was more than work, after all. Still, she'd not want a man involved. After Robert ended their friendship, she'd chosen to concentrate on her work. And now, she lived her life on her own terms just as she'd always wanted.

"How serious are they?" Joan asked, setting her cup on its saucer.

Mary shook her head slowly, but the merriment in her eyes continued. "I think it's quite serious. I'd be surprised if the gentleman in question doesn't ask for her hand before the month is ended."

"We may soon be attending nuptials." Patrice sat up even straighter as she looked at each of the women around the table. "I wonder how quickly they'd tie that knot."

"Does it matter?" Katy chuckled softly, drawing startled looks from her friends. "All I have to say is, no matter when such an event occurs, I'm of the opinion that it will be 'better her than me.' I have no intention of marrying."

Joan blinked slowly, considering her announcement with wide eyes staring at her. "Whyever not?"

She had never talked about Richard and the pain of his passing. Nor of the brief sadness when Robert ended things. What purpose would doing so serve? She didn't want to be pitied or dismissed because of her determination to support herself rather than rely on anyone else to provide for her. So what should she say to satisfy her friend's obvious curiosity?

Katy looked straight into Joan's eyes, letting her smile widen. "I do not believe any man would live up to my high expectations."

The truth emerged into the afternoon quiet a little louder than she intended. But she'd stand by her claim.

Patrice chuckled. "Well, my friend, that probably happens to more of us than you might think."

"You believe so?" Katy refrained from saying more, not wanting to encourage the conversation. She detected some others in the room were paying close attention to the girls.

"Not all men are as kind as they are handsome," Mary said, after sipping her tea. "I've met far too many who think highly of themselves but do not act the part."

Joan nodded as she swept her gaze around the group. "Some men who wouldn't win any awards for their appearance have far more going for them in other aspects of their character."

"Perhaps," Katy interjected, intending to find a way to gently end the conversation. "Does anyone want some tea cakes? They look delicious."

CHAPTER 7

PROVIDENCE, RHODE ISLAND – 1767

*S*now flew outside the front windows of the little print shop. Katy hummed to herself as she worked on completing a new form order for the county government while Paul stoked the fireplace, the scent of burning wood filling the air. She glanced up at the sound of footsteps crossing the floor. Samuel Inslee. He lugged the bucket of ink across to put it near the press. He had fitted right into the flow of the press, despite his slower pace. He'd learned quickly and soon became indispensable to the general work he handled.

She paused in her composing work to look around the room, noting each apprentice and her mother employed in their various tasks. Composing the many kinds of documents required the person doing so to be well educated and capable of not only choosing the right sorts of type but also understanding what the text conveyed. Her efforts to expand on the solid education her mother had given her by reading more had bolstered her own abilities on that front. Thus she kept doing the composing.

Sarah, sitting near the front counter, spent her time

mostly on the content of the newspaper. Perusing other papers from different cities and selecting which items their readers would most appreciate. In fact, she'd made a point of including in this day's *Providence Gazette* William's announcement of the new paper in Philadelphia, *The Pennsylvania Chronicle, and Universal Advertiser*. It would compete with three other newspapers in that town. The first issue of the *Chronicle* was due to be published on the second of January, just two days away. In the middle of the title was an image of the king's arms. William had chosen to use the new bourgeois type on a large medium sheet in folio. The result was an easy to read and aesthetically pleasing newspaper.

"Katy, did you see this?" Her mother strode over to where Katy worked at composing the blank employment application form. She held out a sheaf of papers with scrawling handwriting crammed onto each page. "It's from William."

"What does he want?" She squinted at the writing but her mother folded the letter and tucked it away.

The last time they'd seen William was back in November when he'd come to make arrangements so that they could continue the printing shop and paper mill. They'd divided up the responsibilities such that they were shared among all of the printing shop workers, rotating who traveled out to the mill to check on it. After that William went back to Philadelphia to finalize the partnership agreement between himself and the two other prominent men in that city. The paper he envisioned publishing would be on a far bigger scale than any other, a large folio with four columns instead of the customary three. How would the other printers react to that challenge? She could imagine not well.

"He's detailed the agreement he's made with Joseph Galloway and Thomas Wharton. It sounds like quite a good prospect for William. Apparently, even Benjamin Franklin may be offered a partnership in the venture when he returns from overseas." Sarah crossed her arms and studied Katy. "It may be that William will finally find success and happiness there."

"I pray so." If only he would find both and settle down. "He needs to find a way to fit into the society instead of…"

Her mother held up her forefinger in admonition. "Now, now. I know he can be rather abrupt, but he has found good situations for himself and for us. Don't forget he's made it possible for us to be content and prosperous in service to our community. You've made several good friends, like Miss Wythe, and we couldn't ask for anything."

Chastised, Katy could only nod. She shouldn't think ill of her brother. He was well-intentioned and ambitious even if he did tend to annoy others. He was nothing if not constant in his attitude and ways. Not that those attitudes and ways came across in a friendly or polite manner. But important men backed him so he must not be too abrasive. And he'd sent help to them when they needed it in the person of Samuel.

She glanced to where the man in question wiped his hands on a rag and then met her gaze. He finished with the rag and tossed it on the table, all while maintaining a level look. He gave a slight nod, as if having made a decision, then started toward her and her mother. Something obviously weighed on his conscience.

Samuel cleared his throat as he walked up to stand before her mother. "Mrs. Goddard, I wish to speak to you if you have a moment."

Sarah's clear expression dimmed as her sober gaze met the older man's serious one. "What can I help you with, Mr. Inslee?"

"Ma'am, I've come to the difficult decision that I will retire next month. That will hopefully give you time to find a replacement." Samuel pressed his lips together for a moment. "I am sorry if this leaves you in a bind but I must."

He was leaving so soon? He'd only just started working in the shop three months ago. Concern flooded through her at his unspoken reasons. Was it based on his health that he felt the need to step away? Or something else? Would William blame her for Samuel's quitting for some unknown reason?

"I am sorry to hear this, as well." Sarah regarded him silently for a second, a quick glance at Katy confirming her surprise. "May I inquire as to why?"

Samuel straightened to look down on her. "It's personal, ma'am. I've given you my two week's notice so you can find a good replacement."

Her mother smiled up at the lanky man, a smile tight with affront. "Thank you for your consideration. Please return to your work and I will begin my search for another helper."

Samuel nodded once and then turned to walk slowly back to the press to help Paul with printing the day's paper to send out.

"That was a surprise." Sarah sighed as she placed a hand on her back, grimacing as she turned to address Katy. "I suppose I'll need to put a notice in the paper that we're searching for print shop help."

"Are you feeling all right, Mother?" Her mother's expression hinted at some level of discomfort. "Is your back bothering you again?"

"Yes, some. But I have more to do before we can depart for home."

"When we do get home, I'll put together a warm compress for you. That should help."

Sarah nodded as she started to walk away. "I would greatly appreciate that."

Watching her mother move slowly across the floor sent shafts of concern darting through her core. She hummed to herself. Once again her mother's health and well-being worried her. Despite all of her reading about medicine and healthy practices, whenever her mother seemed unwell, she worried. But at least this time she could help alleviate her mother's pain, a reality which helped to comfort both of them. If only all her worries were so easily handled.

William was at it again. Causing people to attack him for what he published in his new paper. The larger folio made the other printers jealous of its quality and content. And even more toward its content when William had published that caustic piece in March attacking William Bradford's *The Pennsylvania Journal* under the name Lex Talionis. Katy had been dismayed to read it, recognizing how vitriolic a message the lines contained. Surely the men so attacked would respond to such poor treatment. Had William penned the article, or merely printed it? The end result was the same, no matter. Her mother was beside herself when she read what he'd published.

Sarah had written a stern letter to him, one which he surely had received by now. How might he react to her caution and chastisement? She held no hope that anything either of them said would faze him. He couldn't stop himself from reacting badly to perceived slights. Not even his mother's ire or chagrin would make an impression. Several lines of her mother's letter echoed in her mind as she continued working on the day's project.

The opening lines set the tone of the entire missive. "It is with aching heart and trembling hand I attempt to write, but hardly able, for the great concern and anxious fears the sight of your late Chronicles gave me, to find you involved deeper and deeper in an unhappy uncomfortable situation.

In your calm hours of reflection, you must see the impropriety of publishing such pieces as Lex Talionis let the authors be ever so great and dignified, for every one who takes delight in publicly or privately taking away any person's good name, or striving to render him ridiculous, are in the gall of bitterness, and in the bonds of iniquity, whatever their pretences may be for it." Such strong language from such a genteel woman, words that would poke and prod at her brother's self-worth and composure. But would they make any dent?

Now that the print shop had lost Samuel Inslee, there was even more to be done each day. Katy spent long hours at the shop to ensure they met the demands of their customers with accuracy and alacrity. Her mother had advertised for help, and several lads had appeared to apply for the position. However, none had met the standards her mother insisted upon. Slovenly appearance, apathy toward the work, and hints of alcohol were all reasons for sending them on their way. She'd written to William to ask him to send someone to help her but so far no one had appeared.

Paul came over to stand beside her work table. "Miss Goddard, I was wondering if you need further assistance for the move next month? I have some friends in want of work, if you do."

Her mother had arranged to move the print shop from the small house over to a larger place where the post office used to be. The young man had proven over and over again how resourceful and helpful he was. She hadn't thought through how many people it would take to relocate the press and the furniture as well as the supplies of ink and paper. Katy had composed the advertisement that would go into the paper once the move was completed in May, including the fact that the shop was "at the Sign of Shakespeare's Head." That sign amused her, given the reaction to plays in the pious city. Why did they choose to use a playwright's portrait as their signage?

"I believe the more hands we have to make the move go smoothly the better. Please let Mrs. Goddard know of who you're referring to."

"Yes, miss. I'll do that." He grinned at her then, with a little wink for good measure. "I thought as much but I knew you'd have a good idea of how your mother would react to my offer. I'm pleased you agree. Thank you." He tipped two fingers to his brow and then ambled over to where Sarah was sweeping the entry to the shop.

Maybe when they moved and expanded their business, they would finally be able to afford to hire a maid to keep the place clean. She and her mother had endeavored to keep the shop financially solvent and growing, all the better to serve their community. The future seemed bright for the print shop and its associated newspaper and book bindery. She sighed. As long as her brother didn't make more enemies and upturn the cart for everyone.

Several months passed during which the ebb and flow of printing jobs kept everyone on their toes. Katy's mother advertised for help but none suited. William finally wrote that he knew of a young man he thought would work out well for the Providence shop. A man by the name of John Carter. He was expected any moment. Katy wanted to finalize her project before he arrived but simply wasn't satisfied with it. She tapped her index finger on the composing table, staring at the layout spread before her.

"Katy, dear, have you quite finished with the last page galley for that pamphlet you've been fiddling with for days?" Sarah's gentle smile softened the challenge in her question.

Katy had been unhappy with the alignment of certain line elements used as separators and the motif type used for decoration. Time was short, though. The man who'd requested it was waiting for her to finish and print it, wanting to distribute it in a matter of days. But something about the layout irked her and she needed to determine how to make it right.

"Almost, but I must resolve my dissatisfaction with it first. Why? Do you need me to do something else?" Several customers had come and gone, according to the jangling bell over the door, but she'd been concentrating on her work. If she were needed, her mother would let her know.

Her mother held out a neatly written page. "This deposition needs to be composed forthwith so it can be processed by the court."

She'd been working as quickly as she could and still turn out a quality job. She bit back a retort, one born from simmering frustration with the current job. It wasn't her mother's fault she hadn't finished the pamphlet. Katy read the brief sworn statement regarding an apparent threat to another man's business interests. It's short and sweet. So... "Can't Mr. Lancaster handle this one?"

The door jangled open, drawing Katy's attention away from the conversation with her mother. A young man, probably in his early twenties, strode in and looked around with a sense of purpose in his searching gaze. John Carter, most likely. He met Katy's curious eyes with a nod and smiled in greeting, removing his hat. He was a fine looking man, with evident energy and apparently friendly, given the smile still on his face. She had the sense that he assessed her being with one sweep of his intense gaze and liked what he saw. She stiffened her resolve as she straightened her spine. He lifted his chin just a touch, enough to indicate he received the silent warning she'd just sent. Even if she were interested in courting, he was too young and not settled into a career path which would support a family. Not yet.

He stopped beside Katy's mother and performed a half bow. "Mrs. Goddard?"

"You must be Mr. Carter. Welcome. We've been expecting you." Sarah returned his welcoming smile.

"I came as quickly as I could get my affairs in Philadelphia sorted. Your son informed me of your situation, being down a man. I'm prepared to begin work as soon as you'd like." He held his hat in one hand at his side as he turned his head to quickly scan the room. His gaze stopped when he noticed the work space that Samuel had left idle at the far side of the room. Then looked at Sarah again. "What would you have me do?"

"First, let me introduce you to my daughter, Mary Katharine." Sarah waited while Katy and William exchanged a quick nod acknowledging the introduction. "Then I'd like for you take the role of journeyman and start with composing the galley for this deposition. Katy is still working on another project, but this one has some urgency."

"Shall I set up over there?" He motioned to the empty work table. "I'm sure I can find what I need. Mr. Franklin taught me well."

"You apprenticed under Benjamin Franklin?" Katy lifted her brows in some little surprise.

"Years ago, before he left for France. He was very generous and took me under his tutelage, miss. Your brother will attest to my abilities. That is why he asked me to come, so I could readily aid you, Mrs. Goddard." This last with a nod to Katy's mother.

"Yes, he said as much in his letter informing me of your agreement and pending arrival." Sarah handed the paper to John and then indicated for him to follow her. "Come, I'll ensure you are settled as quickly as possible. I do not want to have much if any backlog of print jobs. It's my intent to stay abreast of the work so our customers are satisfied."

Relief flowed into Katy with the arrival of the skilled worker. He seemed sharp and eager to make a good impression in addition to being kind and respectful. He should get along very well. She turned back to her own challenge, intent on solving it as quickly as possible.

John did fit in very well and he and Sarah became good partners. So much so that they announced in the September nineteenth edition a change to the management of the printing business.

> TO THE PUBLIC
>
> The partnership between SARAH GODDARD and COMPANY being dissolved, the PRINTING BUSINESS in future will be carried on by us the subscribers: --And as every proper measure has been Concerted to render the PROVIDENCE GAZETTE as useful and entertaining as possible, the utmost care and Diligence shall not be wanting, on our part, to give general and Entire Satisfaction, so we flatter ourselves the Public will continue to favour this Paper with their subscriptions, and afford such farther Encouragement as its merit may appear to deserve.
>
> SARAH GODDARD
>
> JOHN CARTER

Curious how easily John slipped into the flow of work at the print shop. His quick abilities and attention to particulars ensured the quick completion of one after another of the print jobs. He kept the apprentices on their toes, and had even instituted some improvements to the way they performed their jobs which yielded a more efficient routine for everyone. She'd been asked to dedicate her time to working on broadsides and books, two areas where she excelled.

Having less responsibility at the printing shop meant Katy had more time to spend with her friends, so she did not resent the new arrangement. In fact, she welcomed it. Now she could go to the theater and the parties her friends also attended. But she would obviously continue to work at the Goddard press nearly every day, learning and perfecting her skills alongside the apprentices. After all, she'd come to help her brother's shop and she'd do so even though he wasn't even in the same state.

CHAPTER 8

PROVIDENCE, RHODE ISLAND – 1768

Spring brought both aromatic flowers and a fresh sense of rejuvenation to the city as well as to Katy's soul. She stood at the open window, enjoying the scent of flowers on the breeze as well as the sight of them blooming in front of the houses on her street. A steady stream of coaches and wagons trundled past, now and again the driver of one waving at her in greeting. In the nearly six years they'd lived in the bustling town, she'd made several friends but many more acquaintances through her work with the press. She was content in a way she'd never thought possible before they moved to help her younger brother, both financially and physically. But today she wasn't working. Today, thanks to John's industry, she could spend some time with her dearest friend.

Gathering her shawl and purse, Katy hurried through the house in search of her mother to let her know she was leaving to meet Joan. She'd heard her come into the house while she finished dressing. Poking her nose into each room as she went downstairs from her bedchamber, she finally went down the central hall and out back to find her mother

98

sitting with a book in the garden. Her mother enjoyed sitting in one of the two white metal chairs under a tree, a glass of lemonade on the table positioned between them. It was early afternoon, a light breeze cooling the air but the sun warmed Katy's face as she approached her distracted parent.

"There you are. I thought you were needed at the shop this afternoon." Katy laid her purse on the arm of a chair and wrapped the lightweight knitted shawl more snugly around her shoulders.

"I came home a little while ago." Her mother met her gaze with a calm expression. "I will go back in a few minutes. Mr. Carter insisted I should take a break and he'd oversee everything." Sarah placed a narrow silk ribbon in her geography book and closed it. "I agreed in order to give my back a rest."

"Is it bothering you again?" Katy retrieved her purse while inspecting her mother's posture to assess her discomfort. Her straight spine and easy countenance suggested minimal pain. "I can prepare a compress when I return home after tea with Joan."

"It's feeling much better after a little rest, but thank you for the kind offer." Sarah stood and peered at Katy. "You forget about me and go enjoy your free afternoon with your friend. You've earned it."

"Yes, I'll need to hurry or she'll wonder if I'm coming." Katy stepped closer to give her mother an affectionate embrace. The subtle lavender and vanilla perfume her mother favored tantalized her nose. She'd forever equate the scent to the love of her mother. "I'll see you at supper."

"Yes, now shoo!" Her mother chuckled as she followed Katy back toward the house.

Katy smiled to herself as she turned and strode along the path around the house and onto the street in front. She never tired of the lovely neighborhood they'd made a new home in. As she hurried along as quickly as dignity would allow, she nodded greetings to one after another of her neighbors. The walk to Miss Jenny's Tea House went quickly as she made her way down one street and turned to a side street where the cozy single-story house had been converted into a tea room. She didn't pause to admire the charming exterior of the stone house, but ascended the four stone steps to open the heavy wood door and go inside.

Miss Jenny's was like any other tea house except for the richly sweet scent of the Rhode Island Greening apples she used in her pies and tarts. During Katy's first visit, Miss Jenny had regaled her with the history of the popular cooking apple as well as her reasons for using that specific variety. Apparently, the Greening held its shape when cooked, unlike those used to make applesauce, for instance. She'd learned more about apples than she'd ever wanted to know, but she kept quiet and respectful of the baker's expertise.

The room boasted several round cloth-covered tables, each with a small lantern in the center surrounded by a garland of flowers. Most of the tables were occupied by two, three, or four guests. Except for one near the front window where Joan waited for her with a huge smile of greeting to welcome her. Katy soon took a seat at the table, reaching out a hand to squeeze her friend's fingers.

"I'm so happy to have time with you, Joan." Katy released her friend's hand and folded her hands together in her lap. "Our weekly chats are so important to me."

"They are to me, too." A fleeting worry flashed through Joan's eyes. "I hope nothing happens to intervene so that we are prevented from continuing this new habit."

What worried her friend? Could be her husband, who had become a jealous and possessive man from what Joan had said about his actions. Their wedding three years ago had been a somber affair but she'd seemed happy to be with the man despite his tendencies.

"Nothing will stop us from being friends."

"Agreed. I'm so glad you finally are permitted free time instead of working from dawn to dusk most every day."

"Yes, having Mr. Carter helping has made all the difference. I'm still busy, mind, but not so heavily weighed down with jobs. He also persuaded Mother to bring on another apprentice, so the work is spread out even more."

A young woman in a simple dark blue dress with a white lace-edged apron approached to tell them what the shop had on offer for the day and to take their order. After the brief interruption, Joan turned serious eyes on Katy.

"I need to tell you something. Something I should be happy about but I am concerned about Harold's reaction." Joan laid her hand on the table, palm up in invitation.

Katy placed her hand on top, wrapping her fingers around Joan's hand. "You know you can tell me anything."

The young woman brought a tray ladened with two tea cups in saucers, two small plates, a small bowl of sugar lumps, and a cream pitcher. Katy relinquished Joan's hand while the woman placed the items on the table and then hurried back to the kitchen to bring the pot of tea and apple tarts. Katy reached out again and clasped Joan's hand, a stronger grasp encouraging her to continue.

Joan nodded and moistened her lips. "I am with child again."

"That's wonderful! Why are you concerned?" Surely her husband would be proud to be a father for the third time. They had two beautiful girls already.

"What if it's another girl?" Joan squeezed Katy's hand hard. "He was so disappointed with the first two."

"He wants a son? Most men do." Katy thought about her own father. Had he been upset with the fact that her mother had birthed two girls—even though the first one didn't survive—before her younger brother was born? Had that fact caused a strain between her parents? Knowing her parents, she couldn't imagine such an event. But a man such as Mr. Harold Edward Langley could easily be upset with not fathering a son, what many considered to be a more manly act. "Have you told him of your condition?"

Joan nodded again, tears glimmering in her eyes. "First thing. His reaction was not unexpected but still sends pangs of anxiety through me."

"It's out of your hands, my dear friend. Only God knows whether you will deliver a boy or a girl." Katy squeezed Joan's hand again and then sat back in her chair. "Try to not worry over something you cannot control. It'll make you ill."

The young woman returned with an aromatic pot of Hyson, or what was commonly called Lucky Dragon green tea, and a plate of apple tarts. Katy sniffed appreciatively as she lifted a tart and took a small bite, cinnamon and nutmeg filling her nostrils. Joan poured the pale yellow-green tea into the flowered porcelain cups nestled on matching saucers.

Katy swallowed her bite and rinsed it down with a sip of tea. "These are so delicious."

"Miss Jenny is a marvel in the kitchen." Joan bit into a tart and closed her eyes for a moment as she savored the pastry. "Makes me forget all my troubles."

Katy chuckled as she raised her tea cup, holding it with one hand as she studied her friend's delighted features. "Joan, you know that I'll be here to help in any way I can. You won't be having this baby all by yourself, just like with your other children."

Joan fastened her gaze on Katy and nodded slowly. "I'm counting on my ladies to help me with the lying in again. It's a dangerous time for both me and the little one."

"Definitely. Now, let's enjoy our tea and tarts before I have to go. I want to check in at the shop to see what jobs await me on the morrow."

A little later, Katy parted company with Joan. The beautiful May afternoon could not be any better. A clear blue sky with an occasional white puffy cloud floating by. The scent of the flowering bushes nestled against the houses and shops lining the street. The call of the seagulls above. A light breeze to soften the warmth of the sunshine casting shadows across her path. All capped with having spent a lovely hour with her friend. Life was perfect.

Opening the door to the print shop, the bell jingling above her, Katy found her mother greeting her with compressed lips. What was wrong? Closing the door behind her, Katy hurried to stand beside her mother at the front counter. She seemed upset and severe.

"What has happened, Mother?" Katy clutched her purse to her waist, her stomach in knots at the tension emanating from her mother.

"This." She held out a letter with a shaking hand. "From William."

Katy raised her brows as she unfolded the paper and quickly devoured his words. Then she read it again, not believing what she had read.

"I do not wish to comply with his request." Sarah held out her hand to take the letter back, folding it and putting it on the counter. "I know no one in Philadelphia and do not want to."

"Although it seems his partners have made quite a generous offer, why would he ask us to move to help him with yet another print shop? What of this one?" Katy let her gaze drift across the busy shop, the men each busy with their individual tasks at the composing tables and the press. John happened to look up, his initial cheerful expression trans- forming into a wary one.

"I expect he'd want to sell it if we agreed. Should we?" Her mother leveled her frown on Katy. "I think we should refuse, despite my promise to your father. I'm too old to move again."

"I just learned that Joan is with child and I promised I'd be here for her. So no, I do not want to agree either." Could they refuse him? What would happen to them if he decided to sell out the Providence shop despite their preferences? "What should we do?"

"I'll write to him and tell him that I am too elderly to contemplate leaving my friends and family to move to another city. He'll have to accept my decision." Pressing her lips together, Sarah grabbed a clean sheet of stationary and started writing a short note. When she finished, she turned the paper around so Katy could read what it said.

"I like the way you conclude, Mother. This part where you say, 'my life is almost at a close, and I can hardly think of removing so near the period of my days into a strange part of the world, to launch into a new set of acquaintances, and leave all my former ones, the companions of my youth, and the supporters of my old age, as well as my daughter, who seems by nature designed to take care of her mother in sick- ness, when wanted, which is not so properly in the sphere of sons, and cannot be expected of them.' That should persuade him to accept our decision."

"Indeed." Sarah folded and sealed the letter, then prepared to send it via the Royal Post. "Now, what brings you into the shop on your free afternoon?"

"I wanted to find out what jobs I'd be working on when I come on the morrow."

Katy spotted a stack of papers on the counter with a variety of handwriting evident. Each one represented another job. Then there was a stack of books and pamphlets to be republished through their press. A never-ending workload. She enjoyed doing her part, composing the broadside galleys and printing and binding the books. In particular, she enjoyed sewing the folios together and attaching the leather covers.

She couldn't and wouldn't give up the comfortable life she'd worked so hard to create. Not willingly, anyway.

With the arrival of June came the text for the 1769 almanack from Mr. West. Katy set it aside to tackle later, after she finished with the series of sermon pamphlets they'd received to publish for a local minister. The minister had a particular image in mind of how the pages should be, and he'd specifically requested Katy to create them. An honor and a privilege she refused to fail at. Taken together, the lessons from a variety of religious leaders in the colonies were to be used to further educate his congregation.

Paul and John tinkered with one part of the bigger printing press. Given their language, she assumed their efforts were not proving successful. Something had apparently jammed or become stuck in some way. Her mother chatted with an older woman at the counter, trying to determine what the frail white-haired woman wanted to advertise in the *Gazette*. Katy's gaze traveled to the open door and beyond, noting the steady stream of creaking vehicles and business-like pedestrians passing the shop and post office combined. A light drizzle was falling, making everything glisten. Her mother served as the postmistress in William's absence, drawing on her own experience after Katy's father passed and Sarah stepped in to manage the post office in New London. But everyone knew that William was the actual postmaster. Because of course it required a man to be in charge.

Drawing in a calming breath, Katy concentrated on aligning the type ornaments neatly beneath the sermon's title in the galley. Straightening the last piece a tad, she selected the next type from the lower case where the ornamentals were kept beside the letters. As she reached for the next, strong footsteps sounded from the front of the shop. A frisson of alarm shivered through her. A quick glance showed her that William had suddenly arrived in the city. After the letter her mother sent to him, his abrupt appearance didn't bode well.

All work stopped. Everyone reacted to his presence, a mutual understanding that something important was about to occur.

"William, what brings you here unannounced?" Sarah came out from behind the counter to address her son. "Is something amiss?

"I've come to take you and Katy to White's Tavern for a splendid midday meal." William smiled—smirked?—at his mother. "We need to have a conversation."

He'd come all the way from Philadelphia to have luncheon with them? And talk? She could well imagine the conversation he desired to have with them. Steeling her spine, Katy set aside the composing stick and rose from the stool to cross to greet her brother. After a brief, stilted embrace, she clasped her hands and waited.

"As you can see, we're all very busy today meeting our deadlines." Sarah presented a serene expression to her son. "Perhaps we can discuss whatever is on your mind at supper this evening?"

"I'm afraid that is not possible. My time is limited in this place before I must return to Philadelphia. Please, Mother, allow me to escort you and Katy to White's. Surely you can spare me an hour after I've come all this way?"

He used the tone. The one their mother couldn't say no to. The one that sounded like a cross between a whine and a command. As predicted, Sarah nodded.

"Come, Katy. Let's do as he asks." Sarah met Katy's reluctant gaze. "Let us go now so we can come back and finish here as soon as possible."

In other words, she wanted to indulge her son's demand as quickly as possible in order to get on with her day.

"Very well." Katy forced a smile onto her lips as she noted William's smug expression.

A short while later the three of them were seated at the tavern a few doors away from the print shop. White's had proven very popular and always entertained a large number of customers. The tavern featured a more refined appearance than some other more rustic establishments. More of a cross between those and the tea house Katy frequented with Joan. White's also had a more hearty menu to offer to its customers, promoting stews and pot pies of a large variety. Of course, many relied on the local fishermen's catches. The aroma of fish hung heavy in the air as they waited for the waiter to serve them.

"Now that we're here, tell me what is so urgent that you had to travel here without any warning." Sarah sat straight in her chair, her eyes darting nervously between William and Katy.

William pulled a paper from his pocket and laid it on the table. "This letter you wrote me. I'm afraid I can't accept your arguments. Let me tell you about this wonderful situation that my partners are offering to you both."

Sarah sighed and shook her head. "It's not the offer that I am concerned about. It's the idea of moving at my advanced age. I'm comfortable and settled here. Why should I uproot myself and my household to a strange place?"

Why indeed should they move yet again? Just because he had? She swallowed the angry surge inside. The reason for his sudden appearance, without even a note of warning, meant he wanted to cajole them into moving to Philadelphia. To push them into complying with his wishes. His needs. Without even caring what they'd give up to meet such a demand. Thinking of himself first, as always. She didn't expect him to do otherwise. Surely, though, she and her mother had the option of saying no to his request.

"I do not wish to move away. I have friends here who need me." Katy gripped her hands in her lap, anger making them tremble. "Joan needs me for her lying in."

William met her stubborn look with a blank expression. "I'm sure your friends, including that one, have other friends, and their family, to see to their needs." He blinked and then turned back to regard Sarah. "I need you both in Philadelphia. Please, Mother, don't make this difficult. Mr. Wharton and Mr. Galloway will provide you a house to live in, money to set up a combination book and stationery shop. And will provide an allowance for you both. You'll be much better off, and we'll be together again as a family and in the business. Please, agree to come help me?"

Katy let out a quiet sigh. He'd used the tone again. He'd simply completely dismissed their concerns and reasons for resisting. Their worries and preferences were nothing in his esteem.

"What about the *Gazette*, and the shop?" Sarah glanced at Katy, defeat in her eyes. "Should we offer to sell it to Mr. Carter? He's been instrumental in increasing the amount of customers for the shop and the circulation for the paper."

"That's a fine idea. I'll need to relinquish my postmaster position, but I'll recommend for Mr. Carter to fill it in my place." William smiled broadly at each of them. "Thank you both. I am in your debt and promise you will not regret your decision."

She already did. Her stomach fell at the thought of how she'd break the news to Joan, to all of her friends. To the *Gazette* subscribers, too. They'd come to count on the service Katy and her mother had established and which Mr. Carter had expanded. Starting over yet again meant establishing connections within a new, strange location. Making new friends. All for what purpose? William didn't specify exactly why he needed them there so badly.

Gazing at him, she sensed something not quite right. Something in her brother's expression hinted at some level of deception. What was he hiding? What had they just agreed to?

Miss Jenny's Tea House buzzed with conversation when Katy entered the cheerful building. If only she felt as cheerful as the place looked. She spotted Joan sitting at a table by the fireplace and made her way through the smattering of tables scattered about the room. As she approached, she perused her friend's countenance and demeanor, not liking what she saw.

Joan's usual happy smile of greeting seemed wilted on this summer's day. Perhaps the heat of the afternoon sun had caused her tired expression. Her blonde hair was pulled up into a simple bun, her azure eyes somewhat squinting at her as she reached the table and quickly took a seat beside her friend. She wore a white apron over her bulging dress, the unspoken signal of her condition. The extra layer provided modesty as her waist expanded with the development of the baby.

"How are you faring today?" Katy smoothed her skirts across her lap and then clasped her hands together. "You seem a bit tired. Is it the heat?"

Joan's smile slipped away entirely. "I—What kind of tea would you like?"

"Whatever you're having is fine." The abrupt change of subject sent concern wriggling through Katy like a snake in the grass. "What is the matter, Joan?"

Joan forced her lips to curve a small bit as she poured reddish-brown liquid into a fresh cup. "I am just feeling the baby moving and am worried about the future. But it's not for you to worry about, my friend."

"Your health and wellbeing are important to me. I don't like seeing you look so fatigued. What can I do to help?"

Though she only had a few months before she'd be packing up and moving away. Her mother and William, along with John Carter, had decided it would take time to prepare for the big move. They aimed to leave in the fall as a result. Leaving behind her dear friends, especially Joan with child and fearful. How could she walk away and leave her to fend for herself? Katy mentally shook herself. Joan had her family and other friends to aid her as needed. She wasn't actually going to be left alone to survive the birthing. Still, moving so far away made her heart ache. Perhaps the wee baby would arrive before they departed. A faint hope.

Joan sighed as she studied Katy for a moment. "I do not believe anything is to be done. I must learn to bide my time and bolster my courage for what is to come. But I appreciate your caring."

Of course she cared about her friend's feelings and worries. Soon, her caring would be relegated to being contained in letters exchanged. For how long though? Could they sustain a friendship through weekly missives? She let out a sigh of her own.

The serving girl hurried up to the table with a plate of fragrant cinnamon buns drizzled with white icing which she placed on the table before spinning about and hurrying off again. Unable to resist the mouthwatering temptation, Katy lifted one and took a small bite. A burst of warmed cinnamon flooded her mouth followed by a decadently sweet bread. Delicious.

"So, Katy, what is amiss with you? Why the heavy sigh?" Joan raised both brows as she lifted her tea cup to her lips.

The time had come to tell her, but how? Especially on the heels of her unease about the pending lying in and how her husband might reject the child if it proved to be female. Now to add to those concerns felt like pouring salt into an open wound. She wiped sweet icing off her lips without meeting Joan's expectant gaze.

She took a sip of her tea—something with a hint of orange—and swallowed slowly. Anything to delay for just another moment. Suppressing yet another sigh, she pressed her lips together for a moment and then blurted, "Joan, I have news."

Joan's hand paused in the act of setting down her cup so that she could stare at Katy, obviously to see if she could anticipate the kind of news. "Now you're upset. What news have you?"

"I am…moving." Somehow saying the words made her feel ill. Queasy and sweaty.

"To a new house? That's not bad news, that could be quite lovely." Joan smiled encouragingly at her. "Why do you seem distraught?"

"Because… It's not just… How can we do this? But we are. We're moving to Philadelphia this fall. I must, for my brother, but I don't want to." She leaned forward to peer into Joan's surprised eyes. "I am sorry I won't be here when your baby is born, to help you with your lying in." Tears rolled down her cheeks and she dabbed them away with her cloth napkin.

"Philadelphia? All the way to Pennsylvania?" Sitting back in her chair, Joan grimaced then arranged her features into a gentle smile. "That's so distant. Why there?"

"William has started a newspaper and printing shop there with two partners who apparently insist that Mother and I are needed." She bit off another small piece of bun, chewed and swallowed, all while striving to calm her inner agitation. "Probably to act as a buffer between William's volatile nature and the partners and customers. If only my brother was more like our father, then he would find it far easier to interact with others without such inflammatory remarks and judgments."

"Surely he's really not so ill-behaved. Is he?" Joan lifted the floral tea pot to pour more tea into their cups.

"Indeed he is when the mood strikes." She waggled a hand briefly above the table. "Most of the time he's a gentleman but when he's crossed or feels slighted… Well, let's just say he can be rather a boor."

She'd really hoped he'd grown out of such ungentlemanly behavior but he had not. She'd witnessed his anger and withering dismissal of grown men who came into the shop. Usually he was at least polite to them, but there were times when he was barely controlling his temper so as not to lose the man's business.

"We'll never see each other again, will we? But we can write and tell each other everything that is new and exciting." Joan nodded as she spoke.

She loved her friend for trying so hard to be accepting of the tragic news she'd just shared with her. Joan had a way of seeing the good in every situation. "I do not know. I hope I may be able to travel back or you could journey to visit the city with your family some day."

Joan chuckled as her fake smile grew into a genuine one of mirth. "I imagine that is unlikely. Harry is not enamored with travel. He prefers to behave as a hermit, lording over his dominion."

"I see." Katy smiled as she slowly shook her head. "Then I suppose we'll have to rely upon pen and paper to maintain our friendship."

"As for my lying in, I hope you won't move before this baby comes, but please know that I have my mother and sisters as well as our friends who have all promised to assist." Joan gripped Katy's clenched fist resting on the white cloth-covered table. "I would love for you to be there too, of course, but I understand if you cannot attend me. I will be fine."

Katy opened her hand and turned it over to clasp Joan's. "We'll always be friends despite the distance. After all, Philadelphia isn't the other side of the world."

"Yes, it's miles away not oceans." Joan squeezed her fingers and then released her hand to lift her tea cup in a toasting gesture.

Katy lifted hers to tap brims. "What shall we toast to?"

"To friends who last forever."

They tapped their cups and then sipped their cooling tea. Hopefully, their friendship would continue to be just as warm.

CHAPTER 9

PHILADELPHIA, PENNSYLVANIA – 1768

After several months of preparations, the day finally arrived when they'd board a ship for Philadelphia. The November cold had ushered in snow, making the voyage unpleasant on many fronts. Even the seagulls had left the sky to find shelter from the white flakes whirling through the air. Katy huddled below decks in the small cabin she shared with her mother, striving to stay warm despite the chill. Her mother stretched out under the rough blanket on the hard bed, her back bothering her again. Neither wanted to stand on deck and watch Providence grow smaller as they left its friendly embrace.

Joan's belly had grown large, forcing her to remain at home on the country estate Harold preferred. As a result, they hadn't seen each other since before Allhallows eve. Had she had her baby in the interim weeks? Surely someone would send word when the baby made its appearance. With good fortune, she'd birth a boy to make Harold pleased. Although Joan would be pleased as long as the child was whole and healthy. And that she survived the delivery to be able to enjoy raising it. A wave of disappointment washed through her. She'd not be able to attend, to see for herself the new addition to the family. She'd only have letters to fill the void of their friendship. But for how long? At what point might they grow so far apart as to no longer have any common interests to share in writing? The thought didn't help her mood one iota.

Neither did the fact that all of their meager remaining belongings were stowed in a holding area of the ship. They'd sold off their furniture and most of their possessions. Let go the maid and cook and butler amidst tears and long hugs of farewell. Katy's throat had choked with emotions she couldn't express. With good fortune, their new situation would work out to be a boon for everyone.

The day dragged by, the ship lurching through rough waters along the coast down to the harbor at Philadelphia. Katy didn't bother to eat anything, worried about not being able to keep it down. She'd rather be hungry than embarrass herself.

"How are you faring, Mother?" Katy leaned over her mother's prone figure. "From the sound of things above, I believe we're pulling into port."

Her mother shifted, peeling back the cover and sitting up in the bed. "I could use one of your healing compresses when we get settled in our new home."

"William is meeting us with a coach and four, or so he said in his letter. To take us straight to the house. I have a small supply of the ingredients for the compress, so it won't be much longer before you have some relief."

"Help me up and let's go up top and see what is happening." Her mother held out both hands and Katy took them, gently easing her out of the bed.

Sarah had aged gracefully, still an attractive woman. But of course, at sixty-seven, her joints tended to ache, and her back continued to hurt from time to time. Her gray hair, though, shone like silver in lamplight. Her eyes still twinkled when she laughed, and stilled like a calm sea when she was worried. Like now. Katy pressed her lips together as she wrapped an arm around her mother's waist to assist her up to the deck.

The deck hands were securing the ship to the dock, tossing ropes to men waiting on the pier. The cityscape of the much larger city loomed in the distance. Brick and frame homes and buildings crammed together along crowded streets. The pale blue sky held no clouds, no snow here. For that realization, Katy felt relief. While she liked to watch the flakes fall from inside a warm home, she did not relish traveling while it was doing so. Everything was more difficult under such conditions.

"There's William." Sarah pointed toward the far end of the dock where a coach and four waited, William beside it. "Let's prepare to disembark so we can find out the address of our new home to have our things sent round."

As soon as the gangway was in place, Katy led her tired mother carefully ashore. They hurried as quickly as they could toward William, who stood by the four matched black horses. Unease flowed through Katy at the concerned look on his face. Not even a smile in greeting. Her mother faltered for a step before continuing. Had she sensed something amiss as well?

"Welcome to Philadelphia, Mother, Katy." William half bowed to them as they stopped in front of him. A weak smile finally emerged on his lips but didn't reach his eyes. "I hope your voyage was uneventful."

"Other than being a miserable day to be on the water, all went as smoothly as could be hoped." Sarah straightened to peer into William's eyes. "Is something wrong?"

"Why would you think…"

"William, please. We both know you well enough to read

the concern in your eyes." Katy shifted her grip on her mother's arm, bracing beneath it to steady her. "Can you give the steward the address to send our things around? Then take us home. Mother is hurting and exhausted."

"Well, I suppose if you do not object I'll have them send your baggage to my house for the time being." William started to walk away, until Katy stopped him.

"Why your house?" She had no desire to live under his roof, under his command and demands. "We were promised our own place."

William shook off her hand from his forearm. "Turns out there wasn't a place after all. Mr. Wharton seemingly 'forgot' to arrange for it. I tried to secure an appropriate abode for you but haven't had any success. I'll need to look about and see what I can find for you. In the meantime, there is room at my home nearby. I found an adequate house near the river where you will be comfortable for a time."

"If we must. Thank you for taking us in." Sarah glanced between them, her brows drawn into a frown. "But what about the book shop and stationery shop? We'll need space for those ventures as well. And a press, of course, to create the books and letterhead."

"First, let me convey the address to the steward, then we'll work out the rest of the details." William marched up the pier to the ship and spoke briefly to the steward.

Katy turned to her mother with a huff. "I feared the offer would prove too good to be actually true. What now?"

"We'll find a new place to make into a home, and a business. Be patient. Everything will work out."

Katy could only trust in her mother's confidence because she harbored no such certainty in her own chest. Disappointment and anger warred in her breast as she watched her brother so casually ignore the immense inconvenience that living under his roof represented. Promises made and broken as easily as pie crust. He had not even thought it worth informing them of the change in circumstances ahead of their arrival, as if it were no matter of significance. Would the other promises made be kept or broken as well?

As it turned out, her mother proved correct...eventually. William located a lovely home on a quiet street not far from where his new newspaper and print shop was located at Market and Third and also close to the impressive Christ Church. He also arranged to have a new press installed in a large room on the first floor. But when his partners learned of a competing press so closely located to their own, they objected strenuously. Mr. Wharton had insisted on the press being moved back to the print shop and William had countered he'd confer with his mother before making any change.

Katy and her mother were not happy about giving up the small press for their use at their abode, but they had no choice except to run their business from the other shop. An inconvenience but not too high of an obstacle. But what upset her most was that William's partners had promised them the moon and gave them dust. How could he trust them? Couldn't he see they were self-serving and didn't keep their word? She could only hope that the disruptions to their plans had come to an end. Though that hope stood on shaky ground.

Like her mother had said, everything would work out. And it did. Just not the way she'd imagined. At least they had a workable setup to begin a new stationery and book binding shop. She'd strive to create new friendly connections in this big city and then with good fortune she'd find some new friends as well. She composed in her mind the letter she'd write to Joan once they were well and truly settled. And hope her mother's health didn't decline with the change of residence.

One chilly Sunday morning a few weeks after their arrival, Katy dressed with care in her nicest gown. She'd saved it especially to wear to their first service at Christ Church, an Episcopal parish located near to her new home. She could see the spire from her front door, reaching high into the sky, the tallest building in the city. The imposing façade of the building stirred a bit of unease inside. How welcoming would the congregation be to visitors? She arranged her long skirts with trembling fingers, relishing the silky fabric of the somber indigo gown with white lace edging the neckline and at her wrists. An elegant dress that made her feel respectable if not pretty. She held still in her chair while her maid worked on her hair.

"You look very nice in that dress." Birdie stood behind Katy as she finished putting her hair up into a soft bun. "Mayhap you'll meet some handsome young man among the parishioners."

"Pshaw." That long-ago wish had flown the coop years before. "I am uninterested at my advanced age."

"Why ever would you say such a thing? You're only thirty and still quite lovely." Birdie pushed a pin into Katy's hair and then stood back. "You're ready to join your mother for breakfast."

Katy stood and turned to face her maid. "Thank you for your help and kind words. Still, there won't be any courting of anyone at church or anywhere else. I enjoy living my life on my own terms."

"Ah, well, if you're sure." Birdie gathered up the stray pins arrayed on the dressing table, placing them inside a small cedar box.

"I am. Shall we go down?" Katy gathered her good purse,

the black one reserved for dressier occasions, from the table and looked at Birdie.

"I'll be down after I finish cleaning up in here." Birdie rearranged a powder box on the table. "You go on, though."

Katy made her way downstairs and into the dining room, following the sound of voices. When she entered the room, she found William and her mother enjoying a light repast to break their fast. Their new cook, Holly, had laid out a nice arrangement of sliced chicken, sardines, sliced apples, and hard cheese.

"Good morning to you both." Katy went to the sideboard and added some of each of the tempting items to her plate.

"Good morning. I like that dress on you. It's fitting for going to church." Her mother smiled at her as she lifted a bite of sardine to her mouth.

"I agree with you, Mother." William sliced into his slab of chicken, cutting a piece to eat. "Perhaps you'll find a husband in this city yet."

Katy placed her plate on the table and then settled on the seat. She was not going to have this conversation with her brother. Again. "Could you pour some tea for me, please?"

"Your refusal to admit of your deficiency as to a proper husband and children has been noted by many of my acquaintances. I have the impression several gentlemen have even tested the waters but found them rather, shall we say, chilly? Why do you rebuff their overtures?"

Katy clenched her hands together in her lap. She studied her brother's intent gaze for a long moment, then glanced to her mother's loving smirk. Sighing, she reached for the teapot to pour her own tea. "It is nobody's concern but mine as to whether I wish to marry. You may inform your friends that they are wasting their breath when they attempt to woo me into being courted."

"But, Mary Katharine…"

"William, finish your breakfast as we must start out for church in a few minutes." Sarah smiled gently at her pushy son. "And please refrain from badgering your sister about her choices. You do know her reasons for her decision."

"But—" William snapped his mouth closed and shook his head. "Very well. Katy, I will stop worrying you about such affairs. Shall we retrieve our cloaks and go to church?"

Fifteen minutes later they arrived at the beautiful church and joined the steady stream of people making their way inside. She paused to really appreciate the lovely building. The soaring steeple was topped by the Royal Crown of England. The Georgian spirit of the architecture showed in its symmetry, proportion, and balance of the elements of its design. A very beautiful example of church architecture, to her eye.

"Come along, my dear." Her mother motioned for her to catch up with them.

She joined her mother and brother in a few strides, then they entered the church for the first time. A fair size vestibule connected the front door to the sanctuary, a set of stairs on the right leading up to what she assumed would be galleries where people could observe the service. Inside the immense sanctuary, the furnishings and number of pews combined to stop her steps once more. A beautiful branched brass chandelier hung from the center of the ceiling, ablaze with candles, while matching sconces adorned the walls and central pillars. She eased past the large ornate baptismal font as she trailed after her mother toward an empty pew. Soon the congregation had all settled and the rector, Reverend Richard Peters, appeared to begin the service. He looked like he should be in a courtroom, wearing the powdered wig typical of that profession. But then he had studied law as a young man before being ordained. Talk about him indicated his loyalty to the crown.

As the sermon began, Katy surreptitiously perused the people around her. Everyone appeared to be dressed in their finest attire given the quality of the fabrics and accessories each wore. Thankfully, she'd chosen her own best dress so she did not feel inferior on that front. Still, some of the others met her quick peeks with somber eyes. A stranger among them. She returned her concentration to the sermon, something about loaves and fishes.

After the benediction, her mother led them out of the church. The morning sunshine blinded her for a second and she brushed someone's arm as she came to a halt.

"I'm sorry." She turned to apologize further and met startling green eyes surrounded by blond curls. A smile rested on the other woman's lips, however. "I am sorry for bumping into you."

"You barely touched me, but thank you. You're visiting us today?"

"Yes. I'm Mary Katharine Goddard, and this is my mother Sarah, and brother William." Katy included her family in the introductions.

"Welcome. I'm Brenda Whitman and I'm glad to meet you all." Brenda smiled at them then rested her gaze on Katy. "I hope you found Reverend Peters' lesson encouraging and thus will become a member of our loving and welcoming congregation, Miss Goddard."

The sermon. The one part of the service she least enjoyed. She glanced at her brother's raised brow, his knowing smirk. Then addressed Brenda. "I look forward to becoming acquainted with you and the others over time. I appreciate your welcoming overture despite my inelegant introduction by bumping into you."

"I'm actually pleased you did because that allowed me to meet you all. Are you new to Philadelphia as well, or just the church?" Brenda pulled her ebony cloak closed against the rising chilly breeze.

"We're new to the city. We've only been in town for a couple weeks and thought it auspicious that this beautiful church is so near to our new home." Katy tugged the collar of her cloak up to combat the shiver flowing down her spine.

"Then I would enjoy helping you learn more about our lovely city." Brenda encompassed the three of them with her smile. "If you'll permit me to be so forward as to offer so soon after meeting you all."

William cleared his throat before nodding once. "Miss Whitman, I shall decline your offer merely because I am not new to the city but have been in town for some time now. But please, I fully endorse you taking my sister around. Perhaps you can introduce her to some of your friends as well."

Katy shot him a warning look which he met with a wink. "I'm certain Miss Whitman would not appreciate you instructing her on how she should behave, William."

"I'm sure your brother meant well." Brenda clasped her hands around her small beaded purse. "I have a few friends you might care to meet at some point."

"I would enjoy that." She needed to find new friends to replace the ones that she'd left behind in Providence. Church provided a fine opportunity to do so. Perhaps she'd also discover some appropriate charitable work where she might make more friends.

"I'll decline as well, Miss Whitman, but thank you for the invitation to accompany you." Sarah lifted her chin a touch as she addressed the young woman. "I am afraid the tour would aggravate my condition, so I'll rely on my daughter informing me of her impressions."

"It looks like it will be the two of us, then." Brenda looked past Katy and waved. "My sister is ready to go home, but we'll have a little tour of the city soon. Just tell me where to send word."

"The best place is the print shop at Third and Market," William volunteered. "One or the other of us is usually there during business hours."

"Oh, you opened that new press. I'm glad to have more newspapers in this town, too." Brenda waved again and took a step away. "It's been lovely to meet you all."

As Brenda left to join her sister, Katy released a sigh. Perhaps Brenda would become a friend in time. Sadness sent tears to her eyes, but she swallowed them. She'd always miss her friends, but she must look to the future and move on.

CHAPTER 10

PHILADELPHIA, PENNSYLVANIA – 1768

"We really need to plan for the festivities in honor of Twelfth Night next month." Katy worked on a bit of needlepoint as she sat in a cushioned chair by the blazing fire in the front parlor.

She'd started it the previous winter in Providence but hadn't had time to finish it during the busy spring and summer months. The rhythm of their work day shifted with the sunrise and sunset because they needed all the sunlight possible to do their work. So their work day was longer during the spring and summer. She came home too tired to pick up her sewing during that span of time. Then of course they'd had to pack up everything to make the move to Philadelphia, so progress had not been possible. But in the winter they spent more time at home than at the shop.

"I know it's only December, but time passes far too quickly." She pushed the needle through the fabric, pulling the stitch snug. She was nearly finished with the piece, only one last yellow rose to finish in the picture of a bouquet of them. "Twelfth Night is only a few weeks away."

She could use a bit of a frolic. Twelfth Night marked the

end of the holidays, occurring twelve days after Christmas. A time for one final day of celebration. Many actually chose to get married on this special day, like George and Martha Washington had done. Katy needed a chance to enjoy life. She'd been all about setting up the new press and attracting customers to make it profitable. She hadn't made any friends in the larger city yet. If it weren't for the frequent letters from Joan, she'd be finding a way to journey back to Providence and see for herself how her friend fared. Joan had been delivered of a son, naming him after the father, so her fears had melted away and her husband was satisfied. The young lad was saddled with an imposing name as a result: Harold Edward Langley Junior. Would he grow up to do honor to the name or be oppressive like his father? The idea that Joan had been afraid of her husband sent chills through Katy. What must it be like to live under the same roof with someone you could not trust?

Sarah sat on the sofa before the fire, knitting socks to keep their feet warm over the course of the winter months. "I suppose we should put together some ideas. If only I felt more lively."

"I thought you told your sisters in your last letter that you were feeling better." Her mother had had a difficult time acclimating to their new residence. The very air irritated her chest, making her cough so hard as to send waves of worry through Katy. "You seem much improved."

"I am. But I think it will take a little while for me to fully recover. With good fortune, I'll be back to my usual self before you go for the smallpox inoculation." Sarah's fingers flew with the knitting needles, the sturdy yet pretty dark green sock seeming to flow into being. "Then it will be my turn to nurse you back to full health."

A shiver raced through her at the reminder of the upcoming event. Uncertainty as to the wisdom of allowing the inoculation still quailed her nerves. Not that she feared the goal, but the process itself. She'd been reassured the procedure was not awfully painful and would keep her from falling gravely ill and perhaps dying from the disease. She knew many people who had either succumbed to the illness or had been inoculated and were able to recover from it. That bit of evidence was why she had not canceled the procedure. From her reading about medicine, she understood the importance of such results. Still, a thread of concern wove through her.

She poked the needle into the linen square in her hand, pulling the fine golden yellow yarn snugly into place. "I pray that I don't become awfully ill as a result of it."

"You've a strong constitution so I wouldn't think you would have too much trouble fighting it off." Sarah turned the fabric in her hands to make the final finishing stitches of the sock. "I wouldn't fret over it."

"I'm striving to concentrate on the hoped-for result instead of the procedure." A difficult aim but one she largely seemed to be able to maintain. "Can we talk about something else?"

"If that will calm you, of course." Sarah's eyes twinkled at her, a light smile on her lips. "Who should we invite to our little celebration for Twelfth Night?"

A fine question. Who could she invite? Perhaps Brenda if she did indeed contact her about her proposed tour of the town. Who else might she send an invitation to? Hm. She really needed to make some friends.

"I know who I don't want to invite." Katy snugged the next stitch into place and then secured the tail of the yarn, snipping it off close to the last anchor stitch. "But I fear William would object and insist on their invitation."

"The partners?" Sarah nodded as she finished the sock and set it aside. Only to begin another one.

Katy pressed her lips together at the sight. Her mother's apparent agitation spurred the needles into a faster rhythm. Was she agitated at the idea of hosting the men at their house?

"Why would you not want to invite them when they've supported William's and our ventures for so long?" Her mother's needles clicked rapidly as the yarn wove into another soft covering for their feet.

Katy laid the finished piece on the side table beside the hurricane globe protecting a lit candle, using the couple of seconds to compose her response. She met her mother's curious gaze. "I do not trust them. They have opposing views to ours, even if they're not forthwith about them. They have repeatedly insisted on pieces in the *Chronicle* supporting what the Parliament is doing. And recall their reaction to Dickinson's *Letters* earlier this year."

William had readily taken on printing the first of John Dickinson's inflammatory *Letters from a Pennsylvania Farmer to the Inhabitants of the British Colonies* in a special edition in December 1767, continuing with the remaining eleven letters through February 1768. In the *Pennsylvania Chronicle*, William had explained the reason for the special edition, saying, "Having received a Series of Papers, intitled, 'Letters from a Farmer,' &c. with several other Pieces from our Correspondents, all which we are importuned to publish as speedily as possible; and as we find there will not be Room in our *Monday's Chronicle*, to insert the Whole—from a Desire to oblige, we are induced to give this Half-Sheet containing such of the Pieces as we could get ready, on a Subject of the utmost Importance to the Welfare of our Common Country." The two-page edition, or half-sheet, included the first defense of the colonial cause.

The partners, especially Mr. Galloway, had been outraged, according to what William had written to her, after the man saw what her brother had printed. "They were angry, they fretted, they swore and affirmed, that the letters were too inflammatory for this latitude. Mr. Galloway explained, with a countenance expressive of the deepest envy, that they were 'damned ridiculous! Meer stuff! Fustian! Altogether stupid and inconsistent!' among other invectives." William had wanted to compile the twelve letters into one booklet but the partners deprived him the ability to do so, thereby foregoing the revenue such a product would have generated.

"The partners feel threatened by the ideas contained in his *Letters*, my dear." Sarah paused in the flight of her knitting needles to peer at her daughter and then sent them flying again. "Your brother is adamant that as long as the writing is of a good quality, opposing opinions lead to understanding and compromise that works for all. And he was very upset by their refusal to allow him to print them as a booklet. It's a partnership, so he had to comply."

"It's unfair of them to have done so, though. They are behaving badly, in my opinion." Katy let out a long sigh, frustration filling her with angst. "Look at how they originally promised us a house and then reneged on it. How they manipulated where we could even conduct our book business. Seems as though their needs and desires are far more important than any of us."

"Well, men often act as if they are more important than others. I experienced the same attitude from your father to some extent." Her mother's hands stilled as she regarded Katy. "You've been most fortunate in retaining some independence from a man as a husband, but being a spinster means you'll be solely responsible for your upkeep. When I am gone…"

Katy inhaled sharply as her mother's words trailed off. "Do not jest when you have been ill for so many months."

The front door closing had them looking to the doorway in anticipation of their new arrival. The thump of booted feet on the wood floor echoed in the central hallway, coming closer with each passing second. William soon appeared in the doorway, his great coat dusted with snow.

"Good evening, Mother, Katy." He swung the heavy coat off his shoulders and draped it over a ladder-back chair by the door. His green-gray coat and matching waistcoat and white linen shirt were new, paired with tan knee breeches, white stockings, and black shoes with oval buckles. "I hope you're both faring well."

"I wasn't expecting you today." Sarah set aside her sewing to fully address him. She indicated the melting snowflakes on his coat. "What brings you out on a such a cold and snowy day?"

"Oh, it's pretty much stopped snowing, but I appreciate your concern." William settled on the sofa beside Sarah. "As you know, I need to take care of some business in Connecticut and Rhode Island which I realized will have me away from this place for an extended period. Mainly, I need to collect the money John Carter owes me, and try to sell the properties I inherited from Father. I want to collect also on the annual subscriptions to have the monies in hand to pay expenses, and not tempt either of my partners to lay claim to them."

"We are aware and will manage in your absence as we've always done." Sarah gazed at him, tilting her head slowly as she frowned. "There is more?"

He nodded and stretched out his legs, crossing his ankles as he reclined beside his mother. "I know how you've struggled with your health these past months. So I decided to provide you some relief from worry about the shop business while I'm away."

A rush of warmth flushed Katy's chest, flowing up her

neck to her cheeks. Surely he was not saying what she thought he was saying. "What do you mean, William? You've relied on us for years to manage the business."

William's sharp look suggested he had thoughts on that observation but didn't want to reveal them. "You have and I have thanked you for it. But this time is somewhat different. In exchange for Mr. Galloway and Mr. Wharton withdrawing their interests in the press, they have insisted I take on a journeyman printer. This man is to step in and manage the *Chronicle* piece subject to your oversight, Mother. You'll still be running the shop and managing the overall business, but he will handle the newspaper."

Not only did it sound like it actually wasn't his decision, but he'd already effected the change without even consulting with either of them. Anger simmered in Katy's chest but, as her mother had said moments before her brother arrived, men often treated women as lesser than them. After all the years they had managed very nicely, he still felt they were not up to doing so without a man around. True, it was the way things were, but that didn't mean she had to like it. She would work to prove him wrong once and for all.

"I see. Well, who is this associate?" Sarah asked with an edge to her voice.

"Benjamin Towne. He understands how to handle the newspaper from much experience. I am assured that he'll be an asset, a help to you both."

From her brother's tone, he was anything but reassured the man in question would be helpful. The partners seemed to wield far more influence over her brother than she liked. She didn't trust them. Look at how they'd reneged on the offer which had convinced them to move to the city in the first place. What did they actually intend for this man to accomplish? She'd need to be on her guard in her dealings with him until his true aim came to light.

"When do you leave for New England, William?" Katy peered at him, hoping against hope it would be soon. Maybe her temper would cool before he returned, but she didn't hold out much hope. Yet again he found a way to stir her ire against him.

"In four days. I have a few things to handle here before the ship departs."

"Will you carry a letter and a little gift to my friend Joan?" The idea had suddenly popped into Katy's head as she realized he'd be going back to Providence to try to sell property and collect on some debts. Of course, with the colonies in the throes of an economic depression resulting from the 1763 Treaty of Paris ending the Seven Years' War, whether he succeeded in selling anything, or that those owing him money had any to give him, remained a question.

"As long as it's not bulky. But yes, I'd be happy to." He pulled his feet under him and rose. "I must be on my way. I'll introduce Mr. Towne to you at the shop next time. He'll start on the morrow."

Whether they'd agreed or not, they were going to be working with this unknown man. William tapped his hat onto his head and retrieved his coat. She hoped he had a successful trip to handle his business. She also hoped she would get along with Mr. Towne.

The week before Christmas, Brenda arranged to show Katy around town.

"I had no idea the Library Company held such a large and interesting collection." Katy sauntered past a glass case containing the hand of a mummy, apparently a gift from the artist and almanack creator Benjamin West a year earlier. How did Mr. West come to obtain a mummy's hand? "I thought they would only house books, but they have a wide variety of intriguing artifacts."

"Yes, they have grown their holdings over the decades they've been in existence." Brenda walked with Katy among the various displays in the upper floor of the Pennsylvania State House on Chestnut street. "They had to move the collection here because it had grown so large, but you can see they will likely have to move again before long as it's becoming quite cramped."

Indeed, the large room appeared small because of the plethora of gleaming tables and display cases crammed into every nook and cranny. A tall Palladian case, containing an air pump gifted by John Penn, stood against one wall, surrounded by smaller exhibits. She'd especially liked the elegantly designed case. And one couldn't overlook the many bookcases filled with tomes of all kinds, of course, that took up an entire back wall of the building. Four comfortable-looking chairs grouped together by a front window invited a quiet session of reading from the wealth of information contained in those books. As much as she'd eagerly antici-pated visiting the library, there were other places Brenda had promised to show her, to not only see them but to know more about their place in the city and its people.

"I believe we've seen all of this wonderful diversion, so what is next?" She moved to stand by a stuffed cheetah posed on a low table. All the way from Africa. She had mixed feel-ings about its presence in the library. Surely it would have been better to leave the animal to live out its days in the wild rather than being caught and prepared in such a manner.

Brenda sidled around Katy to lead the way to the stairs. "Let's go over to Market street to the market sheds and see what is on offer today."

"Is the market open every Saturday?" Katy descended the steps alongside of her friendly companion. Would she become a friend as Katy hoped? As they became better acquainted that question would be answered. But for now, she'd merely enjoy the friendly time together.

"Yes, and Wednesdays, too. I always enjoy seeing what the merchants bring into town."

They emerged on the street and started strolling toward the riverfront, turning left at Fourth street to reach Market. A woman and two children hurried across the dirt street as a mounted rider trotted toward the market. A pair of men in business attire strode purposefully toward the courthouse and town hall in the distance. The grand steeple of Christ Church beckoned them, drawing them to the heart of the city's business and civic center. Brenda had informed her that when the city's founder, William Penn, laid out the city plan he insisted that the main street be one hundred feet wide and in the center of town. His aim was to reduce the spread of disease and the spread of any fires, like those he'd experienced in London in the 1660s. The width opened the city up in a way Katy had never seen before, not only more accessible but aesthetically pleasing.

As they turned onto Market, Brenda pointed out a cemetery. "That's the Christ Church Burial Grounds over there. It's been around for some time, since 1719 I'm told. Isn't it a nice spot to spend eternity?"

The burial grounds appeared to be maintained nicely, the grass trimmed and the trees scattered here and there adding shade as well as visual appeal. White marble markers stood in rigid lines across the space. Lying under their spreading branches in a green lawn, kept safe by the brick wall surrounding the grounds, would be a fine way to end your days, and likely comforting to the surviving family members.

"I'm certain those who are buried there will indeed rest in peace." Katy grinned at Brenda, chuckling at her little jest.

"Indeed. Let's go on, it's starting to get late and I will have to be home soon."

"That's a fine idea. I'm curious about the market, too." She'd wanted to visit the merchants but hadn't made time to do so given the amount of work at the shop.

As they ambled down the street, the two stone buildings that comprised the jail at the corner of Third drew Katy's attention. Ever since she'd started working at the print shop on the opposite corner, she'd been intrigued by them.

"I've often wondered why those two are made of stone." Katy indicated the curious buildings. "Most every other building is made of brick."

"Given they serve as the jail," Brenda explained, "that is to prevent or at least deter the prisoners escaping."

"I suppose it would be more difficult than a wood structure, but wouldn't brick also deter escape?"

"I don't know the answer to your question, but they have served the purpose well since 1722 when they were built. Now it's merely accepted as nothing unusual." Brenda picked up her pace as they passed frame buildings housing various businesses, even some booths where butchers sold their meats. As they passed one house, she huffed in disgust. "That's where that traitor Benjamin Franklin lives. I cannot abide his call for the repeal of the lawful taxes levied on us."

Katy glanced sharply at Brenda at her statement. "You mean the Stamp Act? You believe it was a valid tax, even though we had no representation in Parliament to advocate for the colonists?"

"Of course. We are all British subjects and benefit from being so. Now, we're almost to the market, so let's hurry."

Katy fell into stride with the other woman, whose political stance was at complete odds with her own. So much for them becoming close friends. William would be outraged, given his friendly association with Mr. Franklin even if the two men were not close. Still, it wouldn't serve any good purpose to not remain on civil terms with her. After all, they both attended the same church and Katy wouldn't want to do anything to potentially curtail her brother's printing business. Keeping her opinions to herself, she accompanied the blonde woman into the shade of the market sheds.

Beneath the low roofs the merchants displayed their wares on long tables arranged on the outside edges, leaving an aisle between them for customers under the protective cover of the roof. Orange pumpkins and green-and-gold striped gourds mounded on one table. Freshly baked breads and rolls added their scent to the mix of other foodstuffs in the air. A pen of chickens sat in front of a table, ready to be killed and sold for someone's dinner. Many booths sold home wares and material for linens. One merchant displayed children's toys made from wood and fabric.

Brenda paused to finger the silky fabric of a scarf hanging among others from a frame on a table. "How much for this?"

The lady merchant hovered nearby, keeping a wary eye on her merchandise. "Ten shillings, miss." The seller's raspy voice came out rather grudgingly.

"Ah, well..." Brenda released the scarf and turned to continue browsing.

Katy skipped the scarves to peruse a display of fancy writing utensils. Something the book shop should offer as well, especially since they sold blank notebooks. She'd mention it to her brother when she saw him next.

After several minutes looking over the wares for sale, the church bells marked the hour. Katy caught up to her companion standing by a booth of various bird feathers for sale as decoration for hats and other attire.

"I'm sorry, Brenda, but I must go home now. Mother will be waiting on me for supper."

Brenda put back the peacock feather with its startlingly

beautiful colors and nodded. "I as well need to go on home. I hope you enjoyed our little tour of the city."

"Thank you again for showing me the entire town so I have a better understanding of what Philadelphia stands for."

They exchanged farewells, and Katy turned to head for home. She had a new awareness of the city in which she lived, as well as the political divide simmering beneath its genteel population. Would the simmering pot ever boil over?

CHAPTER 11

PHILADELPHIA, PENNSYLVANIA – 1769

Suddenly the winter holidays loomed again. Where had the last year flown off to? Between Katy's never-ending book binding and composing work at the print shop and tending to her mother's recurring illnesses, she had little time for herself. Not that she needed much of that. She enjoyed her work and the interactions with the various customers who relied upon the shop. What she didn't enjoy was the tensions building between her brother and his partners, even though he wasn't in town often. Benjamin Towne didn't help calm matters, either, given his similar temperament to William's.

The new unfavorable partnership agreement William had signed with Galloway and Wharton, which "sold" their shares in the company to Towne, rankled all of them. Since Towne had no money with which to pay the men for those shares, the debt of several hundred pounds fell on William and by extension Katy and Sarah. William had tried to borrow some money from a loyal subscriber but was turned down. So he'd gone to New England for much of the second half of 1769, leaving the management of the shop in the hands of Isaac Collins, a talented journeyman printer. By then Katy had become inured to the implied slight to them. William had yet to return to Philadelphia, still attempting to wind up his many affairs.

At least they had two steady men to work with. Isaac Collins served as journeyman, and at three and twenty years had a good future ahead in the printing business. The other, Shepard Kollock, worked well with Isaac and had a good head on his shoulders. William had been fortunate to find both, in addition to a second runner to deliver the paper to the southern district of the city. The shop hummed right along as a result of all of them. The one man who tended to mess up the flow was the one who came and went at his whim, not working the way a journeyman was expected to work. That on-again, off-again man was Benny Mecom, nephew of the very Benjamin Franklin that William worked so closely with. Currently he was on again, but for how long this time?

Katy finished putting her hair into a bun, tucking in a few strays tickling her cheek. An urgent job awaited her at the shop. First, she must check in on her mother. She'd not been feeling well at all when she retired for the night. This morning Katie worried about which direction her health may have taken. She wrapped a shawl about her shoulders and headed out of her bedchamber to stop at her mother's room next door.

She tapped on the closed door. "Mother? May I come in?"

Her request was met with silence. Perhaps she was still asleep. Katy didn't want to awaken her if so. But what if she'd taken a turn for the worse and... No. That was not possible. She had to know her mother's condition. Otherwise she'd fret throughout the day. As she lingered, undecided, her dark-haired petite maid appeared at the end of the hall, carrying a stack of linens.

"Birdie, do you know how Mother fares this morning?"

"No, miss, I'm sorry." The young woman, not even out of her teenage years, bobbed a quick respectful curtsy and continued down the hall.

She had no other choice. Turning back to the door, Katy drew in a bracing breath and lifted the latch to push the door open and ease inside. "Mother?"

The covers on the bed stirred slightly, a soft rustle of fabric reaching her ears. Relief flooded through Katy. She let out the breath she'd been holding to better listen for sounds of life. She moved closer to the bed, bending over her mother's prone form. Weary eyes peered back at her.

"How are you feeling this morning?" She reached out to clasp her mother's cool hand.

In a whisper, Sarah said, "I don't know yet. I've just awakened."

Katy gently squeezed her mother's hand, concerned at the frailty of her fingers and weakness in her voice. "I'll have Birdie come see to your needs. I must go to the shop to finish the government papers they are expecting to be delivered as soon as practicable. Or, if you'd rather, I can send word to Mr. Towne to handle it."

The very idea disturbed her mind, but she would do whatever necessary to see to her mother's wellbeing. Towne acted as though he owned the shop instead of William, pushing himself into every aspect of the business. Overstepping his role as journeyman to suggest he manage the business, purportedly to give her assistance. Not that she would permit him to do so more than what William had dictated. Most decidedly, she wouldn't let him near the office records including the list of subscribers. She'd brought them home so he couldn't peek into them when she was not aware. He had no need to know the financial status of the shop nor to contact their subscribers. He was tasked with managing the workflow not the cash flow. Following in her mother's foot-steps, Katy paid meticulous attention to the records and keeping them updated so she'd know the status daily.

"No, my dear, go on and take care of your work. I'll rest and recover. Send up some tea and toast, will you? I don't think I can emerge from this bed today."

Torn between her need to tend her mother and the need to ensure the deadline for the government task was met, she hesitated. Her mother's claim of weakness to the point of not getting out of bed sent another wave of alarm through her. Still, when ill, the best thing one could do was rest. She'd ask Birdie and Cook to pay close attention to her and send word if her condition deteriorated even the slightest. Knowing her mother wouldn't be home alone comforted her somewhat and made it easier to do as her mother asked.

"If you insist, then I will go but I will return as soon as I can."

Weeks passed, bringing the end of December and then New Year's Day of 1770. Still her mother seesawed between health and illness. Back on the twenty-third of December she'd written a letter to William, sympathizing with him of his various troubles but reassuring him that the *Chronicle* continued to grow in subscribers every day. Most days she went to the print shop with Katy, but then other days she only felt well enough to be propped on down pillows against the headboard of her bed. Katy fretted continually but had to frequent the book shop and printing press daily to ensure the business ran smoothly and met its deadlines. Every time she left home, she worried she'd not see her mother alive again.

On the fifth day of January 1770, her worst fears came to pass. She was at the print shop to work on some blank forms for the local government when Birdie came running through the door. Katy knew something had happened with Mother by the horrified expression on the young woman's face, but still she reacted calmly. It wouldn't serve any purpose for both of them to become overly emotional in front of the men in the room.

"Birdie, what are you doing here?"

She didn't take time to curtsy, just reached out to grab Katy's hand. "I'm sorry, miss, but your mother… She's gasping for air. White as a sheet. We don't know what to do!"

"You go on home and I'll send for the doctor and follow you in a minute. Be with her until I arrive, you understand? Do not let her be alone."

After Birdie nodded once and scurried back outside, Katy turned to one of the younger apprentices, a lad of thirteen years, and sent him in search of the doctor. Benjamin Towne marched up to her, a scowl on his face as he stopped in front of her. She never liked to have anyone stand quite so close but she wouldn't give him the satisfaction of stepping back.

"Mr. Towne, I assume you heard my maid's alarm."

"I'm sorry to hear your mother is not well yet again. That must prove very trying to you."

Bristling with affront at his patronizing tone, Katy inhaled slowly to manage her comportment before responding. "I will be leaving for the rest of this day. I will send word once I know what the situation at home actually is. Pray strive to have these jobs completed on time and to the best of our abilities."

"Do you wish for me to handle the cash flow in your absence? Someone must."

She peered at him for a long moment, considering her options. None of which she liked. "Make a list of whatever jobs and monies you collect and I will add that to my ledgers once things are settled. Be sure to account for every pence, understood?"

A glimmer of mirth flickered in his dark eyes. "Certainly.

Now go on and tend to your affairs at home. I'll handle everything here."

"Until I return, yes. And thank you." She spun on her heel, snatched up her satchel containing the ledgers the man so greedily sought to possess, and marched out of the shop.

Her mother couldn't die. Not now. But if she did, it would be on her brother's shoulders since he coerced her to move to this place against her will. Hadn't Mother written to him saying she didn't want to leave her friends and family in Providence? She'd already done so once, but then to essentially demand she do so again so late in life proved to be too much for her. She'd been ill more frequently since moving to the bigger city. Now she was apparently at death's door. Hopefully, the doctor would be able to cure whatever was ailing her this time.

When she opened the front door of her home, she was met by silence. No singing from Holly in the kitchen. No patter of her maid's shoes on the wood floors. Not even a meow from the white housecat Holly had adopted off the street. Dropping the satchel to the floor, she flung off her cloak as she hurried to the stairs leading up to the bedchambers. As she neared her mother's bedchamber door, she heard Birdie murmuring inside. She stepped through the open door. Her mother lay on her back, her hands at her sides on top of the quilt covering her.

"Mother, I'm here."

Birdie stopped her prayers to turn to greet Katy. "She's hanging on."

Oh no. Unspoken but understood was that her mother was waiting for Katy to arrive so they could say goodbye. One last final time. Fighting the urge to cry, Katy motioned for Birdie to come to her by the door.

"Any word on the doctor?"

"No, miss. I hoped you were him, in fact."

"Please go show him up when he arrives." Katy prevented Birdie's departure with a hand on her arm. "Thank you for looking after my mother."

"I'll bring the doctor right up." Birdie met Katy's gaze and pressed her lips together briefly. "Be strong."

Katy watched her hurry down the hall and disappear down the stairs before pivoting to occupy the chair by her mother's side. She clasped her mother's hand as she had done throughout every illness her mother had endured. The time they'd lived in Philadelphia had been hard on her but she always bounced back. Each time a little more slowly as her age advanced. Now that she'd reached seventy years, Katy feared she wouldn't rebound at all.

The funeral arrangements and hassling with Benjamin devoured Katy's time the next day. Grieving her mother's death made it even more difficult to concentrate, to manage everything she was responsible for. Starting with Towne, who in her absence had reorganized the furniture and press. Fuming, she confronted the man. He simply told her it helped with the flow of effort. Then the list of jobs and monies he promised to keep had not been started. He said he had it all in his head. His obvious attempt to take over her business furthered her dislike of him and his trickery. But she couldn't immediately deal with rearranging everything the way it was as she had much more to address.

Merely staying upright and not prostrate on her bed, sobbing, proved a major challenge. Tears pressed against her eyes, but she willed them away. Not now. Not yet. Without her brother's support, she didn't have time to let down her guard and cry for the huge hole in her heart at her mother's demise. How could she go on without her love and care and guidance?

She met with Reverend Peters of Christ Church to inform him of her mother's passing. He helped her with the details and obtaining the coffin and much more. Including locating an appropriate spot for her mother to be buried in the burial grounds. That lovely quiet lawn under the shade trees would welcome her mother's body to sleep for eternity. She had not imagined when Brenda had pointed the grounds out to her that she would be laying her mother to rest there so soon. She also dashed off a note to William, urging him to return to Philadelphia as quickly as possible. Perhaps he could rein in Benjamin's mischievous activities as well as help her handle all the important business related to her mother's death.

And give her time to finally grieve in peace.

It was a cold and gloomy day to be standing graveside. A small crowd of friends and businessmen gathered around her. The shop was closed for the afternoon so that all who had worked with Sarah could attend her funeral service. Even grumpy Mr. Towne showed up in a dark suit. Poor Shepard seemed to be having trouble breathing again. She'd have to make sure he saw the doctor. William had not had time to make the journey home, his absence a sore in her heart. The reverend said prayers and talked about her mother's contribution to the community. Katy half-listened, her grief a living, clawing beast in her chest. Tears slid down her cheeks, dabbed away with a damp handkerchief.

How could she go on without the loving encouragement and advice of her dear mother? The two days since her mother died were a blur, filled with a plethora of concerns and decisions. Decisions made without being able to confer with her dear mother. She now would live alone with her cook and maid. The years of shared moments, of their joys and their sorrows, all only memories now. Her mother hadn't wanted to move to this city, not one bit. Yet move they did and look how that had turned out. Her mother buried in a strange city where her beloved friends and family would not have ready means to even visit her grave.

Where was William during all of this? Off to do whatever caught his fancy. Leaving her to manage by herself, which she surely could do better than he ever could. His flighty tendencies led him to flit about like a hummingbird, darting from one nectar cup of endeavor to another.

The more she contemplated how her comfortable situation had metamorphosed, the more she simmered with anger at her brother. Swallowing the lump in her throat, she dashed away the tears as Birdie approached her. Blinking to bring her concentration to the present moment, she noted that the minister had finished speaking and the gravediggers had begun to fill in the grave. The thudding of shovelfuls of dirt echoed in Katy's chest, making her flinch.

"Miss, we should strike out for home as many of your mother's acquaintances wish to gather to commemorate her memory. Holly anticipated such and has been whipping up some refreshments."

She nodded and fell into step beside her maid and friend. "I don't know what I'd do without you and your sister. Thank you."

"These are trying times, I'm aware." Birdie flashed a small smile at Katy. "We'll get through it together."

"I hope William comes soon." Katy glanced to where Benjamin Towne herded the four shop workers in front of him like a shepherd with sheep. His actions continued to vex her in multiple ways. He was not a nice man, rearranging things to suit himself. "I'm not sure how much longer I can fend off the not-so-subtle attacks on the shop's business."

Birdie followed Katy's steady gaze to spot Towne boxing

the ears of the youngest apprentice. She nodded slowly. "I'm sure you can handle whatever he tries to do, miss."

"Now that my mother has passed, and with William so frequently out of town, it is on my shoulders to ensure the enterprise meets with success. With the building tensions surrounding us, it's imperative to keep the people informed of the king's actions. I want to be a big part of making sure everyone knows what is happening to the colonies. I am going to work hard and do my utmost to see that we meet our deadlines and our customers' expectations."

"I'm sure you will do a fine job, too." Birdie picked up her pace. "We should hurry."

"Yes, so we can be there to greet everyone." She needed the townspeople to know they could rely upon her. "Then tomorrow I'll make some changes at the press."

Despite her brother's frequent and often prolonged absences, she had a business to run and she wouldn't allow anything—or anyone—stop her from succeeding.

CHAPTER 12

PHILADELPHIA, PENNSYLVANIA – 1770

The very next day, Katy was back at work, ensuring that the work flowed through the various stages necessary to complete each job. Grief still weighed her down, but having a purpose helped to keep the worst of it at bay. Benjamin Towne went about his own tasks but she felt his regard on her person everywhere she went in the shop. If she greeted a new customer, he was even so bold as to come to the counter to also greet them. Until she'd had enough of his interference and moved to put a stop to his rude behavior.

"Mr. Towne, I'm sure you have far more important things to do than to look over my shoulder." She arched a brow at him with a nod toward the press he'd abandoned moments before. "Your work is waiting over there."

"I—" At the stern look she gave him, he closed his mouth and smashed his lips into a thin line. "Very well."

After the infuriating man had gone back to his own position, Katy turned back to the pastor waiting to submit the text for a religious pamphlet he wished to distribute to his congregation. She finished jotting down the particulars of the design he had in mind, then sent him on his way with a warm smile. The elder man always had kind words for her and appreciated her knowledge and abilities. She appreciated his easy demeanor.

Towne chose that moment to approach her yet again at the counter where she was updating her ledger with the new print job. She finished her entry just as he stopped beside her. Too close, yet again. She kept her pencil in hand as she met his sober expression.

"What is on your mind?"

He leaned closer, peering at the neatly written entries in the ledger book. "You have fine penmanship, Miss Goddard. I am certain all of your records are well in order. If you'd hand them over to me, I will be honored to continue in the same manner. You can trust me to manage the financial aspects of the print shop."

Katy stared at him. Had he lost his mind? "Why would I entertain such a notion?"

"Surely you would prefer to concentrate your efforts within the domestic sphere like most women of my acquaintance. I'm merely trying to facilitate the opportunity for you to have more time in the home where you belong."

She stared at him, struggling to bite back the outrage she felt at his words. "My brother specifically entrusted me to manage the financial aspects of the company." She refrained from slamming the ledger closed, barely, to prevent him reading any more of what she'd written. "Please do not raise the question again. Go back to your work."

Without another word, he spun about and marched back to the work table ladened with work ready to be printed. Was he falling behind? She'd have to keep an eye on his progress. Clenching her fists in her long skirts, she suppressed a sigh. The audacity of the man to suggest she would prefer to spend all of her time at home instead of interacting and communicating with her fellow citizens. She enjoyed knowing what was happening in her community and the colonies at large. Being privy to the ins and outs of the workings of the colonial government and having her finger on the pulse of the resistance to the Parliament kept her interest like no amount of preserving, stitching, or cleaning could ever match. Working on the newspaper kept her informed of events around the world and across the colonies. Simply reading the paper would never serve to satisfy her insatiable appetite for keeping abreast of the times in which she was living. There was a sense of danger and anticipation in the air all around as the Parliament continued to vex the American colonists. She must stay informed and aware, keep her hand in the doings of the city in which she lived. She couldn't do that from home. The domestic sphere indeed.

Working at the printing shop satisfied her need to be useful, to have a purpose for emerging from her warm bed each morning. She did not envy the women who remained at home, constantly tending the needs and desires of their husband and children. Life held far more promise than simply being a wife and mother. Yes, she once thought she'd find a husband and have children with him. Her experience with regard to courtship led her away from that path and toward being self-sufficient. She could and would manage to provide for herself as long as she could continue to work in the print shop and all the other pieces of the company.

Thoughts of Joan's last letter flashed through her mind. She'd relayed all the news of her growing children and their busy lives. Joan had shared that she still wore the silver necklace William had carried to her for Katy. The only real connection between them, living such different lives. The distance between them had grown beyond the miles separating them.

The bell jangled, drawing her attention to the front door.

She pushed back her shoulders and straightened her spine as Joseph Galloway strode into the shop. He declared through his richly attired person just how wealthy he was. He owned many properties in Philadelphia and relished his ability to lord it over others. Pompous as ever. His brown hair was fashioned into side curls and a queue down his back. His dark eyes peered at her with what appeared to be sympathy. His narrow, thin-lipped mouth was pinched as he neared her. What now?

"Good day, Mr. Galloway." She waited for him to reveal why he'd come to the shop on this cold January morning. Why had he decided to visit without any cause?

"Good day, Miss Goddard." He doffed his hat and held it between both hands. "I hope you do not mind my coming unannounced to see you."

"Not at all." She forced a small smile onto her lips. Manners demanded as much. "Is there something I can help you with?"

"My primary purpose is to share my deepest condolences on the passing on of your mother. She was a fine, upstanding, and respectable lady."

His words were polite and correct, but his tone seemed strained, perhaps even hiding some other intention. He'd proven time and time again to have underlying objectives to his actions, ones that often were to the detriment of William's affairs.

"Thank you, sir." She so wanted to walk away and return to the job she'd been about to task one of the apprentices with so that work could begin. Propriety required her to remain to address his concern. "Is there anything else?"

"Well, I did want to have a look at the new press Mr. Goddard purchased a few months ago. Which one is it?"

She stiffened at the disdain dripping from his seemingly polite inquiry. "The one on the right, the mahogany one."

The press was one of the first printing presses built for sale in the colonies. William had purchased it from a clock and watchmaker, Mr. Isaac Doolittle of New Haven, Connecticut, back in September. The notice she'd seen in the *Massachusetts Gazette and Boston Weekly News-Letter* claimed it was "allowed to be the neatest ever made in America and equal, if not superior, to any imported from Great-Britain." She'd been very proud that her brother helped to begin a new industry in the colonies, that of press making.

He strode over to watch the lads at work on the beautiful machine. "As I imagined."

She fought the frown on her face, striving to remain impassive to the umbrage in his tone. "Mr. Galloway, I do not mean to be impolite but I do have work to attend. Is there anything more I might help you with?"

All pretense fell from the man's expression as he studied her for a moment. "I have the utmost concern for you after suffering the severe loss of your mother, my dear. I can well imagine how distraught you must be in your grief."

She studied his pinched features, considering the disconnect between his words and his tone. This man proved over and over he could not be trusted. Her instincts told her to tread carefully. Still, she had a business to run, one in which this man had played a large part in starting. He could also have a part in seeing it fail. Polite manners were called for, so she would do as her mother had taught her and hide her true feelings.

Her mother would have known exactly how to handle whatever Mr. Galloway had in mind. Her chest ached, a tightness centered around her heart. *Oh, Mother. How I miss you already. Please, help me deal with whatever comes out of his mouth next in a manner pleasing to you.*

A sudden sense of calm fell across her shoulders, easing the ache in her chest. She could almost detect the particular aroma of vanilla and lavender perfume her mother wore. Katy glanced around quickly to see if somehow her mother had arrived in the shop. Nothing. Of course she couldn't have come into the shop. Still, the feeling persisted of her mother's comforting presence. Keeping the memory of her mother close, she drew in a calming breath.

Katy aimed her wary gaze at Mr. Galloway. What had he asked? Ah, about her grief. "Yes, her death has been a trying time for me. She was more than simply my mother, but my dearest friend." Tears smarted in her eyes but she swallowed them away. It wouldn't do to become emotional in the shop. "Thank you for your concern, sir, but if there's nothing else, I really do need to get back to the printing jobs that must be assigned."

Mr. Galloway nodded. "Yes, of course, I understand. However, there is one more thing." He reached into his pocket and pulled out an envelope which he held out to her. "It is quite obvious that your brother will not, he cannot return here—you have no friends here—you would live much happier in New England—and may make something for yourself by a sale of your interest."

Startled, Katy could only stare, her mouth falling open. "Interest?"

"Yes, my dear. Your interest in this small print shop." He deliberately looked around the busy shop, six men and boys all working on various tasks throughout the room. Then brought his gaze back to meet her shocked one. "It's a fair offer. You shall be paid annually a certain sum to be agreed on, as well." He thrust the envelope toward her.

Accepting it slowly, reluctantly, she opened it, withdrawing the paper within. She read it quickly, noting the pathetic sum he offered for the profitable business. He intended to remove her from her purpose. To advocate her abandoning her brother. Never. The absurdity of the offer set off sparks of anger in her core. She folded the paper and put it back into the envelope.

"I know this business is very valuable, and I will listen to no such proposals." She shoved the envelope at him, her anger and disdain finally allowed to show on her features. Being polite in the face of such baseness would serve no good purpose.

"Now, my dear, be reasonable." He ignored the envelope as he lowered his dark brows into a frown. "We both know this little shop is not worth more than that. You should thank me for offering to buy your interest so you can move back to where you came from. Your mother would have likely done so if given the chance."

This uppity man had no right to even ponder her mother's actions and motives. He did not know her nearly well enough to have any true insight into what he suggested. Didn't he recall how she moved at William's persuasion to help her son? She would never have reneged on her commitment to support her son. Never.

"Mr. Galloway, although by the sudden death of my mother one half of the interest became mine, by law, yet I would give it all up to William, as it was designed for me to do." She pushed the envelope into his pocket and stepped back. "Now please leave. We have no further business."

"But—"

"Do not make me summon the sheriff, sir." She crossed her arms and stared at him. "I've asked you politely."

"I have never been treated so rudely by any woman." He put his hat back on and shook his head. "You and your brother will regret this."

After he finally closed the door behind him, Katy let out a relieved sigh. She didn't enjoy confrontation even when necessary. But nobody would walk all over her when she knew better. She turned to walk back to the counter but glanced at Towne. That man shook his head slowly at her, his disapproval evident in his expression.

She lifted her chin and kept walking. She'd conduct her affairs as she deemed appropriate. She just hoped her brother wouldn't object with her tactics when he eventually returned—soon, she hoped—to the disquiet all around her in this cold city.

Several weeks later, Katy enjoyed a quiet Sunday at home. Sitting in the formal parlor, she sipped on a cup of tea as she gazed out the front windows. Ever since her mother's passing, she'd been unusually restless. Uneasy about the attempts at work to be chased out by Benjamin or the partners. William had written to her, revealing that a friend had informed him both of his mother's passing and that Benjamin was attempting to steal the records so he could start his own newspaper. She hadn't realized the reason behind the man's attempts, but she was more determined than ever to not permit him to get away with such an underhanded move.

To have had Mr. Galloway also try to trick her into selling for a trifle was flatly unacceptable, as if she was unaware of the true value of the business. She kept the records and knew exactly the profitability of the "little shop." Both men seemed to think she was not capable of running a business, but should spend her time at home. Bah. How boring would that be!

She took another sip and then set her cup on the saucer. Between the saucer and the oil lamp lay a folded copy of the *Providence Gazette*. She'd been surprised by the obituary that John Carter had reprinted along with additional commentary. She wanted to read it through again, slowly.

Whoever had written the piece in the *Gazette* must have known her mother well. But who wrote it? It was only signed "Anonymous." The author claimed he was "no relation to the family, nor very intimately acquainted," but what he had said seemed to indicate he did indeed know her quite well.

Her mother's touch surrounded her in the furnishings of their home. They'd worked together to ensure comfort and a pleasing appearance. Her gaze traveled around the room, noting the wear and tear on the furniture and drapes. After living in the house for several years, perhaps it was time to consider some new furniture covers and nicer drapes at the window. Remake the room more in line with her personal taste now that she was the head of the household. Anyone coming to visit would be assessing her based on her surroundings, the one she created for herself. Not that she had many visitors. Which made her think of Joan. How she missed her. At least she heard from her from time to time via letter.

In fact, her letters had become less frequent to the point that only a couple each year arrived to share news of her now four children, her charity work, and her domestic situation. All of which Katy had never been a part of, hadn't seen her third or fourth child. Katy's life centered around the printing business, something totally foreign to the homey life of her once best friend. She sighed at the thought, taking small comfort from a sip of tea.

One aspect of what Mr. Galloway had raised was the dearth of women she called friend in this city. But truthfully, she didn't feel as accepted in this place, not like she had in Providence. There everyone was warm and friendly. Here, not only was the pace of life more accelerated, but she met with criticism and suspicion. Especially from Mr. Towne and Mr. Galloway. She longed for William to return but in his last letter he said it would be some time, probably summer, before he could wrap up his other business in New England.

Birdie hurried into the room with a huge smile on her face and a white cat in her arms. "Miss, you'll be happy to know that Cotton has caught a mouse in the pantry."

"Happy there was a mouse?" She smiled back at the young woman as she teased her.

Chuckling, Birdie stroked the cat's head. "That it was caught, I mean. This big girl did a fine job, to my way of thinking." Birdie put the cat down and settled on the seat opposite Katy. Cotton didn't linger but stalked out of the room. "Anything interesting in the paper?"

Katy nodded as she lifted the paper and opened it to the obituary. "Indeed. Look at this lovely piece written about my mother's passing."

Birdie eyed the paper that Katy held out to her and then shook her head. "I don't know my letters well enough to tackle that much reading, miss. Could you read it to me?"

"Of course. Let me see…" She peered at the page as she softly cleared her throat. "'Sir, In the last *New-York Gazette*, under the Philadelphia head, I find the following article dated in eighth instant: "Last Friday morning died, in an advanced age, Mrs. Sarah Goddard, late of Providence, in Rhode Island; and yesterday her remains were decently interred in Christ Church burying-ground, in this city, attended by a number of respectable inhabitants. She was the widow of Dr. Giles Goddard, formerly of New London, in Connecticut."' Katy paused to catch her breath.

"That's quite a lovely summary of her life, isn't it, miss?" Birdie dabbed at her eyes with a corner of her apron. "She was a fine woman and a lady."

"Usually, that would be the extent of any obituary, but in this case there is more. Shall I continue?"

"More? Then please." Birdie sat back in her chair and

folded her hands together in her lap. "Who did you say wrote this?"

"It just says 'Anonymous,' so it's a matter of speculation to determine who it might have been. Definitely someone who worked with her. He goes on.

"'This is so very short and simple an account of the decease of a very amiable person, who was really an ornament and honour to her sex, that in justice to her character I think myself obliged, though no relation to the family, nor very intimately acquainted, to mention the following particulars, which have come to my knowledge. Her ancestors were among the first settlers in the colony of Rhode Island, persons in affluent circumstances, and of the respectable characters.' I'll skip over the rest of that paragraph, it's just a summary of who her ancestors all were and covers her early years."

Birdie leaned forward in anticipation. "Is it quite unusual for someone to describe a person's life at such length?"

Katy nodded. "I am still trying to work out who might have written this extraordinary obituary. I wonder if it might have been John Holt. Or James Parker. Either would have been privy to all of the details that follow."

William had been a silent partner to Mr. Holt in New York. Mr. Holt had also worked with Mr. Parker to publish the *Connecticut Gazette* under the name of "James Parker and Company" fifteen years before. Those two had worked together for so long their phrasing mirrored each other's. So she may never actually determine the author. Still, she was highly pleased with what had been published.

Birdie waved a hand to get her attention. "Go on then. I want to hear what he had to say."

"Very well. Let's see... 'Having taken a liking to the Printing business, through her means her son was instructed in it, and settled in a Printing-House in the town of Providence, to which place she soon removed, and became a partner with him in the business, which was carried on several years to general acceptance, the two last years under her more immediate joint management and direction; the credit of the paper was greatly promoted by her virtue, ingenuity and abilities.' You know, after reading that, I really think it must have been Mr. Holt who wrote this. The phrasing sounds like his, at any rate." Katy glanced at Birdie. "But of course, who knows?"

"Go on and read the last of it. I am so intrigued by all of what the writer has to say about Mrs. Goddard."

"The next paragraph just summarizes why we moved here, so I'll skip that one, too. He concludes with, 'Her uncommon attainments in literature were the least valuable parts of her character. Her conduct through all the changing trying scenes of life, was not only unblameable, but exemplary—a sincere piety, an unaffected humility, an easy agreeable cheerfulness and affability, an entertaining, sensible and edifying conversation, and a prudent attention to all the duties of domestic life, endeared her to all her acquaintances, especially in the relations of wife, parent, friend, and neighbour. The death of such a person is a public loss, an irreparable one to her children.' Oh dear, he's so correct on that last point." Katy folded the paper and laid it back on the table, then swiped the tears from her cheeks. "I miss Mother so very much."

Birdie rose to cross to Katy, grasping her hands and pulling her up to a gentle embrace. "I miss her as well. She was a fine lady." Birdie pulled away to peer at Katy. "And you are so much like her. All of those compliments in that piece could just as easily apply to you, miss."

Sniffling, Katy pulled Birdie into another hug for a long moment. Then she stepped back to smile at her. "Thank you for such a lovely compliment of your own, Birdie. I appreciate your very kind words."

Knowing her mother was so well-respected and held in such high esteem comforted her aching heart. The least Katy could do was to continue to follow the example set by her dear mother. Even with regard to her infuriating brother.

CHAPTER 13

PHILADELPHIA, PENNSYLVANIA – 1770

anning herself with a small pamphlet, Katy leaned against the composing table to catch her breath. The July heat and humidity made her feel wilted and tired. The doors and windows were all open to allow any wisp of breeze to flow through the busy shop. The men and lads all were working on the most urgent projects, frequently mopping up the sweat running down their faces.

A couple of changes had occurred in the spring. Namely, Shepard Kollock had removed to St. Croix in the West Indies to recuperate and recover his health. The doctor had suggested the young man would benefit from an extended stay, so Shepard made arrangements to work for a press on the island. Benny Mecom remained working at the shop but only when he felt like it, which frustrated William's attempt to assist him to earn money to pay off his many debts owed to James Parker and others. A happier change came for Isaac Collins, though. He'd moved to Burlington, New Jersey, to assume the operation of James Parker's press upon that man's recent death. Isaac had proved himself to be steady and efficient, so he was progressing on his career path nicely. So she'd advertised for more help, and now they had two new young lads as apprentices.

The one other change she longed for couldn't come soon enough for her liking.

Benjamin Towne cast his eyes her way far too often. Didn't he have work to concentrate on instead of worrying about her actions? He had stopped badgering her about the records but his attitude had deteriorated over the past six months. When William finally returned from running an errand, which could be at any minute, she'd inform him of Benjamin's lack of respect toward her. She wanted him fired after all of the mischief he'd caused, but she hadn't hired him so didn't feel it her place to let him go. She'd make her case, though.

William was well aware of the attempted theft of the forms Towne had lifted when William was away from the shop. He'd tried to stop the paper from being published in order to turn subscribers against William. Katy had gone to him to find out why he'd taken the materials from her brother and he acted as polite as any gentleman. But he denied having any hand in such a theft and claimed he would, of course, recover the form if he knew where it might be. He'd said that he had a bill of cost against William, which it turned out was incurred while William was away. She happened to have that amount on her person and paid it off. She had a plan to make him tip his hand. She issued an advertisement to inform the town of Mr. Benjamin Towne's conduct.

Towne had reacted badly to her advertisement, of course. He'd come flying into the shop and said, "For God's sake, suppress the advertisement, and I will bring back the form. It has played the devil with me." So her plan to flush him out into the open had worked. Once he returned the missing form, they were able to publish the paper but she would never trust him ever again.

He had tried other mischief since then, stealing another set of forms which William found in the partners' rooms. Towne then tried to disrupt things by staying away from the shop, forcing William to threaten a lawsuit if he didn't return to work immediately. Needless to say, a strain existed between the two. At least her brother was in town again and could address the matter.

She straightened on her stool and peered at the hand-written court order the government desired to be made a public announcement in the *Chronicle*. Picking up the composing stick, she deftly filled the channel with the appropriate pieces of type and ornamental bits. She slid the line of text into the galley form and started on the next line. She didn't normally work on the local announcements page of the paper but all hands were needed to meet the pressing deadline.

Her larger than life, boisterous, brash, and innovative brother could irritate and annoy, but his vision for the *Chronicle* had paid off. Since the partners had retired earlier in the year, she'd been free to publish pieces which argued against tyranny and for liberty. Despite the fact that the partners had retired, they still poked their narrow, pointy noses into places they shouldn't. Benjamin Towne seemed to be working with them at times, though she couldn't quite understand why he would.

"Towne, what have you done?!" William marched through the open door into the shop, rage emanating from him like a heat wave. He carried a copy of the *Pennsylvania Journal* in his fist.

"William, what is the matter?" She stood and hurried to catch up to him as he stalked over to Towne's work area.

The heavy scowl on that man's face said much about his

feelings about William's startling appearance. The animosity between them left her wondering why her brother had agreed to take him on in the first place. While the partners insisted, surely her brother had some say in the matter. Was Towne a spy of sorts? Given his actions and attitude, it was likely. He probably thought he could overcome her management of the company in her brother's absence. That had failed, of course.

Towne smirked at William, eying the paper with glee in his eyes. "It's only fair, given the circumstances."

"It's an outrage and you know it." William shook the paper in the other man's face. "I will not stand for such underhanded dealings."

"What is it, William?" Her brother's wrath exceeded any in her memory.

"This—" William cut himself off, apparently struggling to find words to describe the reason for his outburst that were not offensive to her. "He's placed an advertisement in the *Journal*. Here, read it for yourself." He opened the paper to the offensive content and handed it to her.

She quickly read the advertisement, profound shock replacing her curiosity.

Whereas a partnership was some time ago entered into between WILLIAM GODDARD and BENJAMIN TOWNE, which, on experiment, is found to be inconvenient, I, the said BENJAMIN TOWNE, do therefore for legal as well as expedient considerations, decline the connection and desire that no person in future will rely on my credit as a partner in their contracts and dealings with the said William Goddard.

And whereas a person is appointed, on behalf of the principal creditors of the press to receive so much of the subscription money due from the inhabitants of the city and districts for the *Chronicle* as will discharge his debt, the said

Benajmin Towne therefore can only desire the subscribers for the said paper, in other places, to pay their subscription money to him (at Mrs. Marsh's in Second street, near Christ Church) as he has been a considerable sufferer by the partnership, and only wishes to have the company's debts paid.

July 12.Benjamin Towne.

"This is unacceptable, Mr. Towne." She handed the paper back to William as she glared at the scoundrel. "You are not owed that money. You have betrayed our trust in you, what little remained. I do not care to work with you any longer."

"You've exceeded your authority even as a purported partner." William slammed the paper against the table. "You snake in the grass. Galloway and Wharton have been trying to put me out of business for years. With their penchant for defending the abuse by the Crown, I am glad they have retired. Yet I imagine that you are still their puppet and that is why you have acted so basely. Stealing money from the press for all to see, no less."

"You do not have any recourse for my actions as your partner." Benjamin Towne sniggered as he folded his arms over his chest. "We'll see you ruined yet for your stance against the King and Crown."

"You're done here, Towne. Get out of my sight." William vibrated with anger as he pointed to the door. "You know the way."

"This is not over, Goddard." Towne's voice trailed off as his eyes shifted to look at William and then met hers briefly.

She maintained her steady glare at the offensive boor. He would find no help from her side of this sad affair.

William pointed to the open front door. "You have two minutes to walk out that door. Or I will help you out."

"You'll regret this." He snared his hat and suit coat from a peg by the back door. Jamming his hat on, he strangled the innocent coat in a closed fist as he stalked across the room and out the front door.

The silence that followed lasted only for a moment. Then the men and boys who had witnessed the confrontation burst into applause. Katy joined in to show them she stood with them in feeling relieved that the overbearing man was no longer employed in the Goddard print shop.

"All right, now that's over, get back to work." Katy smiled at them to encourage their industry. "We have deadlines to meet and now we're down a man."

"I'll help as much as I can." William huffed out an aggravated sigh. "But honestly, I think it is high time to reveal the dirty dealings of those underhanded, conniving men."

His angry tone made her cringe. "What are you thinking?"

"I'm going to write out everything they said they would do and what they actually did. It will take some time to put it all down on paper, and then I'll publish it for everyone to be forewarned in dealing with them in the future. When I am done, Wharton won't be electable this fall."

"Are you sure? Won't that lead to fueling the fire between you?"

"The public needs to know. I'm going home to begin writing the treatise on the machinations and deceit we've been laboring under for the past two years." He pivoted to face Katy directly. "And I have been remiss in not telling you how much I appreciated your weekly reports of the business. Your reports were more than adequate. I would not have been comfortable being away so frequently if I didn't know you were overseeing everything with your usual efficiency and dedication."

What a lovely thing for him to say to her. Hearing his high regard for her efforts made her heart sing. "Thank you, William. I appreciate the kind words. Now, I must get back to work myself. You go write and we'll see when we can publish it, once it's complete."

"Very well. I will work on it in the afternoons, but will come to the shop each morning to ensure you have everything you and the boys need to accomplish everything."

After he left, she returned to her composing table and resumed her work, humming a catchy tune. Thank goodness she no longer had to deal with the shenanigans of Benjamin Towne so the shop could run more smoothly and without unnecessary drama.

But then, whatever vitriol William included in his diatribe against the partners might just stir up everything even more. *Oh, Mother, send me guidance from wherever you are.*

Over the next couple of months, Katy kept the shop running smoothly while William worked on his pamphlet. From what he'd told her, he intended to lay out every detail of how Galloway and Wharton had mistreated him, how they tried to steal his print shop by lowballing an offer to his sister, all the mischief Towne engaged in, and more. Since the partners' spy, Benjamin Towne, no longer had access to the daily doings of the company, her ability to steer it with a steady hand shone. The only thing she couldn't do was raise enough money from subscriptions to pay off all of the people with their hands out for payment. William said he'd deal with that matter.

She set the straw broom in its corner by the back door and then wiped her hands on her smeared apron. Next, she'd update the cash leger before she called it a day. As she headed back to the front counter, William motioned for her to join him at his work table off to one side. She suppressed a sigh of irritation and forced a smile.

"What can I help you with?" she asked as she stopped on the opposite side of the table from where he perched on a stool.

"I wanted to make sure you are aware of the response I published in the *Journal* to Towne's advertisement of the twelfth. I ensured the reading public knows of the absolute falsehoods in his claim and exposed the two party men backing him."

"Wharton and Galloway, you mean?" She trembled at the thought of the responses which would soon flow in their direction from those accused of misdoings. She couldn't stop the reactions, but she could caution her brother to be as honest and fair as possible.

"Assuredly."

"I hesitate to ask, but what might you have said to them?" Her vituperative brother wielded a savage pen when angered or abused by his peers. She braced mentally for what he'd say next.

"The truth of the matter. I began with, 'It has been my great misfortune to be concerned in business, for some time past, with a very unworthy man, under the name of Benjamin Towne, formerly a journeyman in my office, a person very little known here, till he was drawn from obscurity to be made a scape goat of his superiors, to bear off their iniquity.' Then I laid out what transpired, his stealing and disruptions."

Oh dear, that was quite an inflammatory start indeed. "I see. Well, I hope the men's response is not too abusive of your good reputation."

"Wait until they read what I have to say in my pamphlet. I have much more to share with our community about their actions."

"How is the pamphlet coming along?"

"I'm ready to print the first part in the *Chronicle*, actually.

I'll share the other parts in subsequent papers, then combine them all into a single pamphlet. I want to spread the word of the villainy of my so-called partners immediately to protect others from their deceit. That's why I wanted you to talk to me." William glanced to the press where two young men labored to print the next edition of the *Chronicle*. "Which of the apprentices should I entrust with doing the actual printing job?"

Willy and Jacob were both good additions to the list of apprentices for the print shop. She meant to recommend to William that Willy step into the journeyman position soon. Industrious and honest, she could rely on both boys.

"Let's allow Willy to handle both the paper and the pamphlet and see if the end result might warrant elevating him from an apprentice to the vacant journeyman role." She met William's surprised gaze. "He's a smart young man, a quick study. I think he's ready, but of course, you'll need to decide if you agree."

He studied the two young men for a long moment and then nodded. "If he manages to complete the job to my standards, then I will consider your suggestion."

Katy assigned the task to Willy and over the next weeks he and Jacob worked diligently and efficiently to compose and print the weekly paper plus the seventy-three page pamphlet, entitled *The Partnership: Or the History of the Rise and Progress of the Pennsylvania Chronical, &c. wherein the Conduct of Joseph Galloway, Esq; Speaker of the Honourable House of Representative of the Province of Pennsylvania, Mr. Thomas Wharton, sen. and their man Benjamin Towne, my late Partners, with my own, is properly delineated, and their Calumnies against me fully refuted.* She couldn't suppress the grin at the lengthy if accurate title. William inspected each page, each column, each ornamental element within the pages. Katy held her breath when he turned back to the beginning to peer closely at one of the titles. He pressed his lips together and then nodded as he lifted his gaze to meet hers.

"This is excellent work." William shifted his gaze to Willy's somber expression. "Miss Goddard and I believe it is time for you to be promoted to journeyman printer. Do you accept?"

Willy's sober expression lightened but stayed bland. "Yes, sir. Thank you."

"You're welcome. Now, let's get these pamphlets distributed to our subscribers." William chuckled darkly. "I cannot wait for Galloway's reaction to the truth coming out. He'll lose the next election after the public understands how underhandedly he treats others."

A mix of happiness and wariness fluttered in Katy's chest. Happiness for Willy's promotion, but wary of that reaction her brother so eagerly anticipated. After all, her brother accused his former partners of trying to destroy his business. Which she agreed they had, but publishing this diatribe against them would likely set fire to their ongoing feud. Her mother would be horrified by the way her brother conducted himself in this affair. Katy wrestled with applauding her brother standing up to the men's actions against them, and concern over the resulting war of words.

The feud between the men continued over the following months, stretching into a year of back and forth pieces in competing newspapers within the city. She tried to talk her brother out of continuing it, but he wouldn't listen to her. When her mother had died, she knew it would fall to her to try to contain his tendency toward vitriol and accusations. One of the many reasons she longed for her mother's presence. Her mother had the ability to guide William in ways he wouldn't accept from his sister. She never thought the back and forth editorial jabs would get so bad. Then there was a lull in the attacks and she hoped the feud was dying a natural death. Still, she kept a watchful eye on him as she kept the shop profitable.

Almost exactly a year had passed since the damning pamphlet had been published. She worked on composing yet another sermon pamphlet while William helped Willy repair the press. The front door burst open and two constables strode briskly inside.

Katy froze, alarm shafting through her at the presence of the law in what she now considered to be her shop. After all, William was rarely present or involved in the day-to-day tasks she oversaw. But constables? What could they possibly want? She was unaware of any criminal activity by any of her apprentices. Did William find himself in some kind of trouble that had come home to roost?

Benny and Jacob continued printing the front page of the newspaper, but glanced warily at the lawmen.

"Mr. William Goddard, you are under arrest for not paying your debts." The larger of the two men marched up to William and grabbed his upper arm. "Come with me quietly."

Those debts that he'd promised he'd address. Throwing him into debtors prison to force him to pay them off any way he could. How much did he owe? Was there any way to pay those debts? Thoughts swirled in her head at the scene unfolding before her, like something out of a Shakespeare tragedy.

William yanked his arm away from the constable. "I will not. I have not refused to pay my debts, but only required my partners to pay their fair share. Until they do, I will not be beholden for the entire sum. Who has issued the warrant against me?"

The other constable grunted. "The man who filed the suit saying you owe him money for type and materials, that's who. You have to come with us."

"Sir, I must declare my innocence of this charge." He yanked his arm out of the constable's grasp.

"That's not up to me, but to the judge." The constable grabbed hold of his arm again and started steering him toward the door.

William glanced at Katy, his angry and concerned expression charging her with helping him if she could. He was being dragged off to jail. She didn't have the wherewithal to pay off the unnamed creditor. But William defying the law by resisting arrest wouldn't help his case either.

"Where are you taking me?" William pulled free again and clenched his fists at his sides.

The burly constable noticed the aggressive move and frowned at William. "To jail until you can appear before the judge who will decide your fate." He grabbed hold of William on one side and the other constable grabbed his other arm.

"I'll get you some help!" Katy called after the men as they ushered her brother out of the shop.

When silence announced that work had completely stopped, she swallowed the panic lodged in her throat. They hadn't specified the person or persons who claimed unpaid debt of her brother but she could guess. Here she'd thought the feud had quieted, but in fact those dastardly men had obviously pulled some strings or made false claims in order to silence her brother. To prevent him from publishing the news as he saw fit. As they saw fit, in actuality. She and her brother both believed in the colonist's rights that differed with what the crown held to be true. The people's arguments for no taxation without representation only grew stronger with each attempt by the Parliament to add another tax on the American colonists. Well, she wouldn't let them silence the press. She'd carry on and continue to publish all of the news, not just what they approved of with their loyalty to the crown. The fight for equal treatment must be won and she would do her utmost to keep everyone informed of the front lines. The people of this and all of the colonies were expressing their outrage and dissent over their treatment by Parliament. As was their right.

She swept her gaze over Benny, Willy, and the newest apprentice Jacob, all watching her, gauging her reaction to the startling turn of events. "All right, let's carry on. I need to think about who I can ask for help for William. But in the meantime, we have to keep the press and the paper going. Understood?"

"Yes, miss." Benny nodded and then addressed the others. "You heard her, let's get busy."

It took time, three long weeks, but finally William was released from debtors prison and returned to work. But the experience changed him. She'd watch and wait to decide her next steps until she understood just how much the experience had changed him. Then she had to decide whether she would still stay and help him.

CHAPTER 14

PHILADELPHIA, PENNSYLVANIA – 1772

The chill in the air with the advent of fall couldn't allay the heat in her chest at the unexpected and unwanted revelation she struggled to comprehend.

"William, you can't be serious." Keeping her expression neutral proved a struggle as she considered her brother's latest scheme.

"I am convinced that no matter what I do in this city I will remain a target of my former partners. It's been six months since they caused my imprisonment and they are still causing mischief." He pushed away from the counter to pace back and forth in front of her, his angry strides carrying him to the front door and then to the back door, then the front yet again. "I've tried to operate this press without further antagonizing those troublemakers."

"But Maryland?" She crossed her arms over her chest as he continued his circuit. "Why?"

He stopped in front of her and searched her eyes for a minute. With a sigh, he shrugged. "I cannot continue here and there is only one printing press in that colony. That's in Annapolis, the *Maryland Gazette.* I understand that Baltimore is a growing town, one which would benefit from a press. And far enough from the *Gazette* that it won't be a direct competitor."

"I do not wish to uproot myself to relocate. I am fairly content here." She swept her gaze around the shop, encompassing its entirety in her statement. Benny and the others were busy with their tasks, but glanced at her from time to time as they eavesdropped on the conversation. "I have made a few friends here. And we have responsibilities to those men over there. I'm established, surrounded with good clients and a supportive group of people. Why would I want to disturb all that I've put into place?"

"You do not need to move with me. At least not yet." He studied her for a moment then offered another shrug. "But you know how vital your assistance is to me and my ventures. I will most definitely need your help."

"What of the *Chronicle* and the press?"

The front door opened and admitted a regular customer. She indicated she'd only be a minute with a raised finger. She had to address this matter before she attended to whatever business the gentleman may have. Turning her attention back to her brother, she lifted one brow in inquiry.

"It's not sustainable in this antagonistic climate." William waved a dismissive hand in the air. "Keep it going for as long as you can. This town needs a counter voice to that loyalist rag across town even if they won't admit it."

"I will do my best in your absence, if that is what you want." She lowered her voice and leaned closer to him. "What about Benny and the lads?"

He flashed a look at the workers busy at the press with its familiar rhythmic creak and thump as they operated the mechanism to print the latest broadsides. "They may come with us if they so choose, or we can end their agreements with their parents. I'll leave that to you to decide."

Willy was old enough at eighteen years that making such a change would be relatively easy. He'd likely view it as an adventure, truth be told. Jacob was only fourteen so she'd want to correspond with his parents on the matter. Benny was an adult and she needn't worry about where he'd land if they closed the shop. She'd need to consult with the boys' parents to determine if they would approve of their sons moving with them. But they'd all still be well cared for and would receive a quality education in their chosen trade.

"Very well. I will manage things here while you determine what your new venture will be. Please keep me informed as to your whereabouts so I may keep you apprised of activities here."

"I will be sure to send you word as soon as I have settled on a viable place to conduct business as a press." He straightened his spine, and squared his shoulders. "I need to put my affairs in order, and then decide when it's a good time to travel to Baltimore."

He'd be going alone to the new town where he wouldn't know anyone. Willy, strong and lithe, turned away from the press to retrieve the next galley form from the work table. His shock of blond hair brushed his shoulders as he lifted the frame and turned back to the press. Then an idea struck her. Yes, perhaps that would be a good idea.

"William, what if you took Willy with you to help get things set up? Benny and Jacob and I can manage without him for a while. We're caught up on our jobs for the moment after word got out you were in jail."

"Willy?" He stared at the lad, pursing his lips and then flattening them. "Do you think he'd be an asset? I know he's experienced, but am not certain it's a wise move."

"He is strong and honest. And experienced in the business. I truly believe you'd find him useful."

William crossed his arms as he continued to study the

young man for several moments. Then he shrugged lightly. "If you think so, then I will do so. I'll write to his parents to make sure they're aware of his whereabouts."

"Will you tell him?" She could see in Willy's hazel eyes that he knew they were speaking about him, the uncertainty evident in his expression. "He'll probably find it exciting."

With a nod, William spun around and headed over to talk with the lad in question. Willy's eyes lit with eager anticipation of the pending move.

Katy smiled at his look of appreciation for suggesting he go with her brother to start up a new press. Then she started walking toward the waiting customer, humming softly, her thoughts a whirl.

That conversation did not end the way she'd hoped. She'd be left to try to avoid demands for payments for items and services that she hadn't negotiated herself. She didn't know exactly what other potential creditors may emerge from the shadows once her brother was out of the picture. But she would only honor debts she made.

Her *Chronicle* would include news from all sides of the current affairs circulating through the colonies. The press must continue to air the grievances in a manner which enabled their readers to understand the issues they faced.

And she'd carry on as if she wasn't waiting to be summoned to move yet again.

For the next six months, Katy managed to keep her private vow to carry on with the operation of the printing press and ancillary activities. From time to time she received letters from William apprising her of his progress or lack thereof. He informed her that he'd been encouraged by several prominent townsmen in Baltimore that they'd support the press, and that he'd find the town siding on the more liberal side of affairs. She held onto the hope that he wouldn't actually request her to move yet again, making it a point to appreciate and enjoy every moment in her lovely home a short distance from the offices of the press.

She pulled the front door of her home closed and turned to hurry to the press. Jacob had left an hour earlier to begin the day's work. Benny hopefully would meet them there. Jacob fit right in with her household when her brother had closed his house before leaving town. Her friendly staff had been happy to accept him into her home. She paused, spun around to peruse the façade of her favorite house. Two stories of red brick, a central black painted door flanked by two black sashed windows on either side and on the upper story. Two chimneys, one at either end, emitted a steady stream of smoke into the crisp fall air. Finding this welcoming abode remained a highlight of her life in Philadelphia. One which included much work waiting for her at the shop.

She spun back around and strode purposefully down the side of the street, dodging oncoming people, horses, dogs, and vehicles. Christ Church's steeple rose high into the sky. Reviewing in her mind the many tasks pending, she prioritized them as she arrived and pushed through the shop door. The bell alerted her lads to her presence. She nodded to them as she laid her satchel on the counter, then unfastened her cloak as she went to the row of hooks along the wall by the back door. Swinging the heavy garment from her shoulders, she placed it on one of the hooks and then patted her hair into place.

Facing Benny and Jacob, she motioned for them to stop their work and talk with her. They soon stood before her with curious expressions. She didn't often call a meeting such as this one. But she'd received a letter the day before and she wanted to share its news with them.

"Gentlemen, I have heard from Mr. Goddard and thought you'd like to hear his news." She smiled gently, pulling the folded letter from her skirt pocket. "I won't take but a moment of your time, and then we'll all need to be busy as the bees in springtime to accomplish all of the jobs in the queue."

Benny crossed his arms over his large chest and nodded. "Go on then, Miss Goddard."

Young Jacob mimicked his older example but remained quiet.

Katy glanced between the two for a moment, appreciating their quiet respect and attention. Then she unfolded the paper and began to read the pertinent paragraph. "He says, 'I have settled on starting a newspaper and print shop in Baltimore, Maryland. I was fortunate to be able to purchase a fine press and types from the widow of the city's previous printer, Nicholas Hasselbach, who died a few years ago. I've leased an establishment at the corner of South and Market streets which will serve my needs for sometime to come. I'm calling the paper the *Maryland Journal and Baltimore Advertiser* and will aim to begin its publication in December of this year if all falls in line as I hope.' That is what he set out to do, to begin a new newspaper and print shop."

Jacob raised his hand as if he were in school. "Miss?"

"Yes, Jacob." The lad was so polite and curious. "You have a question?"

He nodded and swallowed. "Will Willy be coming back now?"

Ah, the boy missed his friend. "I am sure he's busy helping start up the press and attaining subscribers for the new paper. So I wouldn't expect that he'd be coming back, no."

Benny looked down at Jacob as he rested a hand on the

boy's shoulder. "Do not fret. I'm here for you and if you need anything, just you let me know and I'll help you out. All right?"

"Yes. Thank you for that." Jacob shrugged. "I miss Willy's jesting, is all."

Katy suppressed a pleased smile. Seeing the evidence in action of the life lessons she'd worked to teach the young man on how to behave and to treat others made her heart sing. The concept of the guys working together to support each other no matter their role or station had sunk in.

"I don't know much about jesting. Let me think on it and see if I can't dredge up some riddles for you, would that suffice?" Benny tousled the lad's hair. "For now, we've work to do."

A few weeks later a messenger came to the print shop with a formal court document. "Is Mr. William Goddard here?"

Katy shook her head at the youth. "No, he's left the city. But I am his sister. Can I help you with something?"

He glanced at the paper in his hand and then up at her. "I was to deliver this to him. When will he return?"

"I do not expect he will return." She peered closer at the tense young man. "What business do you have with him?"

"I was to deliver this to him, but I suppose if he's not coming back then I need to find the man responsible now. So, who is in charge of this newspaper in his absence? Is he here?"

Squaring her shoulders rather than reacting to the young man's dismissal or lack of knowledge, she lifted her chin a touch. "I am running the business for my brother. Anything you have for him I can handle."

The scrawny lad sharpened his gaze as he swept it head to toe and back to meet hers. He opened his mouth and then shut it before opening it again to speak. "I see. Then this notice of demand for payment by several creditors of the *Chronicle* is for you." He thrust the sheaf at her.

"Demand for payment?" Taking the papers, she glared at the man before her. "We'll see about this. If your business is concluded, then I suppose you can see yourself out."

He tipped his hat to her and then left the shop, leaving behind an aura of anxiety and premonition within Katy's soul. Carrying the demand papers to the counter, she laid the packet down and started reading through the legal language. Deciphering the meaning behind the difficult words proved challenging, even with her extensive education and experience with such writing. The gist of the demand seemed to be that several of the men who had provided supplies—type, paper, ink-making ingredients, etc.—had banded together to call for the immediate payment of the debt. The demand was addressed to William Goddard and no one else. Perhaps she could fight back on the grounds that he was not present and was not coming back? It might buy her some time to save up the money to address the debt. Or such a tack might make the issue go away entirely.

She read the pages again and then smiled. Only the newspaper was cited as being in default, not the press as an entity. So if the paper was forced out of business, which seemed the intent behind this legal maneuver, she would still have the press and book shop to carry on with. She'd miss the intensity of compiling the paper but at least she'd still have a livelihood in Philadelphia. She'd be able to continue to support and train her apprentice for the foreseeable future. And no longer would she have to worry about the increasing competition and struggle to increase the circulation of the paper. One less worry was a good thing.

She'd consult with an attorney, then inform her brother of the mischief she guessed was prompted by Galloway and Wharton. Those two men would not let her brother live in peace. Always instigating something against him. But he was out of their reach now. She would have to fend them off her own way. Which they probably wouldn't like one bit.

She smiled to herself as she put away the demand papers. Only time would tell how things would unravel.

CHAPTER 15

PHILADELPHIA, PENNSYLVANIA – 1773

"Benny, Jacob, come look at this." Katy held up the copy of the *Maryland Journal and Baltimore Advertiser* she'd just received in the post. "The first edition!"

"First?" Benny perused the front page of the paper. "This wasn't issued until August 20, 1773. I thought you said he was going to publish the first edition in December of last year."

She shrugged as she turned the paper to assess its layout and decorative elements for a moment. Printed on heavy book paper, each folio sheet measured eighteen by twenty-four inches with twelve broad columns. The type looked to be the new, elegant Elzevir. An engraving of the armorial bearings of Maryland appeared along with the title. The motto he'd chosen as a guiding principle for the newspaper's contents, in a fancy font across the top of the page, was a couplet adopted from Horace:

Omne tulit punctum qui miscuit utile dulci.
Lectorum delectando, pariterque monendo.

She read it again, translating it as she did. "He carries every point who blends the useful with the agreeable, amusing the reader while he instructs him." The colophon declared, "Baltimore: Printed by William Goddard, at the Printing-Office in Market-street, opposite the Coffee-House." So now she knew exactly where he'd set up his new press.

"You know my brother. There were 'delays' and 'challenges' he had to overcome. But he's made his latest venture come to fruition. I congratulate him on producing such a fine paper, as well."

"Seven months late." Benny shook his head and crossed his arms. "I don't wish to speak ill of your brother, miss, but that seems rather a long time to be putting off a venture that one hopes will be a success."

Jacob shifted so he could look at the paper over her shoulder as she flipped to the advertisements page. After a beat, he gasped. "Look at that one." He pointed to one of the advertisements with an inky forefinger. "Do you think he might have actually met Colonel Washington when he placed this advertisement?"

Katy read the offer from George Washington of Mount Vernon, Virginia, to sell twenty thousand acres of his western lands. It must have been a unique pleasure to meet the distinguished military officer. She'd heard many fine things about his abilities and achievements. Despite the failed diplomatic mission that ended in the disaster known as the French and Indian War, he redeemed himself and was elected to the Virginia House of Burgesses not once but twice. He'd married the wealthy widow, Martha Dandridge Custis, in January 1759. They lived at his beautiful and elegant plantation known as Mount Vernon, which he'd renovated and redecorated to suit his new bride and her two surviving children. Indeed, rumor had it that he'd spent a lot of money importing beautiful furnishings for entertaining the many visitors he welcomed. Sadly, daughter Patcy Custis had died recently after having severe seizures. Katy's heart went out to Martha in her grief over losing a daughter. She understood the intense pain of losing a dearly beloved family member, and its lingering aftereffects. She frequently sensed her mother's loving presence, particularly in moments of worry.

"Indeed, I imagine William had quite a conversation with the gentleman and officer. He's always been intrigued by the man." Katy folded the paper. "All right. Let's get back to work. Benny, there are two more pamphlets to be set and printed this week. They take priority over the sermon."

"Yes, miss." Benny tapped Jacob on the shoulder. "Come on, lad, let's get this press moving."

As the day wound down, and the work progressed, Katy's thoughts returned to her brother's new endeavor in Baltimore. Mulling over the challenges he'd written her about, she grew more nervous about her future in Philadelphia. Given his history of starting something he couldn't handle and then crying out for help. She finished the last pressing task of the day and wiped her hands clean on her apron.

At least with him in Maryland he wasn't as involved with the Sons of Liberty in New England. After the Tea Act had passed back in May, he'd become even angrier at the continued taxation of the colonists without representation in Parliament. People had boycotted tea, switching to coffee rather than paying the duty on tea. Tensions kept ratcheting up all across the colonies. The news she reported reflected a growing unrest among the people. She worried as to where they were headed with regard to the king and Parliament.

She retrieved her cloak and swung it about her shoulders, fastening it swiftly as she stopped by Benny's composing table. "I'm heading home. Jacob can come when he's done for the day. Will you lock up when you're finished?"

"Of course. We should be done in just a little while." Benny kept working as he spoke, his selection of types quick and sure as he filled the channel. "Go on. I'll tidy up in a bit."

With a nod, she crossed the shop floor to pick up her satchel on her way out. A cool breeze carried the scents of the river nearby as well as the aromas of stews and roasted meats from the tavern she passed as she strolled toward her home. The city stirred with energy. People hurrying one direction or another about their business. Stagecoaches and dogcarts vied for space on the street. Seagulls flew overhead, their high pitched cries piercing through the rumbling sounds of the traffic. She'd come to love this place. A mournful nostalgia swept through her.

Minutes later she turned up the walkway to her house. After depositing her cloak on the hall stand, she paused to consider her situation. The house itself represented her life in its comfortable furniture and simple furnishings. Her household consisted of her cook, maid, gardener, and Jacob. She kept a few chickens for eggs, and a couple of mousers to fend off the rodents. This situation proved far more comfortable than her previous home, but of course not of the same status as her parents' home in New London. She didn't need such an elevated place as the one her doctor father once enjoyed.

Katy paced down the hallway to the kitchen. "Holly, Jacob will be right behind me in a short while. Will supper be ready at the usual time this evening?"

The young woman greeted her with a wide welcoming smile. Her vibrant green eyes twinkled as she nodded. "Yes, miss. I'm putting the finishing touches on the forced meat now."

"It smells delightful." Katy looked around the kitchen,

noting the bowls of vegetables and fruits aligned on the side work table. A kettle hung near the cooking fire in the large fireplace. Several potatoes were tucked into the ashes to cook slowly. The tantalizing aroma of baking bread wafted from the bread oven. "I will have your pay for you and your sister tomorrow."

"Thank you from me and Birdie both. We've almost saved enough to make the journey to South Carolina to begin anew." Holly bobbed a curtsy with a chuckle. "All thanks to your kind generosity."

Should she tell her employee about the likelihood of her own removal in the not-so-distant future? Not that she desired such a move. Perhaps William will decide he can manage on his own. Then Katy would need to find a new cook and maid when the sisters went on their new adventure in the southern colony. She'd be able to continue the book bindery and print shop and live well in the process. As long as her brother didn't decide to close it down and make her move to help him in Maryland. She drew in a deep breath and let it out silently. No point putting the cart before the horse.

"How soon do you think you'll be leaving me, then?" Katy softened her inquiry with a gentle smile. "I know you're eager to begin your grand adventure."

"Another few months should serve the purpose." Holly turned to the kettle suspended by the fire. Using her heavy apron, she lifted the lid with her left hand and stirred the contents with a ladle in her right. Replacing the lid, she rested the ladle on a stoneware plate and looked at Katy. "We don't plan to leave you in the lurch, though. We have some friends looking for work who might be interested in working with your kind self."

"I appreciate the thought, but we will see…"

Holly frowned and took a step closer. "What is wrong, miss?"

"Nothing. Really. At least not yet." Katy sighed as she shrugged. "I'm just concerned that my brother will ask me to move to Maryland to help his new effort with a print shop."

"Why would he do such a thing?" Holly tilted her head to one side. "Surely he can manage his own affairs."

"One would think. But history suggests otherwise." She chuckled as her brows lifted. "I wouldn't be here if he hadn't insisted he needed my mother's and my help." Not to mention the promise she'd made to her mother. She couldn't forget that day. Although there were moments when she wished she could. If he pushed her too far, well... Time would tell.

"I see. Well, maybe he'll not ask this time."

"Perhaps. I will leave you to finish your culinary efforts."

With a wave, she turned and sauntered out of the kitchen to wander through the rooms of the first floor of the house. Her thoughts wandered along with her steps, always returning to the source of her unease. When would William ask for her help? How much longer would she be able to enjoy living in this lovely, comfortable home?

Turns out the answer to her question was almost six months. She'd known William would eventually send for her to come manage the business while he traipsed off to do something else. His letter insisting she make the move to Baltimore cited his urgent involvement in establishing a new postal system separate from the Royal Post. As the colonies awoke to the oppression by King Charles III and his Parliament, the need to control the flow of information within the colonies became critical. The British frequently confiscated letters and other papers, interfering in the communication within the colonies. He'd started to visualize a new system but couldn't enact his plans if confined to one place. Thus the summons.

With a heavy heart, she had the lads print issue #368 on February 8, 1774. The final issue of the *Chronicle* to ever be printed. In addition to William needing her, the heavy taxes forced upon the print shop finally meant bankruptcy and closure. She'd composed a brief but heartfelt announcement to her subscribers as to the reasons for the paper's demise. Then, after closing the shop for the last time, she'd said her farewells to Benny, and then Jacob had accompanied her home to finish packing their belongings.

"Miss, will you be needing anything special for your last night in Philadelphia? I'm thinking a nice roast and stewed vegetables, perhaps?" Holly dried her hands on her apron as she peered at Katy in the kitchen. "I'd like to fix you something nice this last night in town."

"That sounds delicious. Thank you." Katy drew in a deep breath and let it out slowly, aware of the tension in her shoulders. "I will miss your fine culinary skills."

"Pshaw! You'll find someone with better skills than mine in that new city." Holly winked at her as she pivoted to cross the room to the work table and its scant selection of vegetables in a large bowl.

Winding down a household of her size, merely four people, didn't take long but it still made Katy's heart ache to contemplate. Jacob would accompany her on the morrow in the stagecoach for the journey to Baltimore. Their few possessions would also travel with them. When they arrived in that growing port city, they'd stay with William until she located suitable housing for herself and her servants. Whoever they might end up being. The lad would board with

William and Willy instead of in her female dominant household.

"I really appreciate the fact you and Birdie stayed with me longer, Holly. Delaying your adventure down south must not have been easy." She moved to the kettle suspended near the cook fire and, using her long skirts to protect her hand, lifted the lid to sniff its contents. "This roasting beef smells divine." She replaced the lid and smiled at her cook.

"No, miss, we really didn't like the idea of leaving as long as you needed us." Holly lifted a pair of potatoes and placed them on a cutting board. "But I really am anticipating moving south tomorrow with Birdie. We're all atwitter, to be honest."

"Won't you miss your family when you move so far away?" Four years had passed since her mother's death, and of course her father much longer ago than that. Still a pang of grief, of missing them, always accompanied their memory. And of course her only brother had not been near in a long time, as well. "One reason I'm moving to Baltimore is to be with my brother."

"I can imagine he'll appreciate you being there for him." Holly took up a knife and began to slice the potatoes, placing the pieces into a wood bowl. "I expect you're wanting to freshen up before supper, so go on with you while I finish putting it together."

"Very well." Katy tossed a faint smile to the cook and left the kitchen. She needed air, but with it snowing again, she settled for pacing into the front parlor to peer out the window at the snow muffled street beyond. The familiar scene, of bundled people and lumbering wagons amidst the coaches and dogcarts passing to and fro, made her heart ache.

A meow behind her made her turn around to find Cotton approaching her. She bent down to lift her into her arms, stroking a hand down her head and back. She'd miss the feline but she was more Holly's than hers, so the cat would stay with the sisters. Cotton squirmed to be put down, so she put her back on the floor and the cat stalked out of the parlor. Katy turned back to the scene outside with a long sigh.

Tomorrow a brand new chapter of her life would begin. She'd made her decision so she couldn't change her mind. The very idea of having to pack up everything and once again travel to a new, foreign town where she wouldn't know anyone except her brother quaked her soul. She would do it, of course. She'd promised her mother. But was she really ready to face what the future might bring?

CHAPTER 16

BALTIMORE, MARYLAND – 1774

"We should arrive in Baltimore very soon, so please stop fidgeting." Katy softened her request with a small smile. It turned out that their stagecoach carried the mail, so they traveled faster than a typical stage. But it had still been an arduous trip despite the well defined roads connecting Philadelphia to the young town. Crammed inside the stagecoach on one of three benches, they'd jostled against total strangers every bump in the rough road. In total the coach carried ten passengers plus the driver. Nine passengers inside plus one who rode with the driver outside. The road was so rough that one man had to physically hod his wife in place, she'd been pitching to and fro so much. No wonder the lad felt ill. Trapping an energetic young man in a tiny space for hours at a time under such cramped conditions had proved difficult for everyone.

"We'll go straight to the print shop and then on to William's house which will help you stretch your legs." She met Jacob's tired gaze from where he leaned against the wall of the coach. The poor lad had been sick when they'd first started out, embarrassing himself as well as leaving a lingering unpleasant odor in the coach after they'd managed to clean up his vomit. "Be strong, Jacob. We're almost there."

She peeked out the open side window of the coach, glad they'd managed to secure seat near one. Dusty leather window shades didn't keep out the rain and cold. Beyond, the terrain changed from grazing pastures of occasional plantations and forests to more farm houses as they neared the town. They trundled along the muddy mess of a road, the early February rain falling gently on the wintery landscape. The coach-and-four moved along at a brisk pace despite the slippery road they traveled. With good fortune the rain would stop before they arrived. She checked the small watch she wore pinned to the bodice of her dress. If they were on schedule still, they should arrive in a little while.

"You'll be relieved to know that we should be at the station in about fifteen minutes." She clasped her hands together in her lap. "Once we get there, there will be much to do."

"I'm curious what Willy and Mr. Goddard have established and how everything is set up." Jacob peered out the window of the coach. "And what accommodations we'll have at his place."

"Knowing Mr. Goddard, you'll be quite comfortable, I'd suspect." Her brother always ensured his home met the highest standards he could afford. "At least he was in Philadelphia."

The lad had lived with William for several years before being required to move in with her after her brother had departed that city. He'd been relatively comfortable, but she didn't have quite as big of an abode as her brother preferred.

A little while later they entered the town's limits and the traffic increased around them. Seemed as if all five thousand residents chose that morning to be out in the streets. Perhaps it was a market day. She would have to determine when those occurred so she could best plan her shopping days as well.

Before departing Philadelphia, she'd made inquiries into the situation she would be moving to in Baltimore. What were the people like and what were their attitudes about what was happening in the colonies in general, and Maryland in particular? She'd been reassured by what she'd learned. Now, something warm and fluffy curled up inside her chest as she gazed out the window at what would be her new hometown. She had the oddest sense of coming home as they rolled through the bustling town. The very atmosphere of the city seemed to welcome her.

The quiet energy of the place combined with the neatly maintained houses and then the shops and taverns they passed pleased her. The gentle rain made everything and everyone glisten as they hurried on their individual errands. Some carried an odd-looking contraption, like a shield held above their head by a stick. After a moment, she recalled reading an advertisement in another paper about the new way for people to protect themselves from both the sun and rain. The layout of the advertisement didn't entirely work, to her eye. But the item had intrigued her. An umbrella. How curious. Their use in this growing town indicated the progressive nature of the people, which made her smile. She'd fit right in with them. Even the faintly fishy scent of the air made her feel quite at home, knowing the inner harbor of the Chesapeake Bay was not far off. She'd always enjoyed being near large bodies of water. Indeed, every place she lived had been a port city. Mayhap she'd locate a suitable dwelling nearby as well.

"Look, Jacob, do you see the ladies carrying their umbrellas?" She pointed out the window as she glanced at him. "That's something new to see, isn't it?"

Jacob leaned forward and grinned at her. "Those look mighty funny. Where did they get them?"

"Sit back now, as we must not stare." She leaned back as well, glancing occasionally out the window and then settling her gaze on the lad. "If I remember correctly, they originated in India and were imported here from England."

"Miss, do you know…" Jacob stared at the strange contraptions being held by the disappearing group of women. "Are they made of cloth?"

"The advertisement I saw in an Annapolis paper claimed they were made of coarse oiled linen supported by a rattan stick. I had dismissed the notion of fumbling about with such a thing, but look at how it keeps them dry in this light rain."

"Totally useless in any other kind of rain, I'd think." Jacob sat back with a shake of his head. "I'd rather wear my oiled cape and hat."

The man beside Jacob, still holding onto his wife, grunted in disgust. "Won't catch me with such a silly contraption."

As the coach rolled down Market, she kept an eye out for the Goddard print shop. William had sent her the location and description of the fine building he'd rented some rooms in for the press. What he hadn't bothered to tell her in his last missive was how he expected to receive them upon their arrival in town. If he or one of his lads didn't meet them at the station, then she'd go to the print shop and make plans from there. First, she needed to spot the place. She peered out the window for several moments, finally rewarded by spotting the newspaper's name in large letters on the outside of a respectable building. Now to see what happened next.

The driver called out in his booming voice, "Baltimore station."

Relief and hope swirled together in her chest. "Thank goodness. Gather your things, lad." Katy took hold of her large purse

containing the most important bits and pieces of her belongings, and held it ready to disembark at the earliest opportunity.
Like Jacob, she disliked forced proximity with strangers.

The stagecoach turned onto Calvert and rattled to a stop
in front of the two-story brick courthouse, situated on a
bluff overlooking the town. The spire at its center soared
into the sky, topped by a weather cock and points of the
compass. Ever so grateful to be able to escape the close
confines of the coach and the press of so many bodies, they
were soon standing on the street. She dragged in a deep
breath of cool air, thankful the rain had cooperated with her
desire and had stopped falling. She took in the scene before
her as she waited for her bags to be tossed down from the
roof of the coach. The courthouse was flanked on one side by
a sturdy looking stone jail and on the other by an English
Presbyterian meeting house. Nearby stood the pillory and
whipping post, along with the stocks, thankfully empty. The
muddy street sucked at the wheels of the various carriages
and coaches going about their business in town.

"There's our bags now." She herded the lad toward the
collection of satchels, bags, and trunks piled beside the
coach, away from the passing vehicles which would have
splashed them with mud. "Grab your things and we'll go on
to the print shop which isn't far. Then my brother can help
us get to his home and settle us into our rooms. Agreed?"

Jacob nodded as he reached to grab up her large traveling
bag and satchel to hand to her. "Can you manage both of
those, miss?"

"Yes, thank you for asking. I've packed only essentials.
Get your things and let's go."

She led the way down Calvert to Market and turned back
the way they'd come, but only for a block or two. The print
shop stood on the corner of Market and South. The three-
story brick building impressed her as a fine place to run the

several aspects of the business. A sturdy front door along with pairs of glass windows on each floor created a sense of permanence and importance. She noted that a Mr. Jacob Mohler had advertised his watch and clock-making shop on the first floor. William had told her she'd have to use the outside stairs to reach the upper floor where the press operated. Before long they'd climbed the steps and pushed open the door to the shop and let themselves inside.

Jacob surged into the large, airy room, making a beeline toward his friend. Willy worked at one of the two presses anchored in place by wooden beams stretching from the top of each press outward at an angle to the ceiling. She didn't recognize the type of the press on the left, but she knew from William's letters that the larger one on the right had come from Nicholas Hasselbach's widow. She swept the room with her gaze, taking in the shelf around the upper portion of the rear walls holding stacks of paper, the rods hanging from the ceiling for drying the inked papers, the barrels of ink lining one wall, and the desk by the front door serving as the intake counter. A young man she had not been introduced to continued inking the galley form in preparation to make the impression as Willy rushed to greet his friend. William stood up from the stool positioned by the desk to head toward her.

"You're here!" Willy gave Jacob a brief, welcoming embrace. "Mr. Goddard said you'd arrive today. How was the journey?"

"I'm never taking a stagecoach again. It was awful and I don't want to talk about it," Jacob said as he glanced behind Willy. "I'm impressed. Two presses. Is there enough work to sustain two?"

"Indeed." William smiled at Katy and then glanced at the two boys standing near to him. "I've taken on another apprentice to help with the heavy load. Ralph, come here."

As the scrawny child shuffled over to William, Katy

assessed his condition and attitude. Oh dear. Good thing she'd come. Brown hair fell messily about his shoulders. Pale brown eyes peered from an even paler face. He didn't meet her gaze, but flicked his eyes from one person to another. Why was he so uneasy? Or perhaps afraid? More to the point, what did William see in him to take him on as an apprentice to instruct in the printing trade? Time would tell how efficient he proved to be. And how long he'd suit. He halted beside William without managing to look directly at him.

"Ralph Jenkins, this is my sister Mary Katharine Goddard." William gestured toward Katy and waited for the boy to say something. When he didn't, William pursed his lips. "Where are your manners, lad?"

Katy suppressed an annoyed sigh. She'd have her work cut out for her with this one.

"How do you do?" Ralph said softly, flicking his gaze away yet again.

"Fine, thank you for asking." Katy smiled at him, trying to encourage his confidence. "It's nice to meet you, Mr. Jenkins."

"This lad is also an apprentice." William inclined his head toward Jacob as he introduced him. "I'd like you to meet Jacob Thompson."

The boys shook hands after some prodding by William. But at least Ralph acted more comfortable with the introductions of the other apprentice than he had with meeting her. Which probably meant the boy wasn't comfortable around girls.

"How old are you, Mr. Jenkins?" She lifted her brows a touch as she smiled at him, trying to make her expression easy and friendly.

"Thirteen." He swallowed hard and lowered his eyes to stare at the marble floor.

"Well, then I'd expect you're missing your family, aren't you?"

"No, miss."

Raising her brows in surprise, Katy blinked several times as she assimilated his claim. "I see."

What more could she say? Perhaps the boy had come from a family who had treated him harshly or ignored him. Her own childhood had been filled with love and caring by her family, but not every child had such parents. It was not in her nature to pry into the boy's past, but she'd take into account the possibility of the kind of home he'd grown up in.

William cleared his throat. "All right, you two back to work. I'm going to show these newcomers where they're staying and then I'll be back. Understood?"

Ralph and Willy nodded and turned to go back to the press they'd been working at together.

Then William turned his stern gaze to Jacob. "Once you've settled in at the house, I'll bring you back here to begin. There is quite an accumulation of jobs since the *Maryland Journal and Baltimore Advertiser* is the first newspaper for this town, and our press one of the few around."

"I'm pleased to hear it's been well received." She wanted to be busy and useful, after all. "I'll start helping to manage the register and finances beginning tomorrow, if that suits?"

"Yes, that's fine. But I will be relying upon you to manage all the business tasks as well."

"Are you going somewhere soon?" They hadn't even seen where they'd be living and he apparently planned to depart. The usual reason he handed the reins to her.

"I'll be busy setting up that new postal system for the colonies I wrote to you about. The interference by the Royal Post with delivering our newspapers and letters, often opening and reading them, can no longer be tolerated. We can not entrust our communication into British hands, nor pay the exorbitant taxes they demand." William shook his head as his frown deepened. "I've been in conversation with Ben Franklin and others about what we'll need to do, but it requires my presence to make it happen."

"So, you are leaving when?" She could only assume he was operating this press similar to the previous one. That at least would make the handoff easier. "I've not even seen your home, nor found one of my own."

"I know, and I'm sorry for that." William held up a fore-finger and then went to retrieve his suit coat from where he'd hung it on a peg on the wall. As he shrugged into it and buttoned it, he returned to give her a nod. "Come, I'll show you to the house and then we'll determine the next steps. Will that suffice?"

"Of course. Come, Jacob, let's get settled in." Then she'd have to think through how to go about establishing her own household and finding suitable servants in her new home-town. All while managing her brother's entire business. History repeated itself yet again. She followed the boys out the door and down the steps, both glad she'd kept her promise to her mother and worried about what the future held for her.

"All right, lads, let's keep on top of our chores and tasks." Katy opened the ledger to record several items she'd been carrying in her head. "Mr. Jenkins, please stoke the fire. It's very chilly in here what with the snowfall outside."

"Yes, miss." Ralph hopped off his stool and hurried to the hearth to add another log to the dwindling flames.

"I'll be happy to tackle page four, all the advertisements, if you'll permit me." Jacob peered at her, eager anticipation plain on his features.

"Very well, but if you need assistance do not refrain from asking. We do not have time to redo and repeat efforts."

"Thank you. I won't let you down." He fairly skipped back to his work table.

The lad's enthusiasm for the printing work pleased her. He learned quickly new methods or approaches to the various printing jobs they were hired to accomplish. Some long, some short, but each an important document to the person or entity who awaited its completion. The shop's clientele grew daily along with the growing city.

She'd only been in Baltimore two weeks, but already she'd made her mark on the press. On February 17, 1774, shortly after her brother had left, she'd announced in the *Journal* the reason for her brother's absence and their intentions for the future of the paper. She spent a fair amount of time choosing the proper verbiage, and ended up pleased with the result. The announcement began with, "An affair in a very high degree interesting to the common liberties of all AMERICA, as well as to the Printer of this Paper, having made it necessary for him to repair, for a few weeks, to an Eastern Colony, I esteem it my indispensable duty to acquaint the Public in general, and the Subscribers to The Maryland Journal and Baltimore Advertiser in particular, that it will, during his Absence, be regularly published and delivered every Thursday, and other Printing-work be executed with all possible Punctuality and Dispatch." Her dear mother would have been proud of her phrasing.

As she became familiar with the people who used the press to publish pamphlets and books, as well as those subscribing to the *Maryland Journal*, she had more and more conversations about how the Parliament and King Charles III were oppressing the colonists. Forcing them to pay taxes on things without having any say in the matter. "No taxation without representation" was a favorite refrain, in fact. So when Parliament passed the Boston Port Bill, otherwise known as the Intolerable Acts, in response to the infamous Boston Tea Party, emotions ran high.

The four punitive acts were in retaliation of colonial defiance. They singled out the city of Boston with the Boston Port Bill which closed the harbor until they paid for the tea tossed overboard the year before. The other act that angered the colonists the most was the Quartering Act which had expired in 1770 but was reissued to give colonial governors the right to use unoccupied buildings to house British troops. The other two acts were more administrative and didn't rise to the same level as those two, but taken together the people reacted badly. She could only imagine where the rising resistance might lead. Her overly active imagination kept her awake some nights.

Response to the many essays and articles related to the injustice of the Acts had been great. The citizens of Baltimore did not take kindly to the Parliament punishing them for standing up to what they felt was unfair. That response also increased the circulation of the paper, which gave them even more work to do. But the ledger was staying solvent as a result, so she wouldn't turn aside any of the incoming articles or other matter for the press.

She welcomed items from both sides of the American cause. Including the viewpoints of a local lawyer, Mr. George Chalmers. Word on the street said eleven years previous he'd come from his home in the county of Moray in England to try to resolve a dispute over some land for two uncles who had emigrated earlier. He apparently enjoyed his visit to Maryland so much he elected to begin practicing law in Baltimore, with some measure of success. But his contributions to the paper encouraged the colonists to remain loyal to the king and tried to persuade them to not continue with their ungentlemanly resistance to the governance by Parliament. His pieces were reasoned and well written even if she disagreed with his stance. Freedom of the press to carry all opinions mattered, especially in trying times such as they were living in. She would defend everyone's right to express their opinions. The British loyalist surely had some sharp conversations with the patriots of the town. How long would he feel comfortable remaining in the colonies?

In late March, she finally procured a charming home on Conewago Street. A two-story red brick house, enough windows to permit a pleasing amount of light inside, and a sturdy front door. Inside was a large, cheery kitchen, a sitting room overlooking the street, and four rooms suitable for bedchambers upstairs. A little garden had been started out back and a chicken coop with a couple of hens and a rooster as well. The property was among several cozy dwellings on the quiet street. The place soothed her nerves after a hectic day at the shop.

Next she needed to find a cook and a maid as well as someone to manage the garden and chickens. She must watch her expenses though, so fretted over how to stay within her budget. But first she had to keep up the pace at the shop to meet the demands of the busy press. She'd been very fortunate to find the home a mere handful of blocks from the shop so that she could come and go between the two places as needed.

The shop door opened and a young woman dressed simply but neatly strode inside. Her blonde hair was wrapped up into an elegantly intricate hairdo, one Katy could only appreciate but never duplicate. She carried a folded piece of paper as she stopped by the desk.

"Good morning. How may I help you?" Katy smiled at the woman in greeting.

"I'd like to place this advertisement in the paper, if I may?"

She unfolded the sheet and laid it on the desk in front of Katy. "Is this acceptable?"

"Let's see." Katy read the short notice announcing that Sharon Walker was accepting clients in need of seamstress or mending services. "You're a seamstress?"

"Yes. Will you accept my advertisement?" Sharon kept a steady regard on Katy, waiting for her response.

"Of course, Miss Walker." Katy calculated the cost and quoted the amount to her new customer.

Sharon hesitated, then placed a burlap sack on the counter. "I am hoping you'll except this ham in payment."

Hard cash proved illusive for many residents across the colonies, including herself. While accepting payments in kind, such as the aromatic ham tempting her, didn't pay her bills, it did keep food on her table at home. Over the years of running the printing house and accompanying other ventures in other locations, linen rags, fruits, meats, buttons, and sundry other items had been received. What she didn't use for her own use she added to the offerings of the dry goods part of the shop. The dry goods shop used more bartering and trading than currency. This ham would make a fine supper, though.

"Thank you. I'll put your advertisement in the next edition which comes out Thursday."

"That is vastly acceptable. I only wish..." Sharon pressed her lips together as if not wanting to say whatever she'd started to say.

"Is everything all right?" The other woman seemed suddenly a bit nervous. "You can tell me. I'll not reveal any of your secrets."

Sharon glanced at the apprentices busy at their various tasks, oblivious to the women's conversation. Then nodded. "Times are so difficult. I needed to find some way to make more money to afford what my household needs. But I haven't told my father that I'm doing so. I will tell him eventually, if indeed my advertisement garners income as I hope."

"You should be proud of yourself for taking the initiative to solve the problem facing your family." Katy smiled as she nodded once. "I'd do the same if I were in your shoes."

"Would you? You're obviously faring well here. I see the paper in many hands, at least."

"True, but it hasn't always been easy." More times than she'd care to share. "There is a need for reliable information that we are happy to accommodate in this fine town."

Sharon clutched her purse tightly. "I should go. Before my father realizes I'm gone." She drew in a quick breath and let it out as she winked at Katy. "But I'm glad to meet you."

"I'm Mary Katharine Goddard. I am pleased to meet you as well. I'm fairly new to town and still adjusting to all the changes."

"Oh, then let me show you around sometime. I've lived in this area for years and have watched the town grow. Perhaps we could take in a play down the street?"

"I would welcome that diversion. And I accept your offer to introduce me to the town." Memories of touring Philadelphia with Brenda surfaced but she pushed them away. The friendship she once hoped for never materialized between them. She didn't want that history to repeat again. "Becoming acquainted with what Baltimore offers will benefit my efforts with the newspaper content by becoming more aware of the happenings in and about the town and give me the opportunity to make new connections."

Sharon nodded once. "I will call on you in a couple of days and we'll go out for a little while to do just that."

"I am anticipating getting to know you, Miss Walker." Katy smiled at Sharon. "I do believe I've made my first friend in town."

CHAPTER 17

BALTIMORE, MARYLAND – 1774

rue to her word, Sharon came to the printing shop a few days later and cajoled her away from her work for a couple of hours. Not before Katy had delegated her tasks to the apprentices and journeyman printers. Willy had even ushered her out the door, encouraging her to take a little bit of time for herself.

Spring sunshine warmed her face as the two women strolled at the edge of the dirt street. Seagulls called to each other above, white and gray bodies against the vibrant blue sky. Coaches and carriages and wagons trundled past, pulled by muscular oxen or gleaming horses. The growing city thrived and prospered despite the political tensions everyone contended with.

"How long have you been in town, Mary Katharine?" Sharon asked.

"I arrived in early February, so about two months now." Her initial impression of the town as a friendly and progressive place remained her main reaction to her new home. "Everyone has been so kind to me. To us, really. I am happy to have made the move from Philadelphia."

"I've never visited that city. I hear it's large and beautiful."

"Yes, in its way. But my brother managed to make too many enemies so that we were forced to try anew somewhere else. Here, I feel welcomed by everyone."

Katy paused to let a mother and her two children start across the street in front of where she stood at the corner of Market and Gay. Across the street she admired the two-story market-house which faced Market street. The tavern yards which were in the neighborhood of the market teemed with great wagons and dozing horses. A very busy scene.

"The upper floor of the market-house is where the great hall is located." Sharon pointed to the second floor of the market building. "That's where town meetings and dances are held."

"I hope to attend either of those from time to time. The first for news and the second to have some merriment in my life." She hadn't been to a dance in ages. Not since her mother's merrymaking in Providence, in fact. High time she found ways to be more social so she could make some new friends.

They continued walking. "The peddlers will start packing up their traveling stores of merchandise ere long as it's nearly noon." Sharon glanced at Katy and then indicated the many sellers beginning to do as she suggested. "While market day is all day Wednesday and Saturday, they're only allowed to sell their wares until noon the rest of the week."

"I suppose they have a large variety of wares they bring, given the size of the wagons they've used." From her vantage point, Katy spotted tinware, crockery, clothing, and more. "That's the way it was in Philadelphia, at least."

"Yes, indeed. I enjoy riffling through the hats and gloves and other clothing they bring out for sale." She started walking down the street away from the center of town, passing a popular tavern, and a silversmith's shop. As they neared the river, Katy marveled at the beautiful stone bridge stretching away from her. "We won't cross over the river, I merely desired to show you Philpot's bridge. It's the only stone bridge in town. The other two are of wood."

"Why is it called Philpot's Bridge?"

"Mr. Brian Philpot Jr. owns the house on the northeast corner, that one over there."

"And who might this personage be?" Given the elegant façade of the home, he must be someone of means and importance.

"Someone you should be aware of. He's the Commissioner of Baltimore Towne."

"Thank you for informing me of his importance in town. I am quite struck by the bridge's beauty, to be honest." She perused the apparent craftsmanship of the structure, pleased with the resulting appearance. "I haven't seen many stone structures in town." She chuckled to herself. Really, only the jail.

"Let's head back toward your shop." Sharon sauntered along the street, pointing out who lived where and which businesses she frequented. "One thing I overlooked pointing out is where the theater is located."

The theater. She'd enjoyed going to the theater ever since she'd been a girl. Now at thirty-five she had much more appreciation for the stories told on stage.

"You mentioned there is one but I sadly haven't been yet." Work and settling her household, finding the appropriate help to keep it running, all had taken up her attention. Difficult decisions still lingered as to how she could afford the help she needed. She could not keep a household running by herself when she was at the shop all day. But she had limited funds to pay for the quality of person she wanted. "I do hope we can go see a play together one day."

As they neared Frederick Street, Sharon indicated an imposing warehouse on the corner. "The theater company often sets up within the warehouse to do performances. It's great fun."

"Surely they don't take up all of that space for their play-acting." She marveled at the sheer size of the building. Passersby hurried past her, oblivious to the awe she felt at the sight. "One day we should go."

"If time permits, my new friend, I would enjoy nothing more than sharing that experience with you." Sharon increased her pace as they went on toward the shop at Market and South. "Let's see, what else about the place would be of interest to you? We have a fire company, with two fire engines to respond to any fires. Our prosperity has drawn a bevy of doctors and lawyers, all of which seem to be faring quite well."

"Yes, I've met Mr. Chalmers. He has submitted several opinions for publication in the paper."

"I've read them, but I shall refrain from commenting upon his...opinion." She shook her head, lips firm. "By the way, I like the changes you've made to the paper's format. It's grown both in size and in quality of content. I hope you continue in your role as editor for some time."

"I appreciate your kind words. I'm editing the content but my brother is the real publisher of the paper." And he still claimed the credit for the publication in the colophon, despite his absence. An expected aggravation. "I'm afraid I must return to the paper now and finish some tasks before I can go home for the day."

"As you say, he may be the publisher but you're picking and choosing the content, so you're the one really in charge." Sharon grinned as they walked on.

"Indeed." Perhaps one day Katy would have the opportunity to take credit for her efforts, but she wouldn't be wagering on such an unlikely event.

~

May ushered in gentle breezes and flowers everywhere. The walk to work from her comfortable abode was an everyday joy as a result. She passed vibrant azalea bushes and a multitude of white and pink dogwood trees. She pushed through the door to the printing shop and went to the wall hooks at the back to hang her lightweight shawl, then headed to her desk.

Ralph crossed the room, a letter in his hand. "This came for you a little while ago."

"Thank you." She accepted the missive from him and laid it on her desk while she secured her purse in its spot under the desk. Her brother's penmanship announced the sender. Settling on her seat, she opened the missive and read the short note.

"Well, that's interesting." Katy chuckled as she slipped William's letter into the single desk drawer. Sharon must be a soothsayer.

"What's Mr. Goddard have to say?" Jacob piped up from where he was refilling the ink pan for the inking ball.

Katy glanced at the young man. "Careful you don't spill that. It would be quite a mess."

He replaced the ink-stained barrel beside the others along the wall. "I'm careful, I promise. I don't want you to make me clean it up." He grinned at her for a moment. "So?"

"My brother will be away longer than he anticipated and so has made me sole editor of the *Journal*." His confidence in her abilities to manage the paper, the press, the book bindery, and the dry goods parts of the enterprise made her heart sing. She really hadn't ever expected to be editor in any official capacity. In order to not upset the men in town, she'd use her initials instead of her full name, downplay the fact that the paper's editor was a woman. "So, as of the May tenth edition, I'm updating the colophon to read that the paper is published by M.K. Goddard."

A thrill of pride and accomplishment swept through her. Her friend's prediction had actually come to pass. She now could officially claim her role as editor of the paper.

Willy tilted his head as he looked at her, his mouth falling open. "Congratulations, miss. That's quite the step up."

Ralph lifted a sheet of paper out of the press and draped it over a drying rod. Then he approached Katy and Willy. "You're the official editor now? That's surprising...but well deserved."

She looked sharply at him, hearing the surprise and hesitation in his voice. The kind of reaction she'd expect from others, just not the apprentices. "I've been running this press even more efficiently than the last one."

She hated the defensive edge to her tone but really, who was Ralph to question her?

"I didn't mean to offend, miss. I apologize. I just never thought William would do such a wonderful thing. You're right, you have been running things the best yet. I'm happy to be learning my trade with your example."

"Hello!" Sharon breezed into the room, interrupting the tense conversation. "Miss Goddard, are you ready?"

"Hello. Give me one minute and then I'll be ready." Katy smiled at her friend and then turned to finish the conversation with Ralph. "Then keep your opinions to yourself unless asked. Are we in agreement?"

Ralph looked down at his feet and nodded. "Yes, miss."

"Very well. Get back to work." Katy let her gaze encompass the four men. "I expect you all to carry on while I step out for a little while. Willy is in charge and I expect a full report upon my return."

Willy straightened his spine in response to the new responsibility. "Yes, miss."

After retrieving her shawl and purse, Katy ushered Sharon out the door. They chatted about the weather and other mundane things as they strode together down the street to George McCandless' tavern. Katy suppressed a huff seeing the image of George III on the sign hanging above the door.

Sharon shook her head as they neared the entrance. "I fear Mr. McCandless may need a new sign ere long."

"He very well might, given the growing dissent in town." Katy pushed the door open and they went into the dim interior.

They'd planned to have the midday meal together and make a scheme for when they'd finally be able to see the hottest play in town, *Macbeth* by William Shakespeare. Over the past couple of months, Sharon had made good on her promise to introduce the town to Katy. Now she was happy to benefit from an expanded knowledge of everything the city had to offer. Including which tavern had the best seafood dishes, like lobster bisque, one of her favorite soups. But also she'd discovered scotched and colloped beef, small, tender bites of meat with delicious savory gravy. They chose a cloth-covered table by the front windows and quickly settled on the wooden chairs.

"So, tell me what that young man was apologizing for?" Sharon asked as the serving girl brought two tankards of ginger beer to put on the table.

"It's not worth mentioning. Really. Just a misunderstanding." Katy gripped the handle of the mug and lifted the drink to sip.

"Did something happen? Come now, don't keep secrets from your dearest friend." Sharon chuckled as she waited for a response.

"In fact something did. As you once thought, my brother has given me sole authority as editor of the *Maryland Journal,* effective immediately." She couldn't suppress the elation simmering inside. "So I'll be able to change the colophon to indicate that the paper was published by M.K. Goddard."

Katy didn't want to brag. That would be unseemly. But she did feel a swell of confirmation and achievement at the recognition indicated by her brother's actions. He trusted her competence to carry on the varied aspects of the printing business.

Sharon clapped her hands together. "Good for you! I'm delighted to hear such wonderful news."

"It is wonderful." Her smile widened. "To be in control of the entire venture."

"What will you do to make it your own?"

"After I put my name on it, then I'll be able to select even more articles from various other papers to reprint in the *Journal*. Ones that are more varied and interesting than what William had dictated. Plus I want to expand the book binding part, perhaps even see about creating a paper mill." Since there wasn't a convenient paper mill near town, starting one would ensure ready access to paper for all the press's efforts.

"An understandable change to make to the paper. You'll likely increase your readership as a result."

"Maybe. Since Enoch Story started a print shop nearby on Gay, I've noticed a slight decrease in new customers and subscribers." She bit her lower lip as the anxiety from the competition swept through her midriff. "He doesn't have the same capabilities and experience, from what I understand."

Sharon sipped her beverage and then dabbed a cotton napkin to her lips. "There will be plenty to discuss in both papers given the reaction to the Intolerable Acts. My father is all up in arms over what he calls the oppression by Parliament. He's meeting now with some of his friends to discuss what can be done to fix things in our favor."

Katy paused in replying while the server arrived with a large tray containing two bowls of fragrant lobster bisque and a plate of hot rolls which she placed on the table. After the girl walked away, Katy nodded. "I've received word of an effort for the men in town to start committees of correspondence in order to share information between the towns and cities across the colonies."

"Committees of correspondence? What good will talking to each other do?" Sharon lifted her spoon to stir the steaming soup in front of her.

"That effort to write letters to share between the committees will enable the leaders to fight back against the suppression the king is forcing upon us." Katy studied her friend's confused countenance. "The committees will likely rely upon the new postal service that William is putting together. It's purpose is to enable safe communication between the colonies without the king's men interfering or confiscating the mail."

"Do you think..." Sharon's eyes widened as her mouth formed an O. "Oh dear." She leaned closer to Katy and whispered, "The men are planning to resist which could lead to heated tempers and then to violence."

"We can only hope that it doesn't come to violence, but I do believe they will be forming some form of resistance to the taxation without representation. It's just a matter of what it will look like when it happens."

Sharon sucked in a long breath and let it out slowly. "I am glad to have you as a friend to talk to during these uncertain times, Katy."

Katy reached out to clasp her friend's hand with her own. "I can't agree more. Let's eat and then talk about more pleasant things like, when is the play happening?"

Sharon chuckled and resumed eating her soup. Pausing between bites, she said, "Sadly, they had to postpone the opening due to lack of costumes. But apparently they will be ready in a few days."

Katy selected a warm roll from the basket on the table and broke off a piece. "I adore that play. Especially the witches and their spells. Makes my imagination fly each time I read about them and their prophecies."

"It's rather scary, though, don't you think?" Sharon shivered dramatically, a smile emerging on her lips. "All that talk of battles, blood, and magic, I mean."

Katy merely chuckled in response, the darker aspects of the play's scenes seeming to foreshadow future possibilities in the colonies. She hoped she was wrong and wouldn't voice her concerns to avoid seeming to sound an alarm. But why else would there be a need for a new postal system and men to write letters back and forth if not to plot a rebellion?

CHAPTER 18

BALTIMORE, MARYLAND – 1774

July swept into Baltimore along with high humidity and temperatures. Katy employed her silk fan as she strode briskly down the street toward the print shop. She nodded and smiled greetings to other shop owners and people going about their business. She didn't have time to stop and chat with them though. Too many jobs waited for her at her own shop.

Including the notice William asked her to include in the *Journal* about his new postal system. He had already started twenty-eight post offices in several colonies. Word of his efforts had actually reached London by March, as she'd seen an extract of a letter published in the *Virginia Gazette* in June. The letter had come from the committee of correspondence in Providence. In part the letter stated, "By an Express from Philadelphia, and New York, last Night, we are informed that a Resolution has been come to, at New York, to take the Post Office out of the Hands of Government, and to appoint Regulations themselves; and I think it is probable they will soon take the Custom-house into their own Possession, and ship home the Commissioners." So the secretive effort had

216

been shared publicly. How exactly might the British Parliament react to such news? That question worried her more than she cared to share with even her friend Sharon.

She pushed into the shop and hurried to the desk to place her satchel beside it and her purse in its designated spot. Turning, she quickly assessed what the lads were working on. Ralph worked at the larger press used for printing broadsides and larger sheets of paper which would be folded and stitched into books and pamphlets. Willy operated the smaller press, working on some playbills to be distributed that day. Jacob was in the process of placing reams of paper on the shelf around the upper part of the back wall. He was struggling with the heavy load, though.

"Willy, can you please help Jacob with the paper?" She pointed to where the lad was on the ladder, a pack of paper tucked under one arm. "I don't want to see him get hurt."

Willy nodded and crossed the room to lend a hand to the young boy. Soon, he had Jacob on the floor and handing up to Willy the individual packets of paper to stack on the shelf. The task was accomplished much quicker and more safely, and Katy smiled her thanks to them both.

Then she turned her attention to the notice William left for her to include in the July 2 *Journal.* Scanning the neatly written cursive, she prepared mentally the layout and types she'd use to compose the piece per his instructions. His announcement revealed how busy he'd been on his travels to the New England colonies.

The Printer of this Paper, with great Pleasure, acquaints the Public, that his Proposal for establishing an AMERICAN POST-OFFICE, on constitutional Principles, hath been warmly and generously patronized by the Friends of Freedom in all the great commercial Towns in the Eastern Colonies, where ample Funds are already secured, Post-

Masters and Riders engaged, and, indeed, every necessary Arrangement made for the Reception of the Southern Mails, which, it is expected, will soon be extended thither—as therefore the final success of the Undertaking now depends on the Public-spirit of the Inhabitants of Maryland and Virginia, it is not doubted…but they will cheerfully join….

He had returned to Baltimore and continued to work on establishing post offices around the Maryland colony and setting things up to extend into Virginia as well. She expected him to walk into the shop at any minute.

She carried the page with her to the composing table and settled onto the stool to begin work. Within a relatively short period of time, she had the galley form completed for the front page of the *Journal*. In addition to the lengthy opening, the content included a subscription form that had first appeared in Boston on April thirtieth. He wanted to make it available to any town or city that might want to be on the postal system route.

The door opened and her brother marched inside, all purpose and intent as he hurried to peer over her shoulder. "How goes things, Katy?"

He'd matured over the years into a handsome man of four and thirty years. He'd also become more fastidious about his appearance and manners. Likely influenced by Benjamin Franklin's demeanor and attitude. He'd taken to wearing more cosmopolitan attire, silk stockings and heeled black shoes. Though she doubted William would ever lose his volatile temper when he felt denigrated. Maybe in time his short temper would moderate.

"I've just finished putting this galley together, ready to print for distribution tomorrow as requested. What do you think of the layout? Is that what you envisioned?"

He studied the galley with an expert eye and then nodded.

"You always manage to understand exactly what I intended. I am grateful to you for that."

"What do you anticipate happening next with your post office?"

"Once the Williamsburg office is established and the rider appointed, we'll be ready to take the plan to the Continental Congress that will be held for the first time in Philadelphia this September." His eyes twinkled with pride. "Then the Congress can take control of the system."

"What role will you play in this endeavor? I mean, once it's all set up and running."

"I expect the Congress will make me the Postmaster General since I've put so much time and effort as well as personal expense into it." He smiled with confidence. "It's only right."

"Indeed." Although his management skills did not come close to meeting his visionary talents. Otherwise he wouldn't lean on her skills so very much. "I'm sure they will choose the right person for the job."

"Would you like more coffee?" Katy finished pouring the amber liquid into her porcelain cup and paused with the pot suspended in midair.

She'd invited her friend over for coffee on a sunny Sunday afternoon. Since it was a fine day, she'd elected to entertain her in the garden beneath a maple tree. The last blossoms clung to the rose bushes scattered around the vegetable garden waiting for the spring planting. A task she hoped to be able to delegate to a gardener. For now, the gentle breeze ensured they'd remain comfortable despite the early autumn heat.

"No, thank you." Sharon sat back in her chair to peer at

Katy. "You have only a maid serving as lady's maid, to cook and clean and sew as well?"

"And I have to tend the garden and chickens before and after I go to the print shop." Katy shook her head slowly as she set the pot on the tray on the table between them. "There is always so much to be done. Like this unkempt garden. I think I should expand my servants, but I don't know how to afford to pay them."

"What do you mean? Would you invest in indentured servants or hire local women?"

"I hadn't considered indentured servants, but that's a possibility. I believe there is an auction at the London Coffee-House soon where they will be taking bids on those and slaves as well." Seeing the concern on Sharon's face, she hesitated. Really, if she could she'd like to have her household managed more efficiently by having a cook, scullery maid, housemaid, gardener, and maybe even a butler to oversee all of them. Her day at the print shop was long indeed. But reality settled on her shoulders. "What do you suggest?"

Sharon grimaced briefly and shrugged. "One option is to buy a slave or two to help you. You wouldn't have an ongoing salary to pay out, which will save you money."

Katy could only stare at her friend, blinking slowly as she contemplated what she'd suggested. She'd never considered buying a slave, but it was an option. Sharon was right about the economics of doing so. But she'd been raised in a family that paid their local people to help around the property and homes. In Maryland, she'd come to know more about slavery but she really didn't know how it all worked. Nor did she know if she'd be comfortable with the thought of owning a person.

"I will have to think on that option. I don't need to do anything immediately." She sipped from her cup and swallowed. "While William is away to Philadelphia for that

Continental Congress to pitch his postal system, I have my hands full though."

"Do you think he'll manage to convince the Congress to take on his new system?" Sharon asked.

"I believe so. I mean, why wouldn't they want to put such a system into place, especially when it's already established and operating?" Hopefully, her brother would find success because if not she'd have to deal with his anger and upset. Always a difficult time. She waved a hand in the air, dismissing the negative thoughts entirely. "I'm sure it will all be fine."

"I'm sure you hope so given his proclivities." Sharon winked at her as she rose from her seat. "I will see you later, my friend. I have to pick up a gown from the mantuamaker."

A month passed and still William had not returned to town. She was relieved he remained up in Philadelphia when she learned that patriots in nearby Annapolis on the nineteenth of October had seized and burned the brigantine *Peggy Stewart* when its owner had actually paid the import tax on the tea it carried. Granted, in order to unload the merchandise and the fifty-three indentured servants from what was characterized as a leaky ship, Anthony Stewart, representing Thomas Charles Williams & Company, had to pay the hated, banned taxes. But to have smuggled, under blankets, over two thousand pounds of tea into harbor? What were they thinking? With everyone so up in arms about the tea tax, surely he understood the kind of response he'd receive when word got out. If her brother had been near, she could only imagine how quickly as a member of the Sons of Liberty he'd have been embroiled in the dangerous affair. The Annapolis Tea Party succeeded in sending a very clear message to other loyalists like Anthony Stewart and George Chalmers, though.

She received an angry note from William in November,

lambasting his former partner Galloway for stonewalling his address with the Continental Congress. Apparently, he'd pulled some strings to ensure that although the congress heard William's presentation they tabled it without discussion. All that time and effort for naught. But he hadn't given up. No, he had determined he'd have to work hard to strengthen and expand his postal system to make it more attractive to the congressional representatives.

Wonderful. She mentally shook her head. That meant she'd be running the business on her own for the foreseeable future. She would definitely have to inquire as to options for hiring or purchasing servants to help her manage the house since she'd be spending all of her time at the shop. History repeating itself once more.

CHAPTER 19

BALTIMORE, MARYLAND – 1775

Katy flipped through the daily ledger, pleased with the accounts and the still growing number of subscribers. Despite the competition just down the street in the form of the *Maryland Gazette, or Baltimore Advertiser* being issued under the name of John Dunlap of Philadelphia, but actually by James Hayes in Baltimore itself. The nerve of him to try to steal her customers, using a title very similar to the *Journal*'s. He couldn't actually compete with her, though, since she had established and maintained a network of information sources that flowed into her shop weekly.

Like the full text of the fiery speech Patrick Henry gave to the Second Virginia Revolutionary Convention meeting at Saint John's Church in Richmond, Virginia on the twenty-third of March. She imagined the astonished, perhaps eager reactions of the gentlemen assembled. She happily shared the lengthy speech in the *Journal*, knowing how it would spur others to action in defense of the Americans fight for freedom from oppression. The final paragraph really

inspired her even though she had to conjure the man's into-
nations.

> It is in vain, sir, to extenuate the matter. Gentlemen may cry,
> Peace, Peace—but there is no peace. The war is actually
> begun! The next gale that sweeps from the north will bring
> to our ears the clash of resounding arms! Our brethren are
> already in the field! Why stand we here idle? What is it that
> gentlemen wish? What would they have? Is life so dear, or
> peace so sweet, as to be purchased at the price of chains and
> slavery? Forbid it, Almighty God! I know not what course
> others may take; but as for me, give me liberty or give me
> death!

How could the people who agreed with him not stir themselves to rise to the current state of affairs and affront? Yet another sign of the escalation of the animosity existing between Britain and the colonies. The cry of peace and liberty from tyranny echoed in her mind. No one should be oppressed by their government. No tyrant could be tolerated in a free society.

Although her brother had once again been sent to debtors prison the month before. If he'd pay his creditors instead of arguing with them over the expenses, he wouldn't be in such a fix so frequently. Something she couldn't convince him to give a try.

The shop door opened and a young man in a white work shirt and gray breeches hurried inside, his dusty boots thudding across the floor. Roger Cook pulled his hat from his head as he stopped in front of her. "Miss Goddard, this is for you." He handed her several letters and she reached into her pocket to give him a few coins for bringing the news.

"I wasn't expecting you today, Mr. Cook. What is this?"

She scanned the precise writing on the largest letter, addressed to her at the shop. "Where is it from?"

"It's from the New Haven correspondence committee, and is the account of what all happened between the colonists and the British soldiers in Lexington and Concord last week." Roger shook his head. "The fighting and mayhem were awful, by all accounts."

"Fighting? This is news." A chill pierced her heart. She glanced at the other letters, one from her brother, but set them aside and opened the large one carefully and read the first few lines of the contents. The committees of correspondence had grown into a network that spread important news as fast as possible. "Thank you for bringing this to me so quickly."

Roger replaced his hat and leveled sober eyes at her. "The battle for our rights has begun with those shots. That's what everyone is saying."

"Yes, I can see that. Go on to the tavern and get yourself something to eat and drink before you head out again. Give your pony a rest." She lifted her chin, encouraging him on his way.

"I will. See you next week." Roger pivoted and marched back out the open door into the cool April air.

She paused to read the contents of the communication. Apparently, General Thomas Gage, the newly appointed royal governor of Massachusetts, had ordered his troops to confiscate the colony's military stores in Concord. But his seven hundred men were met on Lexington Green by seventy-seven men. Thanks to the efforts of men like Paul Revere who had ridden through the night to forewarn the minutemen and others of the attack on their munitions, they were able to stand up to the British. After an exchange of gunfire left eight colonists dead and ten wounded, the resistance fell away and the British marched on to Concord. But when they arrived they discovered not only that the military supplies had been hidden or destroyed, but also hundreds of American men stood in defiance. The British were forced to leave, and were harassed all the way back to Boston by Americans shooting at them from behind houses, barns, trees, and stone walls. In all, the estimated casualties were British two hundred seventy-three and American ninety-five. The Americans had defeated the British attack. She drew in a long breath and let it out slowly. This was big news. Historic, in fact.

She quickly penned an announcement for the *Journal*'s front page:

Baltimore: April 26. We have just received the following important intelligence, viz. Watertown, (Massachusetts-Bay) April 19. Wednesday morning, 10 o'clock. To all Friends of American Liberty. Be it known that this morning, before Break of Day, a Brigade, consisting of about 1000 or 1200 men, landed at Phip's Farm, at Cambridge, and marched to Lexington, where they found a Company of our Colony Militia in Arms, upon whom they fired, without any Provocation, and killed 6 men, and wounded 4 others…

Katy finished detailing the events as related to her and then hurried over to Willy and handed him the page. "Let's get this into today's *Journal*. I'll write a note for it in a minute. Got it?"

"Aye, miss." Willy laid the page on his work table and started gathering what he'd need to compose the front page of the newspaper.

Katy went to her desk and pulled out a fresh sheet of paper and her quill pen. Dipping the tip into the inkwell, she carefully penned a note as to how they'd received the news so quickly. She wrote, "The above is a true Copy, as received by Express from New-Haven, &c, attested by the Committee of Correspondence from Town to Town." Below that, she penned her heartfelt opinion as to the importance of the account: "The ever memorable 19th of April gave a conclusive answer to the questions of American freedom. What think ye of Congress now? That day evidenced that Americans would rather die than live slaves!" She sanded the paper and then she carried it over to give to Willy.

As she strode across the room, the meaning and ramifications of this critical moment weight heavy on her mind.

"This is obviously important information to share with the public, Willy. The people need to know what happened from our own people before the British version conscripts the truth." She crossed her arms as the reality of the inherent danger now facing the colonists settled in her mind. "Let's hurry to prepare the paper and distribute it."

"Ralph is about done with the advertisements page, and Jacob is nearly finished with the local news page." Willy lifted his composing stick, holding it in his left hand as he deftly selected type. "I'll work as quick as I can to get this done."

"Oh, and be sure to include the notice of the Committee of Correspondence meeting on the thirty-first of May. Go on now. I'll leave you to your important tasks. Thank you." She nodded as she turned away and headed back to her desk at the front of the shop.

Pride swept through her as she figured out the short time which had elapsed between the battles on the nineteenth of April and the *Journal*'s reporting of them in the edition on the twenty-sixth. One week. She smiled to herself. Mr. Hayes couldn't match the speed with which her sources supplied her with information. Perhaps she didn't need to fear his competition after all.

Her gaze landed on the three other letters the express rider brought to her. She opened the one from William, curious as to how his efforts to expand the postal system were going. Unfolding the sheets of paper, she slowly read his hurried handwriting. Hmm. A slow smile lifted the corners of her mouth. Since he'd been released from debtors prison the end of March and buckled down to work more on his postal system, he didn't want to be tied to any one place. So, he wouldn't be returning to Baltimore anytime soon. Perfect.

Sharon sauntered through the door, left open to let the cool breeze flow unimpeded within the busy shop. "Katy, dear, how do you fare on this lovely spring day?"

"It is a fine day, isn't it?" Katy laid the letter on the desk and rose to cross the floor to her friend. "What brings you here today?"

Sharon chuckled, lifting her brows and widening her eyes in mock surprise. "Can't a lady want to visit her friend without such interrogation?"

Katy laughed at the jest. "Apparently not. But I will share some alarming but not shocking news with you." She went on to tell her about the fighting in Massachusetts. "This is the true beginning of our fight against tyranny."

"Fighting has begun." Sharon pressed a hand on the desktop to steady herself. "I fear what this will all lead to."

"We must do everything we can to support the cause, my dear friend." Katy pointed to the notice she'd received. "Including spreading the news as accurately and swiftly as possible."

Sharon nodded as she straightened. "You're right, I know. I don't know yet how I can help, but I'll find a way."

"I'm pleased to be able to spread the news to my readers so quickly. Only a week after the event happened. I wonder if that's some kind of record."

"Seems like it must be. Only a week? That's setting quite a precedent."

"It is, isn't it? And I have more news." Katy glanced around the busy shop, ensuring the lads were keeping their attention on their work and not on her conversation. Then she grinned at Sharon. "I've updated the colophon again to be more explicit as to where and by whom the paper is published."

She envisioned the new colophon. It read, "Baltimore: Published by M.K. Goddard, at the Printing-Office in Market-Street, next Door above Dr. John Stevenson's." The good doctor wouldn't mind the additional advertisement she would be giving him, either. He was a good man and had helped her more than once when she had a medical need.

"You're having quite a grand day, my friend." Sharon smiled at her, and then sobered. "I wish I was as well."

The shift from lighthearted fun to somber countenance stilled the joy in Katy's heart. "Is something amiss?"

Taking in a deep breath, Sharon nodded as she let it back out. "I've come to ask if I may stay with you for some little time." She laid a hand on Katy's forearm. "Only until I can make other accommodations, that is."

"Why are you in need of a room? What has happened?" Katy placed her other hand on top of Sharon's and squeezed gently.

"Father grew very displeased about my little sewing business. We had quite a row over it. I no longer will abide by his rules. So I have to find another place for me and my maid but that will take some time."

Katy didn't need to think more about her dear friend's request. "Of course you may stay with me. For as long as necessary or even desired. I have plenty of room for you."

"I cannot thank you enough for your kind heart and generosity." Sharon slid her hand free and clasped her hands together. "When shall I have my few belongings transferred to your home?"

"How soon do you need to move?"

"I haven't told Father of my plan, so it depends on how quickly I can find a new place."

"Then let's say after the shop closes tomorrow and I'll have the lads pitch in to help carry everything to my house." Katy glanced at the lads in question, heads down and busy at their tasks. "That will give them something different to look forward to."

"I'll reward them with a good meal at the tavern." Sharon looked at the three young men and nodded. "I appreciate your help and theirs."

Katy gave Sharon a quick hug and smiled at her. "We have to look out for one another, now don't we? It will be fun having you around."

The next evening found the three boys helping load a wagon in front of a three-story brick manor house on Calvert. Katy waited with the driver of the wagon while Ralph, Jacob, and Willy went in and out of the house to retrieve trunks and bags of Sharon's and her maid Yvonne's belongings. She couldn't help but smile at what her friend called a "few possessions." Good thing Katy's house had ample rooms.

"That's everything." Sharon strode up to the side of the wagon where Katy stood, essentially supervising the moving team.

"Are you sure?" Katy winked at Sharon. "There's still more room in the wagon, after all."

Sharon shrugged lightly. "I'm sure. It looks like a spring shower may be about to get us all wet so we should move along."

The boys jumped into the bed of the wagon for the trip to Katy's house while the three women hurried down the street. Katy had already told the lads where to put every-thing once they arrived at her home. Her newly acquitted acquired servants would also help with ensuring the new arrivals in the household settled in easily. She'd been fortu-nate to find good help she could trust. But with the dark-ening sky, she hoped they all made it inside before the storm hit.

"Hurry now before we get soaked." Katy picked up her pace and the other two matched her long strides.

They turned the corner onto her street and she could see the wagon parked in front of her house halfway down the lane. A rumble of thunder urged her on and they soon scur-ried up the steps and into the house just as the heavens opened up.

"Whew! That was close." Katy placed her purse beside the vase of flowers on the side table in the front hall. She saw her new housekeeper Phyllis marching toward her, her dark skin glistening in the light from the oil lamps on the wall. "Every-thing in place?"

"Almost. I believe there's one last trunk to bring in." Phyllis indicated a towel draped over her arm. "I'll dry it off as they bring it in."

"Good. Thank you." Katy nodded to the woman, a slight smile on her lips. "I'd like you to meet my friend, Sharon Walker, and her maid Yvonne. Please help them feel at home for as long as they care to be with us."

Sharon glanced at Katy and then back to Phyllis. "Nice to meet you finally, Phyllis. Katy had good fortune, I under-stand, in finding sufficient help to keep her household running."

Phyllis merely nodded once and continued down the hall to the front door. The door opened as she neared the entrance, admitting Willy and Jacob with a medium-size pine trunk in their hands. Phyllis toweled the rainwater off of the top and then the lads hoisted the trunk to take upstairs to the designated bedchamber.

"Now that all of that is inside, we can have some supper. Penny should be ready for us to eat her fine cooking." Katy adored the woman's delicious and nutritious fare. She'd been grateful to have found such a talented cook. "I'll go check on whether it's ready while you go up and see your room. Phyllis, will you show these ladies to their room, please?"

"Yes, miss." Phyllis waited until Sharon and Yvonne joined her at the base of the stairs and then started climbing to the upper floor.

Katy strode down the hall to the kitchen and swept inside to greet her cook. The woman might be small in stature, barely reaching Katy's shoulder, but her talents in the kitchen proved phenomenal. Her green work dress was plain but attractive, the long skirts brushing the tops of her brown house shoes. Her dark curly hair was covered with a colorful kerchief as she stirred something tantalizing in a cauldron over the fire in the fireplace. Penny turned to see who had invaded her domain, her mahogany complexion glowing from the warmth of the cookfire. Joshua, her handyman and gardener, rested on a bench beside the long table with its bowls containing various fruits and vegetables destined for one delicacy or another. A pungent aroma of baking bread and spices filled the air and made Katy's mouth water.

"Penny, how fares our delectable evening supper?" She grinned at the woman, knowing Penny liked to be flattered about her culinary skills. "We've all worked up quite an enormous appetite."

Penny replaced the lid on the cauldron and faced Katy. "Nearly ready. If you'll gather at the table in the dining room, I'll serve it up in a few minutes."

"Perfect. I'll let the others know." Katy glanced at Joshua and smiled. His work around her house and garden made everything operate smoothly and the garden to grow bountifully. "Thank you, Joshua, for all of your fine labors on our behalf. The house and garden thank you as well."

The black man's full lips stretched into a pleased grin. "I have heard as much from the asparagus just the other day. But thank you for the kindness."

She chuckled as she spun about and left the kitchen to round up the women for supper. She knew by now the lads had likely departed for William's home where they lived. Sharon's offer of supper at the tavern had been politely declined, which was probably a blessing to Sharon's purse. Good thing William had arranged to keep the boys housed despite his long absences. At least he had the sense to provide for their sustenance and shelter even if he wasn't providing their instruction and guidance. Those tasks fell to her to fulfill.

"There you are," Sharon said as she took the last step to the entryway. "We're all sorted out and ready to eat. But tell me, I don't think you ever said why you chose to buy slaves instead of hiring help like you first considered."

Yvonne soon stood beside Sharon, her strawberry blonde hair brushing her shoulders in loose waves. The young woman, about twenty years old, had come from Ireland as an indentured servant. Her green eyes and freckled nose bespoke of her nationality without her having to declare it. Sharon had thought to help the young woman start a new life in the colonies by paying her way across the ocean in exchange for seven years labor. Katy had considered following her example but decided on another path.

"Well, in the long run, it saves me money. But more than that, I want to give these poor souls a safe and decent place to live." Katy glanced about to make sure none of her slaves were within earshot. She didn't want to raise their hopes in case something happened to prevent her goal. She met

Sharon's curious gaze. "Then one day I intend to set them free, once I know a way to make that happen."

"Free them? Is that even possible?" Sharon frowned at her. "I'm sure they'd be ever so grateful, but wouldn't their lives be even more difficult without someone to look out for them?"

"I believe it's possible but difficult. I'll seek guidance and answers before I make any attempts. Mr. Chalmers may have some thoughts on the matter." Assuming his loyalist views didn't force him to flee the town. She studied her friend's reaction. "But one day they will be free. That's my vow to myself."

"A vow I think you should keep mum about until you have determined a viable path to manumission." Sharon shook her head as she fell in beside Katy to walk down the hall to the dining room. "You might find yourself dealing with some unruly servants otherwise."

"A fine admonition and one that I'll adhere to. Now, let us enjoy our evening meal." But one day, she'd find a way to set them all free.

CHAPTER 20

BALTIMORE, MARYLAND – 1775

he last day of May arrived and Katy hadn't spent much time outside enjoying the gentle spring weather. Instead, she'd worked from dawn to dusk in order to ensure the print shop met its obligations to the businessmen and the local government leaders. She valued their high opinion not just of her management of the several businesses she oversaw, but also the quality of the resulting publications.

She also worked hard to keep the public informed of the skirmishes and clashes between the patriots and the British forces. Like the May tenth capture of Fort Ticonderoga. Two leaders, Benedict Arnold with his fifty Massachusetts and Connecticut men, and Ethan Allen of the Green Mountain Boys, stealthily marched to the fort on Lake Champlain in upstate New York. They easily subdued the single man on sentry duty and then captured the fifty sleeping British soldiers inside. They took possession of dozens of cannons and all of the fort's other weapons without a shot being fired. Most considered their success to be the first real victory in the fight for independence.

"Are you finished with the front page, miss?" Ralph hovered at her elbow.

Shaken from her revery, she flashed a smile at him. She selected the final bit of type and placed it in the composing stick before sliding the last line onto the galley form. "Now you may take it to print."

Without further comment, Ralph snatched up the form and hurried over to the larger press to begin printing the next day's edition.

Jacob prepared the horsehair-stuffed sheepskin balls to ink the type while Ralph retrieved a ream of paper the right size for the *Journal*'s pages. She would need to arrange to get more paper soon. Perhaps she should write up an advertisement to collect old rags and linens of sundry kinds to use to make more. William had contemplated starting a paper mill to avoid shortages like the one she feared might happen. But he'd first been in debtors prison in Philadelphia for much of March and then traveling the colonies to refine and expand his postal system. So the paper mill had to wait. He'd informed her that the Second Continental Congress in May had considered the idea of his postal system and ultimately decided that a committee should be formed to "consider the best means of establishing Posts for conveying Letters and Intelligence through this Continent." But no decision had yet been made. So that meant William was still in the wind as far as she was concerned.

She had far greater concerns than her brother's whereabouts. Tension was high as it related to the colonists relationship with their king and Parliament. Since the battles at Lexington and Concord there was another gun powder incident as she'd reported in the *Journal*. She'd provided an account of how on April twenty-eighth in Williamsburg, Virginia, the gunpowder had been removed from the "public magazine, by Capt. Collins and his men, upon order of the royal governor Dunmore, causing a general alarm among the inhabitants." The representative for Spotsylvania was sent for and arrived within twenty-four hours to pacify the nearly two thousand angry residents. Quite a stir in that refined and important town in the Virginia colony. What was the governor thinking?

The front page of the *Journal* also carried several essays by Thomas Paine, a series he called The Crisis. He had some notion of compiling them eventually into a pamphlet or book, but wanted their content before the eyes of his fellow Americans. He was also working on a pamphlet he called *Common Sense*, but she hadn't seen that one come in yet. He told her that aimed to wake his neighbors up to the threats facing them.

She'd reported also that delegates from Virginia and North Carolina had come to Baltimore on May fifth on their way to Philadelphia for the congress convening on the tenth. Specifically, the Honorable Petyon Randolph, Edmund Pendleton, Geroge Washington, Benjamin Harrison, and Richard Henry Lee, all from Virginia, and Richard Caswell and Joseph Hews from North Carolina. Three companies of militia greeted them and escorted them to the Fountain Inn where the delegates were pleased by a triple discharge of musketry in salute of their arrival and mission. The next day four companies of town militia gathered on the Common to be reviewed by Colonel Washington. The delegates stayed in town another day or so, entertained by principal gentlemen of the town at the new courthouse. The delegates' presence in town brought the leaders and businessmen together in common interests, all well aware of the rising tensions in the colonies.

On a positive note, the women of the town had come together to organize a resolution and movement to only use homespun cloth for clothing. In essence, they'd spin home-grown flax and wool, then sew their own dresses and gowns. Also they'd practice frugality, making do with what they could raise, make, or buy from local merchants. Therefore, the importation of goods from Britain and elsewhere would slow to a trickle and have a negative effect on those economies. The women wanted to add their opinion to the international dialogue underway. Using their purchases, or lack thereof, to make the statement crystal clear: they refused to do business with people intent on their oppression. She'd already instructed her helpers at home as to how to proceed in line with the intent of the movement. They'd readily agreed, too.

Katy went to her desk and sat down to review the list of jobs in the queue. So many that she feared she'd never see her home during daylight hours for some time to come. She looked up as the little bell announced a customer. Surprise swept through her as she recognized Enoch Story, a competing printer, approaching her.

"Mr. Story, it's nice to see you." She stood as he drew nearer and turned to face him. "How can I help you?"

"Miss Goddard, I hope you're faring well." He hesitated for a couple of seconds, a parade of emotions marching across his tense features before he seemed to decide to proceed with his request. "I have come to admit defeat. I am getting out of the printing business in this town and moving to Philadelphia to try my luck in that larger town."

Mr. Story's small press had struggled for the past two years. Given that the Goddard and Dunlap presses each claimed the vast majority of printing and book binding business in Baltimore, it really was no surprise. It was more a matter of his personal pride giving way to the reality. Still, failing at achieving one's goal or dream was never easy.

"I'm sorry to hear that, sir. Is there something I might do to help you in winding up your business?"

"I've thought this through and I would like to offer to you my equipment, some of the finest in the country." He shrugged as a small smile crept into place. "For a reasonable price so I can start anew elsewhere."

Surprise filled her but was chased away by the realization of what it would mean to become a three press business. The prestige alone would generate more jobs and income. Still, she'd not make him feel even worse than he already did by stating what a positive influence an additional press would mean. "I believe we can come to an agreement on price. When would you envision this transaction occurring?"

"As soon as you'd like. I am willing to work that out with you."

They discussed what the worth of the equipment was new, and then she haggled with him until they agreed on an amount suitable to both. She sent Willy and Jacob to go with Enoch to attend to bringing the equipment around to the shop, and tasked Ralph with helping her determine where the new press would be placed. Just wait until her brother heard about the expansion of the printing arm of the businesses under her management.

Later that afternoon, the new press and type and the rest of the apparatus and supplies had all arrived at the Goddard print shop. She took a quick inventory of what she'd acquired and added the descriptions and quantities to her records while the lads worked to set up the new press. She'd need to find more apprentices or journeyman printers to operate the additional machine. She'd seek for one at a time until the need was fulfilled. The advertisement would read something like, "Wanted: As an apprentice, an honest sprightly LAD, about 14 or 15 years of age, that can read well, and write tolerably. Enquire at the Printing Office." Yes, growing the printing business would serve the community very well indeed.

Poor Mr. Story, having to face failure, but the boon to her business ensured even more success for her various enterprises.

Moving to Baltimore had proven very beneficial to her sense of wellbeing and purpose. She enjoyed her life in the growing town, filled with such a variety of people and businesses. She didn't know what the future might hold, but one thing she decided would not change. She would not move again, but would stay in the cozy house at 18 Conewago Street for the rest of her natural life. No matter what her unpredictable brother might do.

June of 1775 proved to be replete with more news of skirmishes and out-and-out battles between the patriots and their avowed enemy, the British. Indeed, the Continental Congress made Lieutenant Colonel George Washington commander in chief of the Continental Army, which had been established on the fourteenth. The colonies, now calling themselves states, were definitely gearing up for a fight. She had received a lengthy account of what was being called the Battle of Bunker Hill in Boston. The British had awoken on the morning of the seventeenth to see a thousand patriot militiamen, led by Colonel William Prescott, on the high ground to the north of that city, giving them a perfect view of the British forces. After three separate charges, the British emerged the victor but the patriots had proven they could stand up to what was known to be the world's mightiest empire. That should give the British commanders cause for concern.

She also reported on the attempt to find a diplomatic solution to the situation between the states and the king and Parliament. Dubbed the Olive Branch Petition, the Second

Continental Congress on the fifth of July wrote directly to King George III requesting a stop to any additional punitive measures by Parliament. They'd pledged loyalty to the king in the document penned by John Dickinson of Pennsylvania. Would the king even read the congress' petition?

"Miss, can you review this galley, make sure I got it right like you wanted?" Jacob fidgeted, shifting his dark leather shoes on the wood floor with a raspy whoosh.

"The Bunker Hill report?" She bent over the form he'd placed on the work table.

"Yes, I think I did it right." The swoosh of Jacob's shoes continued as he nervously awaited her assessment.

The lad had improved over time and she was more willing to entrust more complicated layouts to his skills. Take the galley before her. He'd done a fine job of doing the three-column layout she'd requested for the extensive summary of what had transpired in Boston. With carefully done column dividers and appropriately sized indents at the beginning of each paragraph.

She nodded as she met his anxious gaze. "This looks fine, Jacob. Go ahead and have this printed for the July twelve edition before you start on the local news page."

Jacob lifted the form and smiled at her. "Yes, miss, I will right away." He spun on his heel and marched back to the printing press where Ralph and Willy were busily printing page four, the advertisements.

His happy acceptance of her praise made her feel like she'd given him a gift. In some way, she had. How much her opinion mattered to him was still up for debate, but at least for the moment he seemed pleased.

Katy sat back in her chair, folded her arms over her chest, taking a moment to reflect on how far the paper had matured during her time working with its content. As the fighting continued, she'd accepted more and more essays, poems, letters, clippings from other papers in the colonies, all espousing the patriotic cause and some with bitter invective. After much debate with herself, she decided to formalize the poetry content by creating an actual Poet's Corner in the local news section. Her readers had responded quite favorably to the addition, so perhaps she was reading their interests correctly despite all of the varying and vying viewpoints.

Toward the end of July, she received a note from William happily sharing that the Continental Congress officially established his postal system on the twenty-sixth of July. Good news for his efforts, but did that mean he'd be returning to Baltimore? Or would he be taking the postmaster general position? Would he take over at the press? Too many possibilities hovered in the air. One thing was certain. She trailed her gaze around the busy shop, unwilling to relinquish all of the progress she'd made. She wouldn't walk away with a fight.

CHAPTER 21

BALTIMORE, MARYLAND – 1775

*S*he was in shock. But very pleased, nonetheless, in the trust the missive she received a couple of weeks later had conveyed in informing her of her new role. News she couldn't wait to share with her friend. The oppressive summer heat and humidity weighed down her steps as she climbed the stairs, the sound of the new press thumping and squealing in the front room informing her that the new apprentices were keeping to their tasks. She turned at the top of the stairs to walk toward the stationery shop area of the house. She made a point to keep a close eye on the sales of the various and sundry items, some of which she received as payment for the subscription to her paper. With the inflation caused by the fighting and boycotts, more folks had resorted to bartering and trading. Thus its contents changed week to week.

The large room at the back of the upper floor had been carefully furnished to entice people to browse the merchandise. A high counter to the right of the door displayed jars of colorful hard candies, marbles, and buttons. Behind the counter a window overlooked the rear alley and several oak trees. Several square tables draped with beige cloths were spaced around the room, stacked with a variety of blank books, useful items for taking notes and maintaining records. French patented medicines, quill pens, ink pots, and other fancy writing utensils were on other tables. Shelves lined three walls stocked with a wide variety of items, such as writing and wrapping paper, bolts of cloth, spools of thread, and other dry goods. Sharon waited on a distinguished looking man as he considered which weight of writing paper he preferred. After a few moments, he made his purchase and left the room.

She smiled at Sharon as she closed the distance between them. Her lilac day gown with its pale yellow trim showed signs of perspiration, not surprisingly. "Thank you again for agreeing to work with me while I'm taking care of the print shop. How are you feeling on this sultry August morning?"

"I feel as if I'm about to melt, to be honest. Even with the windows wide open, it's warm in here." Sharon fanned herself with a silk fan attached by a cord to her wrist. "Time to do your weekly inventory?"

"Indeed." Katy perused the shelves stacked with reams and rolls of paper, visually assessing the quantities before starting to make her careful list. That task could wait a moment. "And I wanted to share some rather surprising but pleasing news."

Waving the fan slowly, Sharon peered closer at Katy. "Share away."

"I've just received a notice by express rider, dated the twelfth of August, from the Continental Congress via Benjamin Franklin, the new Postmaster General of the Constitutional Post Office that I am the official postmistress for the Baltimore Post Office." Her inner delight at the appointment filled her with a buzzing joy. Her brother, however, had not been pleased with his new role. "William was not happy when he didn't get the Postmaster General position, forced to settle for the surveyor job in order to have any role in what he'd worked so hard to create. At least he has a role, that was important to him. But I didn't expect to be appointed postmistress."

"He must have suggested your name, given your fine work at the print shop." Sharon stepped closer to give Katy a brief hug. "Congratulations. You have earned the respect of everyone in town, as far as I can tell."

"I believe they saw the wisdom of combining the print shop and the post office like we did in Providence because I'm to publish in the paper the postal schedules and a list of any unclaimed letters." An adjustment to the *Journal*'s layout would be necessary to accommodate the additional information. She'd have to talk with Willy about making such a change going forward. "I need to do my inventory and then get back downstairs and set up to handle the mail. At least I have some previous knowledge of how to do so from when my parents were postmaster and William in Providence."

Sharon frowned as a puzzled look settled on her face. "Where? This house seems stuffed to the gills with three presses in operation plus this dry goods store."

"I am not sure. I will have to think on it." Obviously, the post office should be on the first floor to make it easy for customers to access their mail. The first floor of the current location for the press was already occupied, though, by the watchmaker. Perhaps she'd move the dry goods downstairs one floor and adjoin the post office to it, moving the two presses downstairs up to third floor. What a chore to have to tear down and reinstall two presses, though. But maybe she should consider a reorganization to a more efficient work space. That would be very disruptive to the flow of business. But Sharon was right. Every room was occupied. Then a thought popped into her head. "I seem to recall that the cottage next door might be available soon. I will inquire there to see if I could lease it for the post office."

Sharon nodded. "I think that might work."

"I'll solve the problem one way or another. I am so pleased to be entrusted with such an important job."

"As you should be. I think it is wonderful that they see your fitness to handle that responsibility. I do believe that in the time I've known you, you have blossomed into a competent, efficient businesswoman." Sharon gestured to the surrounding tables stacked with a variety of blank books, French patented medicines, and shelves lining three walls stocked with writing and wrapping paper. "I know you need to do your inventory. You've much to accomplish so let us begin."

Her friend's compliment made her review her progress from first learning to compose to all of the aspects of the business she currently controlled. She'd come far in her abilities. Something her mother would be proud of her for accomplishing.

"After I finish my tasks for the day, then I'll meet you at the tavern for a celebratory dinner after we close up shop." Katy smiled at Sharon, happy to have her assistance and her friendship.

"Did you run the notice of our new arrivals from France?"

"Oh, that reminds me." Katy produced a copy of the latest edition of the *Journal*. Unfolding it she laid it on the counter and smoothed it out, turning to page four where all notices and advertisements were presented. "This is what was published in today's paper."

Just arrived from France, And to be SOLD at the Printing-Office, SEVERAL FRENCH PATENTED MEDICINES including KEYSER'S famous PILLS for curing the most inveterate venereal disease, D'AILLAUD'S Universal

POWDER which preserves the whole body from corruption, BOLDUS's STOMACHIC PILLS which evacuates all crud, MEYSEREY WORM-POWDER: the best and fastest medicine that children can take, as well as CUROT's or ITCH ointment.

"Very good. That should bring in some customers." Sharon retrieved the ledger and handed it to Katy. "The earlier notice of the blank books and all the writing and wrapping paper has done the same. I've been busy already this morning."

Katy took the hint as she opened the ledger to a blank page. "Then I will finish my task and leave you to yours." She took the next span of time compiling her inventory and noting their value in the ledger. Then she bid Sharon farewell and went back downstairs to determine where she could set up the post office and what she'd need to run it. Her previous experience with the New London and the Providence post offices served as models for what she must acquire to suit the purpose.

After considering what furniture and supplies she'd need, she concluded there simply wasn't room in the print shop building. She would have to find another place suitable to hold the cubbyholes for the mail, a slate board to hang outside with a list of names of people who had received letters for them to come in and pick up, and a table to hold her stampers, ink, ink pot, and whatever else she ended up needing to perform her duties efficiently. The more she thought about it the more convinced she became that the best solution involved the next door cottage. Not only was it a good size for what she required, but it was also in close proximity to her other ventures. She'd be better able to oversee all the operations with them next door to each other.

"Willy, you're in charge while I run an errand." She stood

up from where she'd been working at the desk, and grabbed up her purse off the top of the cubbyholes. "I shouldn't be too long."

Willy nodded and kept working. They were all busy trying to keep up with the continual flow of articles and essays about the current tensions in the colonies, advertisements for items for sale by businesses and individuals, announcements of meetings of various committees, and notices of runaway slaves. And poetry. She couldn't overlook the Poetry Corner she'd added to the paper, which proved very popular with her readers.

She stepped outside and into the blazing sun, making her gasp at the warmth. Her quick strides had her to the cottage door in moments. A single-story abode, it squatted along the street immediately next door to the three-story brick building housing the printing shop and dry goods store. A single door was at the left end of the small house with one window beside it to the right. A dormer window jutted from the tiled roof with a chimney rising from the right end of the building. It might be a small house, but it would be quite right to serve as a post office. One easily accessible by customers, too, with only two steps up from the street instead of the many they'd have to climb up to the press.

She knocked and waited, hearing light footsteps approaching from within. When the door opened, she was greeted by a woman wearing a white blouse and white apron over long gray skirts that brushed the toes of pink house slippers. She looked like she'd been baking, given the flour on her cheek.

"Hello. My name is Mary Katharine Goddard. I apologize for not introducing myself earlier."

"I'm Mable Hawthorne. Pleased to meet you." The middle-aged woman smiled, her brown eyes twinkling. "Hello. I have you seen you coming and going from next door. You're the highly skilled printress everyone is talking about."

Katy felt warmth in her cheeks at the compliment. "Thank you for the kind words."

"Well earned from what I hear. What can I do for you, dear?"

"I heard gossip that you might consider selling or leasing this cottage. Is that correct?" She mentally crossed her fingers for good luck that she was right.

"Why, no, I hadn't thought about doing such a thing. This is my home." Mable's grin wilted. "Who would say such a thing?"

"I'm sorry. I didn't mean to upset you." Bother. She'd have to look elsewhere, but hopefully something would be for lease nearby. Her heart fell with disappointment. "I understand. I was hoping it was because… No, never mind. Thank you for your time."

Katy turned to leave, already mulling over what other options she had.

Mable called after her. "Wait! Tell me why you were hoping it was available?"

Katy spun back to face her. The sincere curiosity in Mable's brown eyes encouraged her to respond honestly. "I was hoping to run Baltimore's new post office right here, beside my print shop."

"You? You're going to run the post office?" Mable's face scrunched in confusion. "Are you telling me the truth?"

"Yes, I am. Both telling you the truth and I am the new postmistress." She smiled at the other woman, watching her disbelief turn into surprised glee. "Does that make any difference to you?"

"How extraordinary. A woman postmaster." Mable searched Katy's expression in silence for a moment. Then she nodded, as much to herself as to her guest. "That makes all the different to me. I'd be honored to have you run your post office out of my house."

"But it's your home. Where will you live?"

Mable chuckled as she wiped her hands on her apron. "My sister's been after to me to move to Annapolis with her. Just us old cronies living together. She'll be overjoyed if I sell out and do so."

"Thank you, Mrs. Hawthorne. Your generosity is greatly appreciated." Katy regarded her for a long moment. "May I come in? I'd like to have an idea of the interior so I can plan for what I'll need to do to prepare it to be the post office."

"Of course, come on in. There's not much to show you, but I think you'll find it adequate for what you have in mind." Mable ushered her inside, leaving the door open.

Katy stepped over the threshold and into plans for her new post office.

"Really, William, how can you believe that?" Katy stared at her smirking brother, her fork suspended in midair. "The Constitutional Post is putting the entire Royal Post out of business?"

William had recently arrived home again after his round of surveyor business of the new postal system. Riding from office to office to check on the flow of the mail he had plenty of opportunity to talk with men in other towns and cities across the colonies. He'd invited her to his home for dinner so the two of them could catch up on each other's news. His three-story red brick home dwarfed her cozy cottage. He'd furnished it with beautifully crafted furniture and furnishings. He also had a larger staff to manage the household for him. After all, with all the traveling he did, someone else had to run the household. To her mind, he'd chosen to live above his station, but she'd never say so.

"The British system is as good as defunct." He hefted his mug of ale in salute. "Thanks to me."

"You?" How modest of him. "What do you mean?" She scooped up some baked cinnamon apples and relished the delicious taste. His cook's culinary talents rivaled her own cook's.

"We both know it's my vision that brought about the new postal system." His smirk faded away. "I still do not understand why the congress gave the postmaster general role to Franklin."

She put down her fork to regard him in silence for a moment. *Maybe because of your lack of humility, or tendency to excoriate anyone you disagree with or who insults you.* "He probably thought with your intimate knowledge of how the system is to function, you're the exact right person to supervise its operation."

William speared a bite of roasted beef and lifted it to his mouth. He nodded as he chewed and swallowed. "That's a curious consideration. Perhaps you're right."

"Now tell me more about the Royal Post's imminent demise." He'd hinted at the gossip but hadn't elaborated on whether the rumors had merit. Taking a sip of her small beer, she set the silver goblet back on the blue cloth-covered table. "What would that mean to the people of these states?"

"The people took to the new system so quickly that it choked off stamp purchases to the old system. I doubt whether it will last another month. I'm not at all surprised, given that the British post routinely intercepted and read our private correspondence." William cut another bite of roast and dredged it through a puddle of gravy on his gold-rimmed plate. "At this point, the old way's death won't impact us at all since we have a fine network in place and running smoothly."

"That is good to hear that it's running well. However, I've been hearing that the British are increasing the tensions between us. Especially after King George III rejected the Olive Branch Petition in August and issued a proclamation declaring the American colonies to be in a state of rebellion. So he sent his military to put down the rebellion. Just last month, in October, there were ships of war positioned at the mouth of the Chesapeake Bay. I had several merchants who came in to place advertisements for their wares tell me how they'd laid up their vessels for fear they'd be harassed while merely going about their usual business. We were surprised when the *Hornet*, newly arrived from Philadelphia, had a flag flying, the new American flag. I'd heard that a seamstress in that city had sewn the flag but had not seen it until then. It was quite astonishing to see it."

"About time we can identify where our loyalties lie." William laid his fork down to take a quaff of his beverage. Patting his lips dry with a linen napkin, he shook his head. "I'd heard something of that insult. What did they actually do?"

"From what I've been told, the *Hornet* and another ship, the *Wasp*, managed to leave the Patapsco and make it past the capes without the British spotting them." She'd reported on so many confrontations and skirmishes that she feared all out war wasn't far off. She sighed, the daily escalation of the crisis they faced weighing on her. "And of course you've heard by now of the soldiers and sailors who successfully defended the town of Hampton in Virginia against British naval forces the end of October."

"Everyone is talking about that event. Mainly because that clash served to wake up the congress and the men of this land to the onset of fighting. The battle for our rights has truly begun."

She had gleaned as much from the many essays, articles, and even the poems she'd been receiving to place in the *Journal*. "You'll be pleased to know that the *Journal*'s subscriptions are increasingIt's a good thing we have three presses. And I had to take on two more apprentices to speed up the turnaround time for the many jobs."

"I am pleased to hear that. I'm sure you're doing your usual fine job." He scowled at his meal for a moment, then lifted his gaze to meet hers. "You've always been reliably efficient in your methods and supervision."

His tone suggested he had some reservations about what he'd just said. How he'd said it hinted at some level of insincerity. "Thank you."

He peered at her as a slow smile grew on his lips. "I think you need a husband. You're surrounded by men at work and women at home. You need to fix that imbalance and do what comes naturally for women, marry and have babies." He waved a hand in the air then lifted his fork again. "You're thirty-six. What are you waiting for?"

Stunned, she could only gape at his audacity to suggest such a thing. How dare he? She'd loved once and lost the chance of a happy future, a happy family. She'd vowed to never marry and she planned to keep that promise to herself. With her deceased mother's blessing. William had no right to tell her how to live her own life. Especially since the vast majority of her time was spent running his businesses.

"You know why I won't even consider what you suggest." She sipped her small beer, trying to cool the anger seething inside. "Besides, I am quite content with my life as it is. You should be grateful that I do not have a husband and children which would prevent me from managing your businesses so successfully."

William tilted his head briefly to one side and then shrugged. "You're right, as always. I did not mean to offend but to have a little fun with you."

"It was not funny."

"Again, I am sorry. I won't raise the idea ever again."

He'd said that before. She swallowed the small beer along with her ire. The conversation turned to more mundane topics as they finished their meal. But she couldn't help but wonder why he'd raised the specter of marriage when he'd just returned. What was he about now?

CHAPTER 22

BALTIMORE, MARYLAND – 1776

Oh dear. Katy's hands shook as she took on the enormously important task of composing the front page of the *Journal* for the tenth of July. She didn't want to hand off the immense responsibility to one of the lads. The importance of the historic moment weighted heavily on her shoulders. What if the British inflicted some form of punishment for publishing the provocative news? The Continental Congress had been forced into full rebellion against the King of England. They officially declared independence several days ago and now she was composing the text of that declaration to publish for her readers. After the congress declared independence, she'd also reported on "A Declaration of the Delegates of Maryland" who declared that the Province of Maryland was independent as well.

She paused in composing the broadside's galley form to reflect on what the good people of her adopted home city had put down for the world to see. The Maryland delegates hadn't even waited for the Continental Congress to act before writing their own declaration on the sixth of July. It began, "To be exempt from parliamentary taxation, and to regulate their internal government and polity, the people of this colony have ever considered as their inherent and unalienable right. Without the former, they can have no property; without the latter, they can have no security for their lives or liberties."

She retrieved her copy of the Maryland Declaration to remind herself of its contents. Their sentiments reflected her own. She especially appreciated the way they ended with an exhortation to all who agreed with them. The last sentence simply said, "Relying on Divine protection and assistance, and trusting to the justice of our cause, we exhort and conjure every virtuous citizen to join cordially in defence of our common rights, and in maintenance of the freedom of this and her sister colonies."

For a state to declare independence was one thing, but for all thirteen to join together to write the Declaration of Independence was an act of treason. She returned to her work as she mulled the consequences of these brave men's actions. The men who signed that document had to have known the very great risk they faced. Not that she would list their names in the *Journal*. She wouldn't do that until or unless Congress approved disclosing those names. They could be hung or shot in retaliation. Perhaps even their families would be targeted. She shivered as she finished composing the last line of type. Would she and the press be targeted for publishing the text? She pressed her lips together. No matter. The cause was well worth the risk.

She laid down the composing stick and motioned for Willy to come to her. When he stopped beside her, she motioned to the galley form on the table. "That's the front page for the next edition. Are the others ready?"

Willy nodded. "Yes, miss. Do you want me to start printing the paper?"

Although she knew it was not the same thing, she still

hesitated for a brief moment to actually print and distribute the news. But she believed strongly that the American people should be independent, free to live their lives as they saw fit and not under the heavy thumb of a king far away across the Atlantic. "Yes, let's get it ready to send out."

The uncertainty the people faced as they took on the British army and navy, the largest in the world, made her knees quake. The British had been training for, fighting in, and winning battles in various parts of the world. Thankfully, the Second Continental Congress appointed George Washington as the commanding officer of the Continental Army the previous year, and followed that in October by establishing a Continental Navy as well. So the soldiers and sailors had at least some training as war was declared.

The front door opened to permit an older man into the print shop. His familiar features made her start toward the desk by the front door. The apparent quality of his refined suit coat and waistcoat with a pristine white shirt and light blue cravat, knee breeches with a side button, white silk stockings, and sturdy leather shoes indicated his prosperity. The unfamiliar frown on George Blackwell's usually smiling face didn't bode well as he approached.

"Mr. Blackwell, how fare you on this sultry summer day?" Katy strode to the front of the shop to pick up the quill pen, ready to jot down his job details. The merchant routinely placed advertisements in the *Journal* for products he sold at his shop two streets away.

"Fine, thank you for asking." He grimaced as he pulled a piece of paper from the side pocket of his suit coat and laid it on the desk. "You've heard, no doubt, that our congress finally declared independence from the oppressors?"

"Yes, we'll have the full text of the declaration in tomorrow's *Journal*."

"Good. It's high time we stand up and fight back however

we must. If I were a younger man, I'd be joining up some-where, but as it is I'll do my part from here." He placed a few coins on the desktop and then pointed to the paper he placed there. "If you'd be so good as to include this notice of new merchandise just received and that it's not imported but obtained from within our states. I have no intention of sending anymore of my money over the ocean to fund their fight against us."

For ten years, the colonies had tried Nonimportation Agreements to try to force the British to recognize the colonies' political rights. Just last year the last one had failed. Still, not doing business with them seemed right.

"Indeed, I applaud your determination and efforts, sir." Katy perused the brief notice and then set it aside, noting in the ledger the word count and revenue received in payment.

His reference to the fight on their doorstep and wanting to sign up to join the army reminded her of her brother's letter to the congress and General Washington. The fool had told her how he'd requested to be made a lieutenant colonel in the army. While he was definitely a hot head, he didn't have the level of commitment necessary to lead others in heated battle. She hoped and prayed that he'd be turned down, but then would he find another way to enlist? He was deeply unhappy with his role as surveyor of the new postal system, feeling it was barely adequate to support him. But he had the wherewithal to purchase a commission if it came down to it. Or join the local militia. But then what of his job with the Constitutional Post? What was he thinking? Besides, he was her only remaining family in town. What would happen to her if he died fighting and thus lost control of the businesses under her supervision?

"I'll see myself out, Miss Goddard. I know you probably have your hands full with all the news coming and going."

As the gentleman left, her thoughts turned to several key

events she'd reported on over the last several months which clearly reflected the rising concerns of the population. In March, a British war ship, called the *Otter*, commanded by a Captain Squires, had caused general alarm in town by venturing up the Patapsco river. Thankfully, Captain James Nicholson, of Maryland's *Defence*, managed to chase the intruder from the river and captured five of the British boats in the process. Then in June, one of her subscribers, George Somerville, had stormed into the shop and abused her with threats and indecent language because of one of the pieces in the paper he disagreed with the sentiment of. The anger and disdain he'd shown to her could not be tolerated, so she'd gone to the Baltimore Committee of Safety and filed a complaint. The Committee had agreed with her claim of her right to publish whatever news she saw fit and censured the man, placing him under bond to ensure his future good behavior. Looking back, it was easy to see the trajectory of tension in town.

The concept of living and working through a war elevated her nerves to a fever pitch. But she wouldn't show any sign of her nervousness because she believed in their cause. Good men would fight and die to attempt to achieve freedom from persecution but they'd do so because they also wanted to be independent from tyranny. A worthy and necessary aim.

Several weeks passed before William received word from General Washington himself. She let him know that she'd received a letter for him at the post office and would have it for him at the press where she was working. On the twenty-ninth of July he came in to the printing house to collect it.

William's smile showed how eagerly he had been antici-pating the missive and hoping for good news. "Let me have it, Katy."

She lifted it off her desk and handed it to him, her own hopes warring with his. "What does it say?"

William read the letter quickly and then scowled. "I don't believe it."

"What? Tell me." Katy leaned closer, trying to read the letter upside down as William read it again more slowly.

William shook his head as his gaze met hers, disappointment glittering within the depths of his dark eyes. "The good general said that inducting me 'into the Army as Lieutenant Colonel would be attended with endless confusion.' Confusion? What could he possibly mean by that?"

What indeed. So her brother's reputation had reached the ears of the general. And apparently not in a good way. William needed a distraction. "Never mind that right now. Let's all go to the courthouse for the ceremonial reading of the Declaration of Independence that's happening soon. The lads should attend as well, so I'll shut up the shop for a little while. We'll make up the time after the ceremony."

"Fine." Grumbling to himself, William folded the letter and slipped it into his suitcoat pocket. "All right, lads, you heard the lady. Stop work and let's hurry up to the courthouse."

Willy led the other five lads as they all cheered at having a break in the middle of the day. A rarity for everyone. Katy admired the dedication and commitment each of the young men applied to their work. They'd be fine men and able printers to ply their trade as they matured and ventured out on their own.

The group hurried along Market to the corner and up to the courthouse. A large crowd had already gathered in the street in front of the building. An air of anticipation and enthusiasm permeated the men and women gathered to hear the proclamation by the Second Continental Congress. Independent and artillery companies stood at attention, along with several companies of the militia in their striking red coats with turned up buff edges and yellow buttons, and matching buff breeches. Other soldiers wore brown hunting shirts and breeches. The pride each of the men showed as they stood for inspection and to defend their state made Katy's own heart swell.

A distinguished elected official, William Aisquith, appeared at the center of the upper most step and read the entire Declaration. "In Congress, July 4, 1776. The Unanimous Declaration of the Thirteen United States of America. When, in the course of human events, it becomes necessary for one People to dissolve the Political Bands which have connected them with another, and to assume, among the Powers of the Earth, the separate and equal Station to which the Laws of Nature and of Nature's God entitle them, a decent respect to the Opinions of Mankind requires that they should declare the causes which impel them to the Separation." As he droned on, the sense of elation in the crowd swelled.

When he finished reading the many complaints the Americans had against the king, the crowd clapped and cheered with exclamations of joy and satisfaction. Then a discharge of the cannon punctuated the ceremonious moment for everyone.

Katy cheered along with the others but couldn't help but wonder what kind of reaction this Declaration of Independence would draw from King Charles III and his Parliament. And ultimately the military forces at their command.

Snow swirled in the air as Katy strode from the post office to the printing shop next door. Shivering beneath her heavy cloak, she hurried up the steps and inside. No longer were the printing presses in sight, having been dismantled and reassembled in rooms on the third floor. The stationery and dry goods offerings were now more easily accessible by customers on the second floor. And the bookbinding service she'd added recently complemented the book selling she'd offered for years. Sharon was tending to a customer as Katy hurried to a back room to hang her cloak on a peg on the wall.

She strode back to the main room, intent on informing Sharon of the latest news she'd just heard. News she'd make sure was included on the local page of the next edition of the *Maryland Journal*. A mix of surprise and concern bubbled inside as she walked over to the glass display case now serving as the counter for transacting sales. Sharon handed a young woman her change and the customer departed.

"You won't believe what I'm about to tell you," Katy blurted without preamble.

Sharon pivoted to grin at Katy. "Good morning to you, too." She chuckled as she slowly shook her head. "Now, tell me what has you in such a tizzy."

"The Continental Congress has come to Baltimore with haste and secrecy." The man who'd brought word of the distinguished body fleeing Philadelphia had been breathless with worry. "They've convened in Henry Fite's huge mansion."

Mr. Fite's "house" was a spacious three-story and dormered attic brick building, ten windows long, with three doors. The short side was five windows deep with a center door. The house stood on the corner of Liberty and Market. Katy could only try to imagine how many rooms were inside the immense building.

"What are they doing here?" Sharon frowned at the startling news.

"Fleeing the British after they chased the army out of

New Jersey." Katy crossed her arms over her stomach, her innards roiling with the thought of the congress being captured by the enemy. "They're safe here, at least."

"My gracious, what a state of affairs." Sharon shook her head slowly. "I am glad they escaped to safety."

"With the Declaration of Independence. They packed it up in a wagon and brought it with them." She longed to see the actual Declaration to see the men's original words and signatures. What a historic document to behold. If only… "They must have feared for their lives."

"That would have been terrifying indeed." Sharon smoothed down her pale pink apron. "I wonder if they'll need your services for printing their resolutions and such."

"I will offer my services immediately. They may not be aware of this print shop and what we can do for them." Katy nodded and turned to retrieve her cloak. "That's a very good idea."

A week later Katy almost regretted informing Congress of her shop. The three presses never got a rest, nor did the young men operating them. The whole town was abuzz with gossip and news regarding the resolutions and actions of their government. The steady flow of jobs made her glad she'd instituted several refinements to the efficient operation of the presses. Having the Continental Congress in town added greatly to the amount of government work they had to do. She found herself putting the final touches on an official resolution unlike any she'd ever seen before.

December 27th, 1776.—This Congress, having maturely considered the present crisis, and having perfect reliance on the wisdom, vigor, and uprightness of General Washington, do hereby

Resolve, That General Washington shall be, and he is hereby, vested with full, ample, and complete powers to raise and collect together, in the most speedy and effectual manner, from any or all of these United States, sixteen battalions of infantry, in addition to those already voted by Congress; to appoint officers for the said battalions of infantry; to raise, officer, and equip three thousand light-horse, three regiments of artillery, and a corps of engineers, and to establish their pay...

The trust placed upon the shoulders of the commander of the army seemed enormous. The rest of the resolution outlined more actions the government authorized him to undertake, including appointing officers under the rank of brigadier-general; to take whatever he needed for the army if the people wouldn't sell it to him for a reasonable price; and even to arrest and confine people who were "disaffected to the American cause." Thankfully, at least to her mind, the resolution's final paragraph stated, "That the foregoing powers be vested in General Washington for and during the term of six months from the date hereof, unless sooner determined by Congress." There should be some limits applied to such vast powers.

Of course, given his surprising victory at the Battle of Trenton the day after Christmas, he had proved he could be trusted. Washington led his soldiers across the icy Delaware river in the middle of the night during a winter storm, then marched ten miles to Trenton where they surprised fifteen hundred Hessian troops, capturing about one thousand officers and soldiers at the cost of only four of Washington's men. A boost for morale for the Continental Army, most definitely.

Wiping her hands on her ink-smeared apron, she lifted the galley form and carried it from the composing table to the next room where Willy waited to make the requested number of copies. She paused to really look at the man, a journeyman printer in his own right. He'd grown his hair long enough to pull back into a queue tied with a black ribbon. He'd matured into a fine, strapping young man at two and twenty years of age. How long before he enlisted in the fighting? Or would he be content to fight via the printing press's output?

"Here you go, Willy." She laid the galley on the work table near the medium-size press. "This one takes priority."

"I've been waiting for it instead of starting something else." Willy glanced to the new apprentice William had sent to her last week. "Go get more ink and be smart about it."

"How's our paper supply?" Katy glanced to the upper shelf to check on the supply remaining. With the war on, finding paper had become more and more of a problem. She struggled to acquire enough which interrupted the consistency of publication of the newspaper. She'd even had to reduce the number of pages, something she disliked doing because the contents were less useful to her readers.

"We have enough for this broadside and to make the pamphlets, but after that..." Willy shrugged. "I hope we can locate more from somewhere."

"I've advertised for rags but not much is available." How was she going to meet the demands of the community for their printing and publishing expectations? "William is working on a new scheme to try to build a paper mill, but that will take quite some time. Which we don't have."

"In the mean space, I'll work on this." Willy turned his attention to the task at hand.

Katy suppressed an annoyed sigh and went back downstairs. She'd have to see what she could scrounge up at home in the way of rags to use to make the paper, and perhaps her neighbors might have a few about they'd be willing to exchange for something from the dry goods. She might be forced to order some from another town, but the expense may prove beyond her budget. She had to solve this dilemma.

Sharon finished rearranging a table stacked with writing papers in different shades of white. She looked up as Katy approached her. "What's got you frowning?"

"Paper. I need to find more." Not a new worry by any means, but one increasingly difficult to solve. "Never mind. I'll sort out something."

Sharon winked at her. "You always do. That's why everyone relies on you."

"I rely upon your support and friendship every single day." Katy gave her friend a brief hug. "I just hope that we survive and succeed at winning our cause in the end. And I'm glad we have each other through these uncertain and dangerous times."

"Despite the uncertainty, you've flourished and expanded your services." Sharon chuckled and pointed to where the newly hired bookbinder worked to sew a set of pages together to form a tome. "Now that you've added bookbinding, you've brought all the publishing elements together under one roof."

"Yes, now folks can bring their materials to be bound into a book. It's quite popular with the many writers and people who paint and want to gather the pages into one place."

"You're quite the business woman, editor of the *Journal*, printer, publisher, bookbinder, merchant, and postmistress all in one personage."

"A very busy person, but you're right." Katy spent every waking moment working on some aspect of her business. "I can only imagine what additional printing business we'll have as a result of the congress being in town."

CHAPTER 23

BALTIMORE, MARYLAND –1777

She didn't have to wait long to find just how busy she'd be with congress in town. Not only the printing of resolutions and other official business, but the post office saw much more mail coming and going. Each resolution, for example, had to be sent out to the states for their action and awareness. Ensuring the congressmen received their letters and dispatches became a daily challenge. It didn't help that the first month of the new year proved to be cold and snowy.

Katy motioned to Ralph to come to her where she stood by the work table near the largest press. She pointed to the stack of printed resolutions. "These need to be carried to Mr. William Govett, the acting auditor general, down at the Fite House. Can you take them down there, please?"

Ralph glanced out the front window and sighed at the snow falling steadily outside. "Yes, miss."

"Bundle up and be careful with them." She tapped the table with the tips of her fingers. "While you're gone I'll make sure we stay on course with meeting our deadlines."

Ralph placed the stack into a large satchel and fastened

the flap. "I'll try to not be gone too long, once I find Mr. Govett."

After Ralph left, Katy made her rounds of the various parts of the business she managed. Everyone was hard at work, busy with their tasks or serving sporadic customers, given the weather. She finished at the dry goods and stationery on the second floor of the building, glad to have a moment to speak with her friend.

Sharon moved from table to table, adjusting the merchandise into a more attractive arrangement. She glanced at Katy but kept working. Katy didn't fault her for not stopping given how busy the shop had been. Once the snow let up, the customers would return. She shadowed Sharon so she could talk with her.

"I need some advice, my friend."

Sharon glanced at her and then focused on the bottles of patent medicines clustered at one side of the small table. "About William?"

Katy sighed. "How did you guess?"

"Because whenever he's in town you fret and second-guess yourself." Sharon spaced the bottles neatly and then studied the new positions with a critical eye. "I suppose he's causing a stir?"

"Doesn't he always. I wish Mother were still alive and could handle his outbursts. She had more sway with him than I do." But she had a bigger worry than his moodiness. "I think he's actually jealous of my success in his absence."

"He should be. You do fine work and have built a very successful business." Sharon turned to face her, clasping her upper arms with both hands. "Do not let him steal away your confidence in the job you do. Everyone thinks very highly of you, in a way William could never earn with his behavior."

"I just worry about what he'll do. He might try to undermine what I've done, or even take it away. It's all in his name, except for the post office and all of this you're working on. Those are mine entirely."

"Then even if he does try to take control again, you'll still have means to provide for yourself. Just as you've always done." Sharon dropped her hands to clasp them together. "And I'm here to help anyway that I can."

Katy started to speak but then Ralph burst through the front door, the bell jangling as he hurried to where the women stood.

"What is the matter? You look like something awful has happened." Katy peered at him, noting the snow slowly melting on the shoulders of his dark cloak.

"Mr. Govett was very pleased with the broadsides you sent him." Ralph struggled to calm his breathing after apparently racing back to the print shop. "Then he introduced me to the President of the Congress, Mr. John Hancock."

"Why, that is quite an honor for you." Katy grinned at him, happy on his behalf at the opportunity to meet such a fine, respected gentleman. "I trust you were polite."

Ralph bobbed his brown head a couple of times. "He told me that they will be bringing their Declaration to you forthwith."

Katy frowned in confusion. "To me? Why?"

"After General Washington's victory in New Jersey, they have decided to publish it with all the signatures included. And they want you to do it because you've been such a champion of independence even before the fighting began and they recognize the quality of printing you have provided." Ralph beamed at her, his eyes twinkling. "I am so proud to be associated with the Goddard press, miss. It's an honor to work with you."

Shock flooded her for a brief moment, replaced quickly with satisfaction. She would not only get to see the original document, but also replicate it. Printing a signed edition of the Declaration of Independence was quite an honor. It was also a significant moment in the fledgling United States of America's history. And in hers.

"Thank you, Ralph, I am pleased as well. Let's prepare for its arrival." A vision of the layout of the text started forming in her mind. "It's a good thing I was able to scrounge up more suitable paper to print the broadside on then. Sharon, I'll talk to you later."

Just then the door opened again, and several elegantly dressed gentlemen came in, the first man carrying a large portfolio. "Miss Mary Katharine Goddard?"

Katy strode quickly to greet them. "Yes, sir. I presume you're from the congress."

"Indeed." He patted the black leather case in his hand. "Inside is the original signed document and today's order to have it printed with all the signatures for the first time. They've decided it's time to stand by their declaration by name."

He opened the case to show her the contents, a hand-written paper in fine script on top. "We want to add the text of the order to the bottom, beneath the signatures. The design of the broadside is entirely up to your judgment." He handed her the order and then closed the portfolio and handed that to her as well. "Please safeguard that as long as it is in your possession."

"I will not let it out of my sight or possession." Imagine the uproar if something untoward happened to the very original of the Declaration of Independence. She swallowed the bile that rose in her throat at the thought of the weight of responsibility placed on her shoulders. Nothing untoward could be allowed to happen to the precious document. "I promise."

"I'm afraid your promise is not enough. I will be staying with the document until you are finished with it." The younger, brawnier man glanced at his compatriots. "If that is acceptable to you?"

One older man nodded. "That's a good prevention to mishaps." He met Katy's gaze with his sober countenance. "We'll need at least thirteen copies of it to send out to the states. How quickly might you have this accomplished?"

Katy knew the length of the original Declaration from her previously sharing the text with her *Journal* readers. Adding the text of the order in her hand didn't significantly add to that estimate of time and type required. She peered at the order, which read simply, "Ordered, That an authenticated copy of the Declaration of Independence, with the names of the members of Congress subscribing the same, be sent to each of the United States, and that they be desired to have the same put upon record. By Order of Congress, John Hancock, President."

She swept her gaze around the group of men and then nodded. "I'll have fifteen copies of this ready by tomorrow morning. Will that suit your needs?"

"Yes, that will be soon enough. Until tomorrow, then." The men tipped their hats to her and then turned to depart back into the cold air outside.

She turned back to address the guard who had remained with her. "Now, I expect you'll want to stay in the room with this, so follow me upstairs to the presses." She turned and led the way to the third floor and her composing table. "You are welcome to sit at my desk over there while we begin on this job." Katy pointed to the wood chair and desk near the back of the room.

"Very well, Miss Goddard." He crossed the floor to perch on the chair and supervise.

Having such an attentive audience didn't settle her nerves one iota as she contemplated the important job that had suddenly been thrust upon her. "I'll do the composing, to shield you and the lads from any potential backlash." Katy stared at the portfolio in her hands, realizing she held history. How proud her mother would be of the opportunity to truly contribute to the cause for liberty. She looked at Willy and then said, " Come along and let's get this started. This is our highest priority."

Willy nodded. "You start composing and I'll get the press ready. What size paper do you plan to use?"

"It's a broadside size." She laid the portfolio on the work table and opened it, the original signed document was, of course, handwritten by a careful hand. "I'll get started."

She set up at the composing table, reading over the complete text to get a feel for the contents. She envisioned the title in larger type, followed by the full text. She considered how best to display it, then decided to make it two columns. Below would come all of the signatures, including the largest one by John Hancock. The signatures were grouped by state, which would make setting the type easier to align as well. Below the signatures she'd include the text of the order. Below that would be the colophon she always placed on her work.

Only… Instead of using her initials, this most important work would bear her full name. She'd separate the colophon from the rest of the document with a line. Then, "Baltimore, in Maryland: Printed by Mary Katharine Goddard."

Yes. That would be fine. She'd sign the Declaration of Independence as well, as a patriotic printer honored by congress with this significant work. Without further delay, she picked up the composing stick and began the most important printing job of her life. The Goddard Broadside of the Declaration of Independence.

HISTORICAL NOTE

Mary Katharine Goddard continued to run the printing press until William forced her out of the newspaper business in January 1784. She was apparently upset with the way her brother treated her, filing five law suits against him in November of that year, though there is no record as to what they were specifically about. She focused instead on the bookshop and post office. In the fall of 1789, Mary Katharine was ordered to resign as postmaster by the postmaster general because as a woman she couldn't be expected to travel as part of her duties (something the postmaster never did anyway). A petition by more than two hundred and thirty businessmen from Baltimore calling for her reinstatement was ignored. She maintained her bookshop, moving it to 28 Chatham Street in 1803, until she retired in 1809/10.

She lived at 18 Conewago Street with one slave, Belinda Starling, until her death on August 12, 1816. She was 78 years old. Upon her death, Belinda was freed and inherited all of Mary Katharine's property.

All of the quoted material came from primary and/or secondary sources I used in writing this story. The facts surrounding what she accomplished and where she lived also come from those sources. However, there are no sources regarding who she was as a person, her likes and dislikes, her reasoning and motivations. That's where the facts end and the fiction begins. All references to her friends, her pets, her home are informed fiction based on my research. I also do not know why she never married, so invented the reasons she used to defend against questions related to her marital status. Some of the apprentices names (not descriptions) are from sources, but most are fictional characters.

Mary Katharine, Katy to her friends and family, is an important figure in American history. I hope you've enjoyed getting to know her as much as I have.

ACKNOWLEDGMENTS

I couldn't have written this book without the amazing assistance of a plethora of professionals. After I'd exhausted every source I could find, I reached out to these folks who each provided me with a new piece of information or source. So my deepest appreciation goes out to Jessica Shainker, Archives Specialist, National Archives and Records Administration; Pat Schaefer, New London (Connecticut) Historical Society; Meg Bowersox, Manager of Gallery Interpretation, Museum of the American Revolution; Tristan Bella, Access Services Librarian, Historical Society of Pennsylvania; Darby Nisbett Schini and Morgan Miller, Reference Archivists, Maryland State Archives; Jennifer L. Galpern, Senior Manager, Robinson Research Center, Rhode Island Historical Society; Maria Paxi, Librarian, Connecticut State Library; Benedict Leca, Executive Director, Redwood Library and Athenaeum; Colin T. Braun, Technical Services Librarian: Circulation and Operations, Redwood Library and Athenaeum; Josie Breck, Library Associate, Periodicals Department, Enoch Pratt Free Library; and from Historic Annapolis (Maryland) Kaelynn Bedsworth, Development Outreach Director; Elizabeth Fox, Curator; Mary-Angela E. Hardwick, Vice President, Education and Interpretation; Carlea West, Lead Visitor Services Specialist.

I'm also indebted to the five beta readers— Brandi, Chris, Danielle, Dani, and Deidre—who read and critiqued Katy, providing invaluable insights and feedback so I could improve the story to be the best I could write. Thank you for your time and honesty.

Finally, I'd like to thank my loving husband, Chris, of nearly 40 years for all of his support and encouragement. He is truly the wind beneath my wings!

ABOUT THE AUTHOR

Award-winning author Betty Bolté enjoys writing authentic and accurately researched historical fiction with heart and supernatural romance novels. A lifetime reader and writer, she's worked as a secretary, freelance word processor, technical writer/editor, and author. She's been published in essays, newspaper articles/columns, magazine articles, and nonfiction books but now enjoys crafting entertaining and informative fiction, especially stories that bring American history to life. She earned a Master's Degree in English in 2008, emphasizing the study of literature and storytelling, and has judged numerous writing contests for both fiction and nonfiction. She lives in northern Alabama with her loving husband of more than 35 years. Get to know her at www.bettybolte.com. Be sure to check out materials for book club discussions at https://www.bettybolte.com/book club.

9 798986 045078